THE COMPANY YOU KEEP

The Bishop Smoky Mountain Thrillers
Book 9

LAUREN STREET

STERLING & STONE

THE COMPANY YOU KEEP

Chapter One

THE IMAGE OF ROBERT REDFORD THAT HAD STAMPED A smile on Jeremiah Johnson's face had been on the cover of one of those magazines for halfwits in the checkout line at Walmart, where he'd gone to buy toilet paper. Pitiful to have to depend on civilization just to wipe your ass.

Jeremiah had studied it — the magazine cover, not his ass — and determined that he was a helluva lot better looking now than Robert Redford was. He took a perverse but profoundly satisfying delight in that.

Of course, Jeremiah was a lot younger. Robert Redford was eighty-seven and Jeremiah was only seventy-seven. And truth be told, *both* of them looked like death on a cracker — two cadaverous old men on a downhill slide to the boneyard. But Jeremiah had aged better than his namesake, could still do damn near anything he'd ever done. Could Robert Redford say the same? Jeremiah doubted it. Robert Redford had been a cardboard cutout of a mountain man, while Jeremiah was the real deal.

The checker caught his glance at the magazine cover. "Whatcha grinnin' at, Jeremiah?"

Jeremiah ignored the remark, same's he did the checker. He had never admitted to anybody that comparisons to Robert Redford, who had played the part of the mountain man, Jeremiah Johnson in the 1972 movie, made Jeremiah's skin crawl.

The movie had come out right after Jeremiah got home from two tours in Vietnam. One he was forced to serve, but the second he'd re-upped for out of spite. Worst mistake he ever made. Got back home to the mountains and suddenly people he'd known his whole life were coming up to him and teasing him about his name.

In truth, he'd ought not to begrudge that movie for using his name, because it had changed the whole trajectory of Jeremiah's life. If not for that movie, he would never have gone looking for the story of the *real* Jeremiah Johnson that the movie was based on. And that story had so inspired him that he'd pretty much spent every day since then living it out in the Smoky Mountains.

Well, living it out best as he could. He didn't go out and kill Indians and eat their livers like Jeremiah Johnson had done. But the real Jeremiah was a man to admire and respect, nothing like the cartoon character that Robert Redford had played in that movie.

Not that Jeremiah was out looking for anybody's admiration or respect. He had given up on the human race years ago. Moved deeper and deeper into the mountains, saw fewer and fewer people the older he got. He suspected he'd just get killed out in the wilderness one day and wouldn't nobody know or care. Struck by a timber rattler. Or lightning. Fall in a creek and hit his head on a rock, drown in six inches of water. At least it wouldn't be something as ordinary as cancer or a heart attack.

And when he did die, it wasn't likely anybody was going to find his body any time soon. Which was also just fine. He liked the prospect of his corpse providing a meal for scavengers and his bones scattered in the mountains somewhere wild and free.

The real Jeremiah Johnson had come out of the Civil War as jaded and disillusioned and disgusted as Jeremiah had felt when he got home from Saigon. They'd both come back to the mountains they loved and wanted to be left alone. The real Jeremiah Johnson — not the pale shadow of him that Robert Redford had played on the silver screen — had been a remarkable human being. His wife was a member of the Flathead Indian tribe, and one day when he wasn't home, she was killed by a young Crow brave and his fellow hunters. That set Jeremiah on a vendetta that lasted three decades. He set out to avenge his wife, and in the process, he killed and scalped more than three hundred Crow Indians. Then he ate the liver out of every one of them — raw.

He was a constable, a log cabin builder, a wood hawk, a whiskey peddler, a sailor, a scout, a soldier, a gold-digger. But more than anything, Jeremiah Johnson had been a hunter and a trapper who lived his life on his own terms. His life story had inspired the also *real* Jeremiah Johnson in Yarmouth County, Tennessee, to do the same.

Moving as silently through the woods as smoke, Jeremiah stalked his quarry. A raccoon. A big sucker. He'd been tracking this one for damned near a week now, always half a step behind, and he had developed a grudging respect for the critter, a cagey little bastard that had slipped his snares one after another.

Jeremiah stood stock still, didn't even breathe, his eyes clawing through the undergrowth for that little masked marauder. Raccoons were primarily crepuscular — active at dawn and dusk — as well as nocturnal. But a raccoon's go-to life skill was adaptability. They'd come out at noon to raid a chicken house while the hens were nesting in the heat of the day, or every afternoon at three o'clock to eat the dog's food when Fido ran into the front yard to greet the kids getting off the school bus.

Jeremiah earned what he called walking-around money by selling their skins to a shop in Pigeon Forge that made authentic coon-skin caps. Not the fake fur ones that every kid who came to the Smokies went home wearing, boys and girls alike. He drew the line at making real tomahawks, though. The tourist kids would kill each other if they got their hands on tomahawks that weren't rubber. He lived on his government pension, which wasn't much, but he didn't need much. The reason he was pursuing this particular wily rascal with such determination was that he needed *extra* money. He'd finally decided to break down and buy himself some damned hearing aids.

Jeremiah could see just fine. If he couldn't, he wouldn't be able to hunt. But over the years, the world had grown muffled. He missed things now, couldn't hear the scramble of critters in dry leaves anymore, or the cooing of doves on a tree limb. That doctor fellow at the Veterans Hospital in Nashville had fitted him with a pair of sample hearing aids, let him try them for a few days just to see if he liked them — and damn! He heard birds in the trees, tree frogs and crickets, even mice scratching in the wall — all kinda sounds he didn't even know he'd been missing. Of course, his benefits wouldn't pay for the hearing aids. VA benefits wouldn't pay for anything he really needed. So he was socking away his walking-around money to get him a pair.

If Jeremiah had been wearing hearing aids, that fella hiding in the rocks wouldn't have gotten the drop on him.

"Freeze!" a voice called out, and Jeremiah 'bout shit his britches in surprise. "Lay that rifle down on the ground easy or I'll put a bullet in your back."

Jeremiah did as he was told, nice and slow.

"I don't know who you are, mister," he said to the man he couldn't see. "But you'd get a lot more bang for your buck snatching some tourist lady's purse in town than you're gonna get robbin' a broke old man like me. I bet I ain't got two bucks in my pocket."

"Get into the sunlight where I can see you."

Jeremiah moved out of the shade, into the open space beside the pile of boulders, then looked down and spied a red smear on one of the rocks. His eyesight was just fine, thank you very much. He didn't have to bend over and squint to tell it was a drop of blood.

He heard the man let out a breath then, and the voice that spoke after that wasn't nearly as strong or forceful.

"Sorry. I just had to make sure. Look … can we pretend this didn't happen, you just pick up your rifle and go?"

Jeremiah relaxed, but he made no move toward the rifle on the ground.

"Ain't none of my concern, but 'pears to me you might be hurt. You need some help?"

"You can help me by not telling anybody you saw me. Don't dial 911 or call the police or report an emergency. Just walk away."

His voice had the breathy quality of a man in pain.

"If you're hurt—"

"I'm fine … just please, don't report this." There was a pause before the man spoke again, his voice pain-clotted. "They'll kill me if they find me. I'll just disappear. They tried, but they can't protect me."

"Who might 'they' be?"

The man didn't reply for several breaths, finally said grudgingly, "Just … government agents."

If that fella had meant to send Jeremiah Johnson an

engraved invitation to his Help-a-Wounded-Stranger party, he'd just put the stamp on it.

"The gub-mint." Jeremiah spit the word out because it tasted foul in his mouth.

Jeremiah had figured out some foundational truths during the seventeen months he spent in a cage as an honored guest of the Viet Cong. Not just that the depravity of the human heart knows absolutely no bounds, but that there was something rotten at the core of the United States government. The older he got, and the more he watched the country he had gone to war for fall apart around him, the more convinced he became that there did exist a "Deep State" and that its goal was to destroy America.

When he finally came to that understanding, he figured he had two choices. He could join some kind of resistance — or start one of his own — and take the country back. But he was too old for that. Besides, in some ways, he thought the country was getting what it deserved. If you were so stupid and easily gaslighted that you'd elect the assholes running the country now, you deserved what you got. His second option was to drop out. About ten years ago, he had opted for Door Number Two. He figured when the whole house of cards finally collapsed under its own weight, he could survive on his own in the mountains. And when they came for him, if they ever did, he would make the sons of bitches pay dearly to take him down.

It appeared that Jeremiah and the fellow hiding behind the rocks was singing from the same sheet of music.

Saying nothing, Jeremiah walked slowly around the rocks, not believing this fellow would actually shoot him, if he even had a gun. And if he did, well, it was better way to go out than drownin' in the creek.

Leaned up against the backside of a big rock was a man clutching a pistol in his right hand, though his arm was limp, so the gun was useless in his lap. He was blond, hair cut high and tight, dressed like a tourist in jeans and a t-shirt that was gratefully vacant of idiotic Pigeon Forge sayings like: "You couldn't handle me if I came with instructions," or "Whoever said diamonds are a girl's best friend never owned a dog," or "There's no reward for stupid, so stop competing."

It was a plain black tee with blood all over it. And a piece of fabric wrapped around it, like a sleeve ripped off a shirt.

The fellow was all tore up, had been in some kind of accident. If Jeremiah had to guess, he would have figured that the fellow had a broken left arm, and maybe his leg was broke too. He was cut up and bleeding in half a dozen different places. He wore shoes but only one sock, and Jeremiah saw a lump under his tee shirt, like maybe he'd used the missing sock as a pressure bandage to stop bleeding there and the piece of fabric to hold the sock in place. His eyes were closed, but they popped open like a window shade you'd let loose at the bottom to flap around and around at the top.

The man didn't appear to actually look at anything, just closed his eyes again, but he said softly, "You can't tell."

"Tell what?"

"That you found me."

"You need a doctor."

"No!"

Jeremiah knelt on the ground beside him. "It ain't like I can dial 911. There ain't no cell coverage where we are. It's a mile and a half up the mountain before you can even get a couple of bars. But I ain't gonna just walk away and leave you like this. I gotta go get—"

The man reached out faster than he ought to be able

to, given the shape he was in, and grabbed Jeremiah's shirt, dragging him forward.

"No, listen, you have to listen to me. They're after me. If you call for help, they'll know. They have informants everywhere. They'll come for me and they'll kill me. *I'm not the bad guy. Please…*"

Jeremiah had always considered himself a pretty good judge of character. And he believed the guy. No reason he'd ought to, but he did.

"If I leave you here and walk away, ain't nobody gonna have to *kill* you — you're gonna die your own self. You got to get help, son, or you ain't gonna live to see another sunrise."

The man was silent, his eyes closed. Maybe he passed out.

Then he said two words: "Mitch Webster."

"The sheriff?"

"Yes, Sheriff Mitch Webster. Just him, don't tell anybody else."

"Exactly who is it I'm supposed to tell him I found?"

"No names."

"You think he's gonna drop whatever he's doin' to come help some nameless fella he don't know?"

Turning pain-filled eyes on Jeremiah's face, the man spoke slowly and distinctly. "Oh, he knows me. Tell him that. He'll remember who I am if you say this … that when he met me, *he didn't have to unzip his pants.*"

"What?"

"Tell him that. Exactly those words. Say it back to me."

Jeremiah obediently repeated the phrase 'bout the sheriff not unzipping his pants.

"When you say that, he'll know who you mean. He'll remember."

Then the man closed his eyes and didn't speak again.

Chapter Two

"HAVE EITHER ONE OF YOU EVER ACTUALLY SHOT A squirrel?"

It was a simple enough question, but Rileigh couldn't get a straight answer out of either Gus or Mitch.

"I shot a gopher once," Mitch said. "Isn't that the same thing as a squirrel?"

"No, a gopher is not the same thing as a squirrel." Rileigh sighed. "Gophers live in the ground. Squirrels live in trees."

Rileigh Bishop, Mitch Webster, and Gus Hazelton were walking through the woods together, their .22 rifles pointed at the ground as they trekked across Hanging Chicken Hollow to get to Hanging Chicken Ridge, where they were going squirrel hunting.

Mitch had asked, and Rileigh hadn't known the answer: what's up with the *Hanging Chicken* thing? It was one of a hundred different places in the Smokies that'd been named by somebody sometime for some reason nobody remembered anymore, but the name stuck. What she did know was that it was squirrel-hunting heaven. What she didn't know was why there was such a high population of squirrels in Hanging Chicken-dom. You would think that, since it had the reputation of being the best place in the county to shoot squirrels, the squirrels would have figured that out by now and moved to Florida. Or that all the hunting there would have decimated the squirrel population. Apparently, neither one of those things had happened, because when Mitch had inquired around among his deputies about the best place to go squirrel hunting, they had confirmed unanimously what Rileigh had already told him — go to Hanging Chicken Ridge.

"I shot a brush-tailed phascogale a few years ago." Gus said.

Both Rileigh and Mitch spoke at the same time. "What's a brush-tailed phascogale?"

"Well, the Australian natives call it a T-U-A-N," Gus said. "Or the common wambender, or the black-tailed mousesack, or the black-tailed phascogale. Or they just refer to it as an arboreal rat-sized carnivorous marsupial."

Rileigh rolled her eyes. "You ask the man what time it is and he tells you how to build a watch. Can't you just answer the question? Have you ever shot a squirrel?"

"I guess the answer is technically no, if you don't count the phascogale."

"We don't count rat-sized arboreal carnivorous marsupials from Australia as squirrels," she said. "Not in Yarmouth County, Tennessee."

"Wait, wait, wait," Gus said. "I *have* shot a squirrel. A ground squirrel."

"A ground squirrel is not the same thing as a squirrel," Rileigh said.

"The hell it's not," Gus said.

"The hell it is," Rileigh retorted.

And so the discussion went on, with Gus pointing out that he had grown up on the high plains of Texas, the home of ground squirrels uncountable.

"Is it our fault we didn't have any trees?" he added. "If you were an aspiring squirrel in West Texas, you had to innovate, think outside the box, adapt. In short, you had to live in a hole in the ground — essentially, become a *ground* squirrel. And I've shot one."

"Squirrels live in trees," Rileigh insisted.

Gus wasn't ready to let it go.

"There are no squirrels native to Australia," he said, "so the locals consider the brush-tailed phascogale a squirrel."

"The natives thinking something is a squirrel and it actually being a squirrel are not the same thing," Rileigh said.

"The hell they're not," Gus said.

"The hell they are."

"I shot a chipmunk once," Mitch chimed in.

Both Rileigh and Gus turned to him in surprise.

"You *shot* a chipmunk?" she asked.

"Don't look at me like I bludgeon baby seals. Chipmunks are not squeaky little creatures named Alvin who sing Christmas songs. They're small rodents, and they're the same thing as a squirrel."

"No, they're not. Chipmunks live in the ground—"

Mitch and Gus completed the sentence for her. "And squirrels live *in trees*."

"Let's ask Siri," Mitch said.

"Siri's an idiot," Rileigh replied. "I tell her to 'Call Mama,' and she says, 'Here's everything I can find on the web about 'Call Mama.'"

Mitch still inquired, and Siri replied that ground squirrels "are small mammals that generally live on the ground or in burrows. All chipmunks are ground squirrels. But not all ground squirrels are chipmunks."

"Well, *that* was helpful," Gus said.

"I never dreamed Mama's squirrel request would launch us into such zoological consternation," Rileigh said.

Mitch laughed. "Say that three times fast."

When Mama had first brought up the subject of making squirrel stew, both Jillian and Rileigh had given her a *sure, Mama*, believing that in ten minutes, she wouldn't remember that she'd asked. But for some reason, squirrel stew hung on a nail in Mama's head, and the more she mentioned it, the more determined she was to make it.

Finally, Rileigh had given in, telling her, "If you'll just stop talking about squirrel stew, I'll go out and shoot you some squirrels so you can make it."

So she had enlisted Gus in that endeavor. After all, Gus was something like a professional hunter. He'd been on countless safaris all over the planet. He had an office full of stuffed trophies — elk and deer and moose and antelope and mountain goats and more on his walls. He was a gun aficionado, and his arsenal had more firearms than the armies of some Third World countries. Going to his home was like going to Cabela's. About six months ago, he'd decided to forego shooting big game with anything except a camera and a three-hundred-and-thirty-millimeter lens, which was why there was a life-size picture of a white rhinoceros in his office waiting room.

And she had invited Mitch because, well, duh. Mitch.

Her mind paused there and smiled. Can a person's mind smile? Hers did when she thought about Mitch. And her body responded to him almost of its own volition, pebbling her arms with goosebumps whenever he was close.

A smiling mind and self-actualizing goosebumps. *Rileigh girl, you have been hit hard!*

Gus suddenly stopped in his tracks and held up his hands. "I have it. I can answer the question of what is and is not a squirrel — definitively."

"We're listening," Mitch said.

"With bated breath," Rileigh added.

"A squirrel," Gus said dramatically, his voice Shakespearian, "is a rat with good PR."

That settled it.

They had come to the top of a hill, less than half a mile from Hanging Chicken Ridge. Rileigh turned to Mitch, the squirrel-hunting newbie, and said, "Squirrels may be ground squirrels or gophers or chipmunks or phascogales or rats with good PR, but there is one thing they are not — deaf. In fact, those little twitchy ears of theirs can hear very well. So from here on, channel your inner squirrel and consider the spiritual ramifications of what squirrel-ness means — in silence."

Rileigh crept quietly through the woods with Mitch, Gus behind him. Stopped beside a large oak tree, she held up her hand, signaling for Mitch and Gus to stop too. Then she pointed up at the limbs of a sycamore tree about 30 yards away. You could see a squirrel there. A big fat gray one. If they could bag a dozen of those, there certainly would be plenty of meat for a mama to make a batch of squirrel stew. She pointed to Gus and gestured for him to take the shot, and he shook his head and pointed back at her. She lifted the .22 rifle to her shoulder, seated it firmly, though a .22 didn't have a whole lot of kick. Sighting down the barrel at the squirrel on the limb, she drew in a breath, let it out slowly, and squeezed the trigger.

Pop!

The squirrel dropped like a rock out of the tree, and

the three of them rushed to the base of the trunk to find the body where it lay — twitchy, but dead.

"Now what?" Mitch asked. "Do we just stuff it still warm into the game bag and keep going? I'm no expert on the decomposition rate of a … creature that is *not* an arboreal rat-sized carnivorous marsupial. But won't it … start to stink in there?

"No, we're good," Rileigh said.

"For big game, we'd field dress it on the spot, get the blood and the guts out ASAP," Gus said.

Mitch wrinkled his nose. "That sounds like a pleasant activity."

"If you can't stand the heat, stay out of the kitchen."

"Clean them any time within 24 hours and you're fine," Rileigh continued. "I've shot squirrels in the morning, then gone hunting again in late afternoon and cleaned the whole lot of them at one time — some of them have been dead more than twelve hours."

"So if you're going to wait until we get back to Mama's, there's still a chance I can come up with an excuse and get out of helping."

"Not anymore there isn't."

The afternoon wore on, the squirrels predictably plentiful. And there was, of course, absolutely *no* competition among the three of them to see who could shoot the most squirrels.

Right … like every time a bell rings, a moose gets run over by a dump truck.

Maybe it was a testosterone thing for the men. For Rileigh, she was showing off in front of Mitch, trying to impress him. When she realized that, she was embarrassed, like some sophomore in high school. But when she cast sidelong glances at Mitch, she began to wonder if maybe he wasn't doing the same thing. Which would make them two sophomores in high school. She shook her head. They really did need to sort this relationship out. That wasn't going to happen until they could finally have the, *drum roll please*, big date. Which had been put off more times now than she could remember. All for valid reasons. One of them being that she was shot and hospitalized. There were others, too. Unfortunate scheduling conflicts. Mitch had a conference of sheriffs. Mama got an infected ingrown toenail and Rileigh had to haul her back and forth to Knoxville for treatment three times a week.

But next Saturday, they were *on!*

When the sun began its slide down the western sky to hide behind White Mountain, Rileigh decided to call the hunt. They had 21 squirrels now. Mitch had shot four of them. Gus had shot ten of them. Rileigh had bagged seven.

The three headed back through the woods to where they'd parked, wound through the trees until they came to — yup, Hanging Chicken Creek — fast rushing water so clear you could see the minnows darting around in it. Rileigh took a deep breath, thought how good it felt to be here now with Mitch and Gus and not be smack dab in the middle of a crisis. Unfortunately it was smack dab in the middle of that thought that a crisis called out from upstream.

"Yo! Sheriff Webster, been looking for you."

The three of them turned to see an old man with a Santa Claus-sized beard and a rifle in his gnarled hand he carried as naturally as if it were an extension of his arm. His pants were made from deerskin. He wore a vest of some other kind of skin over a ragged camouflage tee shirt. His shoulder-length gray hair stuck out under a for-real, no-kidding coonskin cap.

"That guy looks like a mountain man out of a movie," Mitch whispered.

"Not out of a movie," Rileigh said. "He's the real deal. That's Jeremiah Johnson."

Chapter Three

Cody Whitlock had been mucking out Midnight Angel's stall when he seen Ben Carlisle come running toward him. Ben's eyes were open way too wide and his face was flushed and he was yelling before he even stopped running. That's when Cody first got scared.

"Did you hear what happened to Alex?"

Alex Spaulding had gone missing, and Cody had been dreading this day — when he'd find out what'd happened to him. Whatever it was, it'd put a look of terror on Ben's face.

Cody, Ben, and Alex worked together, farmhands in the barns on Willow Creek Farm, cleaning out stalls and making sure the horses had hay and fresh water and such. The farm employed hundreds of workers — Cody didn't even know how many, let alone their names, but him, Ben, and Alex was friends. It was a good job if you liked horses, and there was nothing that Cody liked more. Never wanted to do anything else with his life but become a trainer, teach them horses how to lift their legs up high, like Tennessee Walking Horses was supposed to. He'd been five years old the first time his daddy set him up on the back of one — Black Mystery. He felt like the king of the world that day, sitting up there so tall, feeling the horse between his legs, all that power and strength in an animal with a soft nose and when you give him a piece of sugar, he'd nuzzle your cheek. Soon's he could save up enough money from odd jobs, he'd got a great big tattoo of a Tennessee Walker on the back of his head. Cost a fortune and hurt like hell, but his only regret was he didn't put it on his chest so he could admire it in the mirror.

It looked like Ben didn't even try to stop running, just smacked right into Cody, damn near knocked him on his ass, kept babbling the whole time.

"What the—?" Cody sputtered, staggering back.

"They found his *body*!" Ben gasped.

"What are you talking about? Whose body?"

"Alex's! He musta died right after he vanished, cause the body was ... you know..."

Cody didn't like imagining that.

"But even so, they could tell he'd been all tore up."

"Tore up?"

"Bones broken — *on purpose*. Like finger bones crushed with a hammer! And worse."

Cody couldn't think what could be worse. But Ben provided plenty of other gruesome details about the condition of Alex's corpse, enough to make Cody want to throw up his breakfast.

Ben's revelation had come to Cody yesterday morning, and he thought about it all that day, hadn't slept last night neither, thinking about it, scared about it. Because he'd been there that day when they come and got Alex. Didn't nobody know Cody was there, but he'd seen the whole thing, how that fella came striding into the barn, that bad fella. Cody was in the back, loading up some hay when he seen this big black car come rolling up to the barn real slow. And that was odd.

What was more odd was the men who got out of it — foreigners. Mexicans, he supposed, with dark skin and black hair. But one of them had a strawberry birthmark on the side of his chin across his jaw, and that there was a *bad man*. Cody knew he was. Cody was like that. He had always been able to see things and understand things other folks couldn't. Important things like whether a man was lying. And Cody could always spot a bad man.

The men who'd arrived in the black car went into the workshop beside the barn. Cody sneaked around so he could see and hear what was going on. He heard what musta been keys on a ring jangling on that fellow with the birthmark as he walked along.

Jangle, jangle, jangle.

And then the man had stopped where Alex was working, said something to him, and Alex put down his tools and went off with that fellow and *never came back.*

Cody had been shocked by what Ben had told him about Alex's body being all tore up, but he couldn't lay claim to being surprised because that was a *bad man* who had took him away. Cody had known the day he went to work for Mr. Griffin Davidson at Willow Creek Farm that *he* was a bad man, too, and it'd be dangerous to work for a bad man. But Cody did so love horses that he took the job anyway. He was always looking over his shoulder, though, always wondering if something bad was going to happen just because of where he was and who he worked for.

And all of that had been even *before* he'd done *the dumb thing.*

Of course wasn't no way to be sure that what happened to Alex had been because of what Cody had seen Alex do the night Cody had been doing the dumb thing. Maybe that didn't have nothing at all to do with Alex getting killed and being all tore up. Probably wasn't no connection at all. By about lunchtime, Cody had talked himself into believing that the two things didn't have nothing to do with each other. Nothing at all.

Just as he was about to take his lunch break, Cody looked up and seen a car coming down the road from the big house. It was the same kind of car, maybe even the same car, that'd come down that day for Alex. Cody dropped down behind a stack of hay, burrowed his way into it, lay there, his heart hammering. He couldn't see out through the hay. But he could *hear.* He heard footsteps coming into the barn. And then he heard the sound of keys.

Jangle. Jangle. Jangle.

Panic exploded in Cody's chest, and he busted out of that pile of hay like a rabbit and raced into the woods. He knew those woods like he knew the back of his hand, and he ran for dear life, more scared than he'd ever been, all the way down to the creek, then upstream to the wildflower meadow and across the meadow into the Burkett's chicken house.

They had a big flock of chickens. And they'd just got in some brand-new ones a couple of days ago. Cody knew that them new chickens, the young ones, wouldn't want to go out of the coop in the daytime, they'd be scared so they'd stay inside till they got used to their environment. So that chicken house would be jammed full of chickens. It was the only place he could think of to hide.

The chickens squawked and fussed and carried on for a bit when he first went inside, but he talked to 'em soft and gentle like.

"Hey chick, chick chick, s'okay chick, chick, chick, whoa there, settle down, chick."

The birds calmed slowly and stopped fluttering around. The dust and feathers they'd stirred up with their outburst settled out of the air back to the floor and it got quiet.

Cody hunkered down in the back, breathing the acrid stench of concentrated chicken shit through his nose. If he breathed through his mouth, it was like he could taste it.

And he waited. After a while, he lost all track of time. It could have been an hour. It could have been three. The whole time, he thought about the dumb thing he'd done that had got his ass in such a sling.

Chapter Four

IT WAS OBVIOUS RILEIGH WASN'T JOKING ABOUT THE MAN who was hopping from one rock to another in the creek, as agile as a mountain goat. As he drew nearer, Mitch noticed that he smelled a little like a mountain goat, too. He wondered if the man was delusional, thought he really was Jeremiah Johnson — and acted out that persona. But maybe it was the other way around. The man really was Jeremiah Johnson — it wasn't that uncommon a name — and built his persona around his name. Mitch would ask Rileigh which it was when he had a chance, because it was clear the two of them knew each other.

"How do, Miss Rileigh. You and Lily doin' a'right?"

"Can't complain. You?"

"I was doin' better 'fore I found the fella in the woods who sent me looking for the sheriff."

The old man fixed Mitch with a stare from eyes as pale blue as a cloudless sky, and the gaze was piercing, questioning, and challenging all at once.

"I take it you're Sheriff Mitch Webster."

"I am. Who sent you looking for me?"

"I ain't got no idea who he is, but he says you'll know. I was out hunting this morning, tracking a coon on the back side of Seminole Ridge." He looked at Rileigh then. "It was down in that hollow under the bluff, couple of miles from where August Spring spits out that little waterfall."

Rileigh nodded, while Gus and Mitch shook their heads.

"The state road's up at the top of that ridge, so maybe…" The old man thought for a moment, then took up his tale where he'd left off.

"When I come upon this man." He paused, seemed reluctant to continue. "He surprised me … I didn't know he was there until he told me to freeze and drop my rifle." He shook his head, mumbled to himself, "If the damned gub-mint would pay for them hearing aids…"

"He got the drop on you, had a gun?" Mitch asked.

"Yeah, but he might as well a'been unarmed 'cause he wasn't in no shape to use it. He was hurt, all tore up. Looked like maybe he'd been in a car wreck or something. He was bleeding pretty bad. But he wouldn't let me help him. He wouldn't let me even bandage him up, though he'd already done a fair job of that his own self."

"So this man was holding you at gunpoint when he told you to go find me?"

"More or less. Like I say, he wasn't in no shape to use it. I told him I was gonna go for help and he lost it, told me not to dial 911 — as if that'd do any good in that hollow — then he begged me to go on about my business and not tell anybody I'd seen him."

"Why didn't he want you to go for help?"

"He was on the run, said if they found him, they'd kill him."

"They who?"

"He wouldn't say. Just" — the old man spit in the creek — "the gubmint. I'm just telling you what he said. Then he asked me to come get you. Not to tell nobody else. That you would help him."

"Me?"

"Yep. He said as soon as you found out who he was, you'd help him."

Mitch was thoroughly confused at this point. "Well, who is he?"

""'Parently, he didn't want to give his name, 'cause he wouldn't say."

"He said I'd help him as soon as I found out who he was, and then he wouldn't tell you his name?"

"He told me that you'd know. Then he told me what to say to you so you'd understand and help."

Mitch looked at Rileigh and Gus, then shrugged. He very much didn't like riddles.

"Okay, lay it on me."

"He said to tell you…" The old man paused then, recalling so he'd get the words exactly right. "…that when you met him, you didn't have to unzip your pants."

Mitch made a little involuntary choking sound. Rileigh looked shocked. Gus grinned.

"What? That when he met me, I — *what?*"

"That's what he said. I'm sure of it. He made me repeat it — when you met him, you didn't have to unzip your pants."

Mitch shook his head. Who in the world did he meet … and then he remembered.

~

THE TALL, *blond man standing in Mitch's office wasn't exactly patronizing, but he was very damn close to it.*

"I value your input," the man said.

"Is that code for we could use your help in crowd control?" Mitch shot back at him. "Because if it is, that's bullshit. It'll take your whole crew half a day's work to find out what I already know. That's a waste of resources. And if you think the locals in a little East Tennessee mountain town are going to open up to a bunch of suit-and-tie strangers, you best get used to disappointment. "

The man looked at Mitch with a new respect. "Look, Sheriff Webster, I'm not interested in getting into a pissing match with you over jurisdiction. "

"I'm fine with the pecking order. You're running the show and my deputies, and I will do whatever you think's necessary. But if you try to sideline us in parking lot duty when we're the most valuable resource you've got right now, then yeah, I'll start unzipping my pants."

~

"DEVEREAUX," Mitch said, shaking his head.

"Who's Devereaux?" Gus asked.

"Senior Special Agent Lamar Devereaux, out of the Nashville FBI field office."

"That smug agent?" Rileigh asked.

"He wasn't so bad once you got used to his style. He was the consummate FBI agent, cared about only one thing — finding those missing children. And he would have run through brick walls and parked cars to do it."

"Are you talking about the FBI agent who worked with you when that little girl — Chloe Morgan, wasn't it? — and Mason Stump were kidnapped?" Gus asked.

Mitch nodded.

It had been a strange case. A little girl disappeared from a school carnival — where every adult and child was local, from Yarmouth County. A couple of days after that, the youngest son of Rileigh's best friend, Georgia Stump, disappeared from Walmart. Mitch had called the FBI, and Agent Devereaux had arrived by helicopter in less than half an hour — and took over the investigation.

Mitch had only worked with the agent for a couple of days — but he could tell when the agent asked him "tell me everything you've done so far" that his response had pleased him, that the FBI agent believed Mitch had done a thorough job in the critical early hours after the children went missing.

Then the kids were found, the case was over, the FBI left, and Mitch hadn't heard from the man since … until now.

"I want to hear way more about how you came to tell an FBI agent that you … well, to consult him about unzipping—" Gus began.

"It's simple. I—"

"But not right now." Gus turned to the old man, Jeremiah Johnson. "You said this man was hurt — bleeding, is that right?"

Johnson nodded. "He might have had a broke arm, maybe leg, too. It was hard to tell."

"Did he have an open wound you could see?"

"No, he was cut up and scratched up like, but his shirt was all bloody and he was missing a sock. I 'spect he used it to stop the bleeding, but I couldn't see where."

"We need to get to this guy now!" Gus said, then headed through the trees in the direction they'd been traveling to where they'd parked.

Mitch realized he'd never seen Gus as "Dr. Gus Hazelton" with a live patient. Everybody Mitch had taken to him was already dead. "How far is it?"

"It's a right smart piece," Johnson said. Mitch had

26

heard Mama use that phrase and kinda, sorta knew what it meant. "I cut through the woods to find you."

"How'd you know where to look?" Mitch asked as they hurried along.

"Wasn't no cell coverage where I found him, so I went up to the top of Seminole Ridge and called the Sheriff's Department. They said you's off today, gone squirrel hunting with Rileigh Bishop. So I knew where to look."

He went on to say where he'd come out of the woods, the route he'd taken to the spot where he figured they'd parked their cars, described landmarks and turnoffs. Rileigh nodded along, probably knew exactly where he was talking about. Mitch shook his head. He had been totally lost and disoriented for hours, had had no idea where he was.

"And you … just walked into the woods and found us?" Mitch couldn't help asking.

"Well hell, it's not like you folks is hard to track." Johnson pointed to the footprints Mitch had just left in the dirt. "You got a pair of shoes that's got a split place in the heel," he said to Mitch. "And you sure got little bitty feet, Miss Rileigh."

"They always seemed huge to me," she said.

"How about we compare shoe sizes some other time," Gus said impatiently, making a come-on gesture, and they followed the old man into the woods.

When they emerged from the trees at the spot where they parked, Rileigh said she would ride with Jeremiah Johnson, and Gus and Mitch could follow. Gus was in full-on doctor mode now. He ran to his SUV — he'd met Rileigh and Mitch here — opened up the back, rummaged around for a few moments, then pulled out a collapsible stretcher. Why did the county coroner drive around with a stretcher? Mitch would ask when he got the chance. And

he'd explain the "unzipping his pants" thing then, too —
whether Gus asked or not.

Rileigh fired a glance up at the mountaintop as she ran
to Jeremiah's dilapidated pickup truck, and he knew she
was calculating how long it was until "sunset." It would be
nightfall soon. Could even Jeremiah Johnson find Agent
Devereaux in the woods in the dark?

Chapter Five

As they bumped along the steep mountain roads together, Rileigh asked Jeremiah how far it was from the road to where Devereaux was holed up in the rocks. He answered in typical mountain fashion, telling her time rather than distance because it really didn't matter how far point A was from point B in the mountains. The only thing that mattered was how long it took you to get from point A to point B. And even though the distance between them was a constant, if point A was at the bottom of the mountain and point B was at the top, then the time to get there was considerably more than if you were going the other way.

"Least an hour to get there," he said. "Pro'lly more'n that."

It hadn't taken him that long to come down, but down was down and up was up. And Rileigh calculated that it would take considerably longer than that to bring the injured man down the mountainside on Gus's collapsible stretcher.

There had been no discussion at all about calling in the

troops. She could tell by the look on Mitch's face that he was considering it, considering whether he ought to call the rescue squad and an ambulance, whether Lamar Devereaux liked it or not. She wasn't sure exactly why he decided to abide by Devereaux's wishes. She would ask him about that when she got the chance. But if she had to guess, she'd say he was extending to Devereaux the same respect and confidence that Devereaux had displayed in dispatching Jeremiah Johnson to Mitch.

Rileigh was sure there was an active discussion going on in the car behind that carried Mitch and Gus along the winding mountain roads, the two batting around ideas about what could possibly have happened to Agent Devereaux that he had ended up injured, hiding in the rocks on the mountainside, and pleading with Mitch not to tell anybody he was there.

"So he said that he wanted you to just go on about your business and leave him there, injured like that?" Rileigh asked.

"That's what he said. Just go on and pretend like you never found me."

"And he said, 'if they find me, they'll kill me.' Right?"

"That's two for two, Miss Rileigh. And if you ask me, he had every right to be scared shitless."

"How do you figure that?"

"I s'pect you don't know the dark things that's going on in the guts of the government of this country," Jeremiah said.

Rileigh remembered then Mama talking about how the old man was a conspiracy theorist and paranoid and anti-government to the point that he had gone off the grid, as they say. He didn't really exist in any official capacity, or so Mama claimed. He didn't use his Social Security number and he had set up his veteran's benefit check to come to his beneficiary, a mythical son, Jeremiah Johnson, Jr., who had set up the bank account into which the money was electronically transferred every month. She didn't know whether or not Jeremiah paid taxes. She would think he'd have to pay taxes on his pension money, that the government would know that somebody got it and somebody needed to be taxed for it. But she didn't know, and it was none of her business. Jeremiah was a smart man who had lots of very smart friends who believed the similar kinds of conspiracy theories that he did. And she was sure that if that's what he wanted, he could vanish off the books of civilization and just not exist.

When Jeremiah had come out of the woods after he found Devereaux, he'd caught a ride back to where he'd parked his truck, and now he pulled off the road and parked in that spot.

Mitch carried a high-powered flashlight in the glove box of his car and Jeremiah had a kerosene lantern in the back of his truck. They grabbed both and they hurried through the woods as darkness settled around them in the trees ... silently, almost magically, small puddles of shadow reaching out fingers of darkness to join hands with other small puddles.

As the darkness thickened beneath the trees, Jeremiah led the group with his lantern. He never faltered, apparently knew exactly where he was going. He had explained to Rileigh as they drove to the spot that there was a creek at the bottom of the hillside where he had found Devereaux in the rocks. The creek, of course, led downhill, merged with a larger creek, and then came out beside the county road at the bottom of Black Rock Mountain where they parked.

The rescue party retraced that route, followed the creek that ran along beside the road up the mountain to a spot where a smaller creek poured into it, then they climbed the hill where that creek came down. It was slow going in the dark. But Jeremiah never once hesitated as if he didn't know which way to go, never backtracked or found his way blocked. The lantern light shone out into the dark woods, casting harsh shadows that danced and contorted as if they were living things.

They could have been walking for one hour or three, Rileigh wasn't sure, when Jeremiah turned off the creek bank they had been following and started up the hillside. He got about halfway up and stopped. He lifted his lantern up, not so he could see better, she realized, but so that he would be illuminated.

Then he called out in a loud voice, "I'm the fella who found you. The man you sent to go get Sheriff Webster. Well, I done what you asked and I brung him. He's right here with me. I'm hollering 'cause I don't want you to shoot us."

There was no response of any kind from anywhere and Jeremiah simply moved on up the hillside. Eventually, his lantern lit up a pile of rocks. He slowed, then turned and held up his hand to the others to stay where they were. He went on by himself another fifty feet or so and looked down at the rocks he was standing next to. Then he got down on one knee, turned, and motioned for the others to come.

Rileigh and Mitch and Gus hurried up the hillside with Gus in the lead. Reaching Agent Devereaux, Gus knelt beside him and placed two fingers on his neck, feeling for the carotid artery.

"His pulse is weak and thready," he said without turning around. Then Gus slapped him gently on the cheek. "Hello. Can you hear me?"

The man was unresponsive.

Gus asked Jeremiah for the lantern and held it up close so he could examine the man in its light. He was indeed "all tore up," scratched up and banged up, a large gash on his head with dried blood on his face and beneath his nose. He cradled his left arm in his lap. In his right hand was a pistol. When Gus took it out of his hand, the man's eyes popped open and he jumped, pulled back, his eyes wide in the glaring light.

"It's okay, Agent Devereaux. It's all right."

"Who are you?" he asked Gus.

"My name is Dr. Gus Hazelton, and I have come with Sheriff Webster." Gus looked over his shoulder and nodded. Mitch came and knelt down beside him in the lantern light so Devereaux could see.

"Hello there, Agent Devereaux," Mitch said. "I understand you want to talk to me. What happened to you?"

The FBI agent looked confused by the question and then obviously remembered something and sat more upright, tried to straighten up on the rock.

"Don't move," Gus said, "or you're going to start everything bleeding again."

"What happened to you?" Mitch asked again, but Devereaux only looked around with wild eyes.

"You didn't tell anybody, did you?" he demanded. "Where's my gun? What'd you do with it?"

"It's all right. We're here to help."

He looked at Johnson. "I told you not to tell anybody — just the sheriff. They'll kill me."

"Who will kill you?" Mitch asked. "Who are you talking about?"

"If they know I'm still alive, they'll come after me." He reached out a hand with dried blood on it and grabbed Mitch's arm. "You won't say anything, will you? Promise me you won't."

Mitch looked into the man's eyes. "I won't tell anybody."

The man relaxed back against the rock when Mitch said that and closed his eyes.

"Now, tell us what happened to you."

The man didn't open his eyes.

"Agent Devereaux? Lamar?"

"He's out again," Gus said.

Rising from where he had squatted down beside the man, Gus began to unfold his portable stretcher. "We need to get him out of here. I'm not going to touch those bandages or I'll start the bleeding. Let's get him down the mountainside where I can see how bad this is. We might have to call an ambulance, whether he likes it or not."

Chapter Six

It was the stupidest thing Cody Whitlock ever did in his whole life, and he knew it was stupid at the time, and he did it anyway, which he supposed made it double stupid. Or stupid squared.

But when Annalise Henderson looked at him the way she could look at him, with her chin tilted down, looking up through her eyelashes, Cody just melted in a puddle. He'd do anything that girl wanted him to do. And she had promised to do all kinds of things to him — wondrous *sex* things — if he would grant just one itty bitty favor. She wanted to see one of Willow Creek Farm's famous Tennessee Walking horses up close. She wanted to *touch* one.

Cody had held out long as he could, but after the night in the backseat of her car where she gave him a *sample* of what she would do for him, he finally gave in, sneaked her onto the property one evening, into the back side of the barn, and finally into the stall of one of the horses.

Of course, that girl couldn't tell the difference between one horse and another. She didn't know that he took her to the barn of the horses that didn't make the cut, the losers Mr. D was getting ready to sell. He kept the champion horses under lock and key on the other side of the corral from where he took Annalise to pet Doggy Dancer. That girl had fallen all over that horse, fed him an apple and some sugar cubes while Cody stood at the gate, watching.

Suddenly, he saw two men walking down the pathway from the big house to the barn.

"Get down on the floor," he told her.

"No! There's horse shit down there."

He grabbed her by the arm and yanked her down, pointed toward the two men. Nobody ever came to the barns at night. But the one night he picks to sneak Annalise into the barn, here comes somebody from the big house.

He and Annalise watched through the slats of the corral as Cody realized in horror that one of the men was Mr. D. himself. Him and another fellow went into the barn. They left the big bay doors open and there was a light high up in the ceiling in the center of the barn. Mr. D brought out the horse that'd just arrived that afternoon from his other horse farm in Europe somewhere, Belgium, maybe. Him and that man were bending over, looking at the horse's right front hoof when Alex came around from the other side of the barn and froze just outside the spill of light coming out that door. Cody didn't know what in the world Alex was doing there at night. Probably something as dumb as what he was doing. All he knew was that Alex only stood there for a second. Maybe Mr. D seen him, maybe he didn't. Cody didn't know 'cause Alex turned instantly and bolted, run for all he was worth around the corral, right past where Cody and Annalise lay. Cody didn't know if Alex had spotted them or not, but he grabbed Annalise's hand and made her crawl through the horseshit on the floor all the way out of the barn and through the tall grass halfway to the woods. She was furious at him but waited until they got to the trees to unload. She only got a few words into her tirade when all hell broke loose in the barns behind them — like a bomb had gone off! Lights came on and yelling men ran around. Then they heard gunfire and that scared the holy hell outta both of them and they ran all the way back to his car. Annalise wouldn't speak to him after that, and Cody had assumed that Alex had got away, that nobody'd seen him, or nobody knew who he was if they did see him. He'd assumed that until the day the bad man came jangling his keys in his pocket and left with Alex.

A chicken by the door fluttered up and squawked. Cody stopped breathing.

At first, he thought he was imagining it. But he wasn't.

Jangle. Jangle. Jangle.

He heard them keys on that bad man as he come walking up to that chicken house. And Cody had never been so scared.

He'd never understood how that fella got away with taking Alex out of the barn in broad daylight and nobody said nothing. He supposed it was just 'cause Alex went quietly. Cody did *not* go quietly. He kicked and hollered and screamed when them men dragged him out of that chicken coop. The Burketts wasn't home. He was making such a racket, some of the other neighbors ought to have heard, though, but they didn't. Then one of the men hit him over the head. And when he woke up, he opened his eyes to a world he didn't recognize. A barn somewhere. A warehouse maybe.

The man with the keys in his pocket and the strawberry birthmark on his cheek got right down in Cody's face. His breath smelled like cigarettes and rotted teeth, and he said, "Pablito wants his bubbles back."

"I don't know anybody named Pablito," Cody said. "And … I ain't got nobody's … what are bubbles?"

"That's what Señor Davidson calls them." The man's accent was thick. "And you know what bubbles are, *hijo*. You saw where he hid them and when nobody was around you went back and stole them. They belong to *mi jefe* and he wants them back."

"I swear to God," Cody sputtered. "I swear on the soul of my mother and my grandmother and my sister, I swear I didn't take nothing from Mr. D. I didn't see him hidin' nothing. I don't know what bubbles are."

But that fellow with the birthmark didn't believe Cody, thought he was lying. And it wasn't long before Cody found out why Alex's body had been so tore up when they found it. The bad men had been asking Alex about them bubbles and if he didn't tell them what they wanted to know, they hurt him. Just like they was hurting Cody.

He screamed and pleaded, told them everything he did know, told them about Alex and Annalise and petting Doggy Dancer and the apple and the sugar cube, but he couldn't tell them about the bubbles they were looking for because he didn't know.

When the world finally did go black, Cody was in such agony, he was grateful. The fellow put the pistol to Cody's forehead, and he had time to think that he wished he could ride a horse just one more—

Chapter Seven

RILEIGH LED THE LITTLE CARAVAN CARRYING FBI SPECIAL
Agent Lamar Devereaux on a stretcher down the mountainside. It was slow going. She held the lantern high so she
could light the path in front of her and in front of Mitch,
who was carrying the front end of the stretcher where
Devereaux lay. Gus was carrying the other end and Jeremiah Johnson was behind him with Mitch's flashlight,
shining it on their feet so they wouldn't stumble.

As they hauled Devereaux down the mountainside to
the creek bank and then followed the creek downhill, the
three men switched off where they were carrying, rotated
— Gus would take the front, which was heavier, with
Mitch at the back and Johnson behind him for maybe a
hundred yards and then they'd swap out, with Mitch at the
heavy end, Johnson at the lighter end, and Gus behind
carrying the flashlight. Mitch lost his footing on the mossy
rocks once, fell hard on his knee, but managed not to drop
his end of the stretcher. Jeremiah was by far the most sure-
footed of the bunch, but he was also wearing handmade
moccasins. Rileigh knew that being able to feel the ground

beneath his feet was part of what enabled him to move quietly through the trees and to keep his footing. Gus was wearing street shoes, and Mitch and Rileigh were wearing running shoes, which gave them good support, but they certainly couldn't feel the ground through them.

Again, Rileigh lost track of time. She was exhausted. They had spent the whole day walking through the woods hunting, and then the evening trekking up the mountainside and now back down it. But she knew she wasn't nearly as tired as Mitch and Gus and Jeremiah must be, hauling that heavy man between them. Jeremiah was the only one among them who never looked tired at all. Spend five minutes in his presence and you forgot how old he was. It's not that he was full of energy like a teenager, but he exuded a strength and stamina that was remarkable. He carried his full load when it was his turn at the stretcher just like the two men who were at least 30 years his junior.

When they finally got back down to the road, they laid the stretcher in the bed of Jeremiah's pickup truck, and Gus climbed up beside him with the lantern, checking to make sure the movement hadn't started any of his injuries bleeding again. But Devereaux appeared stable. They had agreed to take him to Gus's office, and though it was a long way on the road, as the crow flies it wasn't terribly far — measuring distance in time, not feet and inches. Jeremiah trekked up logging roads and down shallow creek beds to get to Gus's office faster.

Once there, they hauled Agent Devereaux into Gus's examination room and laid him on the table where he laid out dead bodies to perform autopsies. Only then, when he had bandages and instruments handy, was Gus willing to start removing the agent's clothing and bandages.

Rileigh and Mitch remained with Gus after they brought the agent in, but as soon as he was sure he had done all that he could, Jeremiah Johnson gathered up his lantern and took his leave. Gus had three or four other vehicles on the property Rileigh and Mitch could use to get back to where they'd parked this morning, a lifetime ago.

"I'll be going on home now," Jeremiah said.

"Jeremiah, do you realize that you just saved that man's life?" Rileigh said.

She might as well have touched him with a hot poker. He almost physically leapt back.

"Don't you be saying a thing like that. You save a man's life, and you wind up becoming responsible for him. And I don't want to be responsible for nobody on God's green earth except Jeremiah Johnson."

"Alrighty then," Rileigh said. "How about — Agent Devereaux would have been just fine if he'd never laid eyes on you. He'd have gotten up when he woke from his nap and walked out of the woods under his own steam, probably would have signed up to run the Boston Marathon the next day."

Jeremiah smiled at her. "You tell Miss Lily I said hello."

And there was something about the way he said it. The pause. Rileigh thought she saw it then — an explanation for the old man's sudden appearances on their porch every now and then with a brace of rabbits, a fat wild turkey, or a string of fish. Rileigh caught something in his attitude or his words or his body language, telling her that Jeremiah Johnson had ... how would you put it about a man in his 70s? She certainly wouldn't say Jeremiah had the hots for her mother — something more gentle ... he had a crush on her. And that was just fine with Rileigh. Jeremiah Johnson was a good man. And that was a hell of a lot more than you could say for J.R. Bishop, who had been married to her mother for more than twenty years. Rileigh's father was a monster in a human being suit.

After Jeremiah drove away, Rileigh went back into the examination room where Gus was caring for the injured FBI agent. He had cut away the man's left pants leg up to the knee.

"Jeremiah thought his left arm might be broken because it's hanging at an odd angle," Gus said. "It's not broken, but the shoulder's dislocated and I'm going to have to pop it back in place. Jeremiah *might* be right about the broken leg, though." Gus pointed to the swollen, discolored leg below the FBI agent's left knee. "The bones aren't displaced and I'm hoping the bone's just cracked. There's no way to way to tell for sure without an X-ray, so I'm going to splint it as a break. But those aren't the most urgent needs right now."

Gus picked up the scissors then and began to cut away the piece of fabric that was wrapped around his chest. It had been soaked in blood, dry now, and was just what Rileigh had first thought it might be — the arm torn off a long-sleeved shirt. Then he cut away the T-shirt Devereaux was wearing. "I need to find the source of the bleeding." He gently pulled the fabric of Devereaux's shirt off where it was stuck to his skin by dried blood. A wadded-up sock was shoved tight up against his upper right chest, held there by his shirt and the shirt-sleeve bandage. When Gus peeled the sock away, the blood began to flow again. And he looked up at Mitch in surprise.

"This is a bullet wound," he said.

That was definitely a conversation stopper.

Gus gently turned the man over and sighed with relief when he saw a matching hole, smaller, in his back — an *exit* wound. Absent the exit wound, Gus would have had to go digging around to find the bullet — which he absolutely would not have done. If there had been a bullet lodged in Devereaux's body, Gus would have called an ambulance, whether Mitch and the agent liked it or not. As it was… they could take him to an emergency room where they'd bandage the wound — but Gus could do the same thing.

Gus stitched up a nasty cut on the man's forehead and another gash on his left upper arm. He also pulled his dislocated left arm back into the shoulder socket. All of that would have been terribly painful if the FBI agent had been conscious. Gratefully, he was not.

It was at least two hours before Gus was finally finished. He stood up and straightened his back, and Rileigh realized that he hadn't been aware of a moment's time passing. The FBI agent who lay on the examining table was clean, had been washed, his wounds bandaged, and Gus had started an IV with fluids laced with antibiotics to prevent infection.

Rubbing his stiff neck and shoulders, Gus looked at Mitch and Rileigh, who had been at his beck and call, cutting off pieces of clothing, handing him instruments, getting him bandages.

"You guys missed your calling," he told Rileigh. "You should have been an OR nurse."

"Oh, I don't think so," Rileigh said.

"You didn't pass out."

"I've seen way more blood than this." Her mind flitted briefly to gory battlefield injuries, then closed the door on the images. "It just isn't my favorite substance in the world. Blood and I are not on good terms."

"We can move him now to the guest room," Gus said.

"A guest room in your office?" Mitch asked. "For corpses too drunk to drive home?"

"Guest room sounds more user-friendly than what it really is — a storage room with a bed in it. Nothing fancy, but I call it home — when I have to work late."

The room was, indeed, nothing fancy. Storage boxes,

filing cabinets, and miscellaneous flotsam and jetsam was pushed up against one wall. Against the other was a single bed, a bedside table with a lamp, and two straight-back chairs. The bed was made, with a hand-made quilt bedspread spread over neatly tucked sheets.

Mitch and Gus eased Devereaux onto a rolling gurney and pushed it down the hallway to the guest room, then transferred him to the bed. His pistol had been lying beside him when they found him, and Mitch had stuck it in his belt. He took it out now and put it in the top drawer of the small chest in the "guest room."

Rileigh appeared at the doorway. "I just made a big pot of coffee. How about you sit down, Gus, and I'll bring you a cup."

"Sitting definitely sounds like a plan."

After they filled up coffee cups in the little kitchenette, Gus led the way to his office, opened the door, and immediately closed it back. Rileigh got a brief view of the chairs in the room piled high with … whatever. Instead, they filed into the waiting room — under the watchful eye of a life-sized white rhinoceros, keeping the door open to the guest room down the hall in case agent Devereaux came around.

"That damn bullet certainly puts a fly in the butter-milk," Gus said as he eased himself down into a comfort-able chair and allowed his muscles to relax with a sigh. Rileigh and Mitch nodded. It was state law in Tennessee that every doctor had to report to the authorities any bullet wound he was called on to treat.

Gus's face suddenly brightened.

"Sheriff Webster, sir," he said to Mitch. "Please consider this my official report: I treated a bullet wound tonight." He relaxed back into his chair. "There. I've reported it, met the letter if not the spirit of the law."

The three were silent, sipping coffee.

"You realize what we just did, don't you?" Rileigh said. "We just allowed ourselves to be dragged into somebody else's drama."

"Like that's something new," Gus said.

Mitch sighed. "And that's the least of our problems."

"The *least* of our problems?" Rileigh asked.

Mitch gave her a "well, duh" look and wrinkled his nose. "We've got a sack of long-dead squirrels to clean."

Chapter Eight

As Rileigh, Mitch, and Gus sat exhausted next to the white rhino in Gus's waiting room, Rileigh refused to allow herself to look at her watch. She didn't want to know how long they'd been out scrambling up the side of the mountain to find the FBI agent and then scrambling down again to get him to Gus's office.

Gus guzzled two cups of the coffee Rileigh had made before pointing out that she had either a) put twice the amount of coffee into the little bowl thing as was required or b) put in only half the amount of water. Either way, the result was road tar.

Rileigh shrugged. "Making coffee isn't one of my primary life skills. Mama won't let me touch the coffee pot."

"Which explains why Lily Bishop is still alive."

"I noticed you didn't have any trouble swallowing it."

"A parched man will drink anything — up to and including rhino piss. Please don't ask me to explain how I know that."

All three of them fell silent then, too tired to launch barbs at each other.

"So, who wants to hazard the first guess about how Agent Devereaux got that hole in his chest and why he doesn't want you to tell his superiors in the FBI that you found him?" Gus finally said

"Well, when you hitch up those two facts, one behind the other, it kinda, sorta gives the answer — the people he's afraid are going to kill him are the ones who tried and failed the first time."

"The FBI," Rileigh said.

"So, why did Agent Devereaux come looking for *you* in his hour of need?" Gus asked Mitch. "I didn't know you guys were blood brothers."

"Actually, we were conjoined twins separated at birth." Mitch paused and shrugged. "I don't have any idea."

"I do," Rileigh said.

"Lay it on me, baby."

"I'm not trying to say Agent Devereaux was harboring a, whatever they call it — a bromance, that he had a man-crush, or anything like that on you," she said. "Just that I did notice Agent Devereaux held you in very high esteem."

"And you noticed that how?"

"Do you ever watch anybody's body language?"

"Well, yeah. Sure I do … sometimes."

"Meaning 'No, I don't, because most of the time I'm too busy busting heads.'"

"So you were watching his body language. And you could tell by that that he admired me?"

Lifting his head from the back of the couch where he had been resting it, Gus said, "The whole body language thing's woo-woo."

"It's *not* woo-woo. You can't possibly believe that, Gus."

"Just pulling your chain," he said. "I got your back on that score."

Then Gus did what he so often did, and it amazed, surprised, impressed, and intimidated Rileigh every time. Of course, she understood that the man was brilliant, on a scale far above even the mortals who'd scored 1600 on their SAT tests. He had a handful of degrees. She told him once that he could play Scrabble with all the letters he had dangling off the end of his name. But it was at times like these, when he provided a peek at that didactic memory of his, that she had trouble for a while afterward treating him as a normal person.

Gus proceeded to spout information about body language that sounded like he was reading off a Wikipedia page, looking as much like a savant as Buddy Henderson had the day he told Rileigh the make, model, and year of every vehicle that'd been parked in the elementary school parking lot during the festival.

"Body language is a type of communication in which physical behaviors, as opposed to words, are used to express information — facial expressions, body posture, gestures, eye movement, touch and the way a body takes up space," he droned. "Nodding the head in conversation may be a sign of approval, whereas a single nod acknowledges respect, similar to the Asian practice of bowing."

"So Agent Devereaux nodded his head once at me and you interpreted that as a ceremonial bow," Mitch teased.

"Stop it," Rileigh said, cocking her head to the side and giving him a look. "You know what I mean." She turned to Gus. "You do, don't you, Gus?"

"I'd know if you kept your head still. In India, a head bobble, tilting the head from side to side, is a totally ambiguous movement, whose interpretation is context dependent."

"Both of you stop it. I had a slumber party once when I was eight years old and we stayed up all night. About four o'clock in the morning, we all started giggling and couldn't stop. Mama said we had 'the simples.' Is that it? You guys are so tired you're loopy?"

"Yeah, the simples is a good term for it." Gus straightened up on the couch and grew serious, talked a little about how to read body language, how reliable it was, how it was used effectively in everything from psychotherapy to police investigations.

"So from his body language, you could tell Agent Devereaux respected me, and you think that's why he came to me?"

"I think it's more than that," Gus said. "I think he came to you for help because you are not associated with the FBI in any way."

"There must be other people in his life who aren't."

"True, but relationships are webs," Gus said. "You can trace a person along the strands of his relationships, one to another. And there's a break in the transmission line between you and Agent Devereaux. You don't know any of the same people. Nobody in his world knows he has any connection to you. He worked with you for two days on a case months ago. I think he came to you because he trusted you, believed you were a straight-up guy, but mostly because he couldn't be traced here. He needed a place to hide, and he thought you'd give him one."

"Right," Rileigh said, her voice tired. "Which brings us full circle to: who was he hiding from, and why was he hiding at all?"

All of them fell silent, considering. The silence drew out. Rileigh relaxed back into her seat, Mitch and Gus into theirs. They might all three have nodded off into an exhausted doze if Mitch hadn't tossed a hand grenade out into the midst of them.

"In other news," he said, "I got the results back from that DNA test."

They didn't have to ask which DNA test. They knew.

Right after she got out of the hospital for a bullet wound of her own, Rileigh had received an anonymous mailing envelope. Inside, wrapped in a newspaper, were the two bones of a human thumb. On the newspaper in which it was wrapped, someone had circled a small story in red magic marker. It was about a man who had been murdered, his body dumped into Lake Michigan, and when they fished it out, he was missing the thumb on his right hand. Mitch had sent the bones in the envelope to have them analyzed.

"You had the DNA results and you didn't say anything all day? Why?"

"Because we went squirrel hunting and I didn't want to spoil it with a downer." He looked around and sighed. "We're definitely not having a good time now, so there's nothing to spoil."

Mitch pulled a crumpled piece of paper from his pocket and began to read from it.

"The thumb bones are those of one Mr. James Spencer Mason, aka Trey Mason, Fats Mason, and FatBoy, 36 years old, 1282 112th Street, Chicago, with a jacket as thick as a large-print Bible and sealed juvie records dating back to 1985 — when he'd have been nine years old."

"Career criminal," Gus said. Mitch nodded.

"So given the guy's record and his line of work, what does a bullet to the back of his head and the body dumped in Lake Michigan sound like to you?" Mitch asked, a rhetorical question.

"A hit," Rileigh said simply.

"And the only person who could have removed the bones from the murder-*ee* would be the murder-*er*," Gus said.

"So a hit man somewhere in Chicago kills a slimy criminal, cuts the guy's thumb off, and sends it to me. How did I get on some hit man's Christmas card list?" She stopped as an awful thought struck her. "You don't suppose the little finger bone that came last month was … did somebody commit a murder and then send me the victim's little finger?"

"Well, whoever the person is who's no longer in possession of their little finger bone might very well still be alive," Mitch said. "Or not. Either way, the person is/was not a known criminal, has never been in the military or entered into the national database for any number of other reasons." They'd checked the DNA registries.

"So where does that leave us?" Rileigh asked.

"Nowhere." Gus sighed. "I hate to break up this party when we're all having so much fun, but I need to set up a cot in there." He motioned toward the guest room. "So I can keep an eye on him." He stood. "Take my jeep — keys are on the peg by the back door — and we can sort the cars out tomorrow."

"Works for me," Rileigh said, rising.

"But we're not finished," Mitch said.

"Finished what?"

"Squirrels," he said. "We've got dead squirrels to clean."

"Never saw anybody so damned concerned about dead rodents," Gus said.

"They'll keep until tomorrow," Rileigh said. "Unless you're volunteering to clean them all by yourself right now."

"I couldn't get the skins off those little critters if they had zippers."

Chapter Nine

RILEIGH AND MITCH ARRIVED AT GUS'S OFFICE EARLY THE next morning to return his jeep and to find out what was going on with the man they had rescued off the mountain the night before.

Passing through the waiting room, Rileigh said, "'Mornin', Beulah." She had decided to give the life-sized white rhino on the wall a name. No reason. In some strange and probably psychotic way, she had grown attached to the creature. After all, they'd spent hours in its presence last night. It had kept an eye on their discussions about everything from the FBI agent's condition to U.S. Postal Service-delivered thumb bones.

"Beulah?" Mitch asked.

"She looks like a Beulah, don't you think?"

"That's a singularly ugly name."

"What? You think she looks like a Debbie? Christi maybe? Susie the rhino?"

"Hermione would work. So would Agatha. But how do you know she's not a he?"

Good question.

"Beulah if it's a she rhino, Cornelius if it's a he."

They found Gus in the mini-kitchen of his office making breakfast — scrambled eggs and bacon.

"How's Devereaux?" Mitch asked.

"He had a good night, all things considered," Gus said. "I kept him pretty knocked out, so he could get some rest — and so could I." Gus reached up and felt the whiskers on his chin. "Actually, I only woke up about half an hour ago. I need a shower and a shave. You guys want breakfast?"

"Are you fixing all that for you, or Devereaux?" Rileigh asked. He was scrambling a black iron skillet full of eggs. What looked like a pound of bacon lay draining on a paper towel on the countertop.

"Both," Gus said. "Well, mostly for me. He's not likely to come around enough to be hungry until the pain medication I gave him wears off."

Mama often commented that "Gus eats like a field hand."

"Did he wake up at all during the night?" Mitch asked. "Did he say anything?"

"Nothing coherent, mumbled about how somebody was going to kill him, and then about hot-wiring a car."

"Hot-wiring a car?" Rileigh said. "I didn't even know you could do that anymore."

"You can if you find an old enough car," Mitch said.

"Do you think that's what he did? That he hot-wired a car?"

"We haven't given a whole lot of consideration to how he got up onto the side of that mountain," Gus said.

"The state road traverses that ridge, two switchbacks, to the top of the mountain. If he wrecked a car up there, he could have staggered down that far," Rileigh said. "But he could have walked a long way before he made his home in those rocks. The woods there have been logged, so the brush is thick under the trees. The wrecked car he 'allegedly' hot-wired could be anywhere."

Suddenly, Gus cocked his head. Shoving the spatula he was using to scramble the eggs at Rileigh, he hurried out of the room and across the little hallway to the room occupied by Agent Devereaux. Rileigh heard him say, "Well, good morning," as she found a bowl and scraped the eggs into it. Then she went to stand in the doorway of the room where the agent was lying in the bed they'd settled him in last night after Gus had patched him up.

Devereaux was awake, looking around, confused.

"Where am I?" he asked.

"In my office," Gus said. "I'm Dr. Gus Hazelton, the Yarmouth County Coroner. Remember me? I took care of you last night."

"The coroner? *You* took care of me?"

Gus smiled. "Yeah, most of my patients are dead before they get here, but every now and then I get a live one. *You* came close to leaving here with a toe tag yourself. You ready to tell us what happened?"

The FBI agent was still wary and disoriented.

"So I'm in your office? How'd I get here?"

"A man named Jeremiah Johnson found you in the woods yesterday. Do you remember Jeremiah?"

"The guy with the beard. Yeah, I remember him."

"You told him to come get me," Mitch said, stepping forward for the first time, "and not to tell anybody that he'd found you. Just to come get me."

Reality seemed to download into the agent's head then. "Sheriff Webster. He found you." Relief washed over his face and then his eyes clouded again, and he looked around fearfully. "Did he tell anybody else about me? Did you?"

"Nobody knows about you but the people in this room," Mitch said. "And Jeremiah Johnson. Why don't you want anybody to know you're here? We need some answers."

"Who is it that you are afraid of?" Rileigh asked.

Mitch was more direct. "Who shot you?"

"Shot me?"

"Yes, who put that bullet hole in your chest?"

The longer the man was awake, the jumpier he became. "Listen, I need to get out of here." He tried to rise up off of the bed, but Mitch restrained him.

"You're not going anywhere," Mitch said. "Your leg is broken."

"No, you don't understand. They're going to come for me. I've got to get away."

"Who is they and why are they coming?"

"I have to run. They'll…"

He was growing more upset by the second.

"They *who?* Who's after you? Who shot you? Answer that one question — who shot you?"

"I don't know who shot me. What difference does it make which one?"

"You have to tell us who you're running from."

"It was supposed to be a safe house…" He coughed out a strangled laugh. "Safe. Riiight. Nowhere is safe now. I don't know who it is, but they bought somebody, found out where I was. When they find me, they'll kill me. They killed all the others, one after another, left me the last man standing." The agent had gotten more upset and combative as he spoke, his eyes open too wide, wild. He was struggling weakly, trying to get up. "I have to hide."

Gus put a syringe into the joint of the IV tube and injected something into it. The man began to relax immediately. Gus stepped between Mitch and the agent.

"That's enough for now. He's having a reaction to the pain meds. They're making him agitated. I've given him something to calm him. Hopefully he'll be lucid when he wakes up."

The agent had settled back on the bed, his eyes closed. Gus ushered Rileigh and Mitch out of the room. They sat around the small kitchen table, sipping cups of Rileigh's awful coffee while Gus ate the cold breakfast he'd prepared for his patient.

"We know a little more," Rileigh said. "He was in a 'safe house' that wasn't safe."

"He didn't even know who shot him," Gus said between bites. "Said it didn't matter 'which one.' That would seem to imply bullets were flying."

"The mysterious 'they' went after 'all the others' until he's the only one left," Mitch said. "And somebody was 'bought off.'"

"I've been meaning to mention this," Rileigh said. "Remember what Jeremiah said Devereaux said — 'I'm not the bad guy'? What if bad guy doesn't just mean generic dude in the black hat — but a specific bad guy?"

"Yeah, maybe somebody in a case he's working on," Gus said. "Or has worked on."

Mitch looked at Gus. "You know how long that list would be? Every case has a bad guy."

"So where does that leave us?" Rileigh asked.

"When will he come around and make sense?" Mitch asked.

"He should have his marbles mostly gathered up by this afternoon."

"Then we'll come back this afternoon, try again."

"So between now and then, we are … what?" Rileigh said. "Hiding an FBI agent from somebody who wants to kill him? We don't know who the killer is, or why he wants to kill him, and we're *not informing the FBI*. Are we all agreed that that's what we *ought* to be doing?"

"We won't know for sure what we ought to be doing until we can get some answers out of Devereaux," Mitch said.

"So you're okay with us just pretending we never found an FBI agent in the woods who, oh, by the way, had a bullet hole in him?" Rileigh asked. Mitch and Gus exchanged a look.

"For the time being, yes." Mitch got to his feet. To Gus, he said, "Your jeep's parked outside." He fished in his pocket for the keys and set them on the table. "Rileigh's going to take me back to town. Then I suggest she and I do some discreet sniffing around. We both know people in the bureau. Let's shake some trees, see what falls."

"You're not gonna *out* this guy, are you?" Gus said.

Mitch laughed. "The FBI has something like fifteen or sixteen thousand field agents." He looked at Rileigh for confirmation and she nodded. "And they're pretty siloed — the left hand doesn't know what the right hand's doing."

"He said there were 'others,' that 'they' went after the others. There could be 'others' out there somewhere in as much danger as he is," Rileigh said.

"Or not," Gus said. "He said he was the last man standing."

Chapter Ten

"We didn't have this conversation," Mitch said, and the voice on the other end of the line chuckled.

"What conversation? Hell, I haven't talked to Mitch Webster in, what, two, three years maybe?"

Mitch had met Bill at a Nashville Police Department seminar that brought the FBI in to make a presentation, and Bill had been one of the agents there. He hadn't been making the presentation, was still a minion with the FBI, just like at that time Mitch had been a minion with the Nashville PD. But the two had ended up on the same panel discussion, went out for a beer afterward, and ended up inebriated enough to indulge in an If You'll Tell Me Your Story, I'll Tell You Mine session that lasted almost all night. After that, they got together whenever Bill was in Nashville, and kept in touch.

"So what is it you want me to tell you that you don't want anybody else to know you're asking?"

Bill Larson always did cut right to the quick of things.

"I just need to know a couple of things in general terms. Talk to me about safe houses."

"The sheriff of Yarmouth County, Tennessee, is calling the Federal Bureau of Investigation to find out the location of our safe houses?"

"Oh, I don't care *where* they are. I just want to know *what* they are."

"They're just exactly what they sound like. They are safe places."

"Who do you put there?"

"In the broadest terms, anybody that we think might be in potential danger. Specifically, it tends to be witnesses about to testify against somebody with enough clout to hurt them if they wanted to."

"So mostly witnesses?"

"Or anybody else involved in a case that we think might be in particular danger. Where are you going with this, Mitch?"

"This is just a hypothetical," Mitch said. "So what if I knew somebody who'd been put in a safe house and it wasn't safe?"

"Meaning…"

"Meaning the bad guys he was running from found him there."

"If that's not just a hypothetical, we need to renegotiate the terms of this conversation. Because if you know somewhere that a safe house wasn't safe, I need to know about it."

"The honest truth is I do not know of such a safe house. The underlying truth is I believe there *may* be one. And what I want to know from you is how likely that is."

"There's only one way that a safe house would not be safe, and that's if there's a leak somewhere. And I don't want to say that the FBI is leak-proof — we certainly aren't, but usually in the cases where somebody's testifying against some powerful figure, if there's a leak, it's in the administration, it's in the courthouse, it's in the clerk's office, it's in some place where paperwork happens. Or it's a hack if it's electronic, and don't ask me how all that works because I don't know."

"I take it from your concern that unsafe safe houses are rare occurrences."

"They'd better be! If we can't count on a safe house being safe, then, like I said, Mitch, I need to know—"

"I'll make a deal with you. If I find out for certain, I'll call you and let you know. Right now, it's all speculation."

"I hold you to that, Mitch."

"You can count on it."

"We're a little touchy, I guess, about security. A number of agents have … gone missing since last summer. I don't suppose you know about the two whose bodies we *have* found. It was ugly."

"What kind of ugly?"

"Mexican drug cartel ugly."

Mitch cringed.

"One was Agent Hector Gutiérrez. He worked out of the Memphis field office, and he literally vanished in a puff of smoke. Left work and never made it home. They found his body a few days later. Somebody tried to sink it in the Mississippi, but it bobbed up. I'm glad I didn't see it. I'm glad I didn't know the guy, but they said he had been brutalized in the way the cartels use to instill terror. And Agent Sullivan's body was just as bad. "

"Motive? Suspects?"

"Zip and zip. Something like that, you know, it makes us all jumpy."

Mitch sat, drumming his fingers on his desk after he completed the call to Bill Larson, trying to work things out in his head. He had an injured FBI agent who said he'd run from a safe house that wasn't, and Bill Larson said that other FBI agents had vanished and been murdered. Did the two things have anything to do with each other? Mitch had no idea. Truth was, he wasn't going to have any real understanding of what was going on with FBI agent Lamar Devereaux until Devereaux was conscious enough to explain himself.

Mitch thought about getting in touch with a couple of other friends he knew in the bureau and decided against it. He didn't want to kick up dust. Even in a huge agency like the FBI, there were grapevines. He'd promised Devereaux that he would keep silent about finding him in the woods. If he realized he couldn't keep that promise anymore, he'd tell Devereaux before he told anybody else.

"WE DIDN'T HAVE THIS CONVERSATION," Rileigh said to her friend Shelly, who chuckled on the other end of the line.

"You're pregnant, right?"

"*No!* I'm not pregnant. But if I were, why would I be calling you about it?"

"You probably wouldn't. But if you *were* pregnant and you *did* call me, you'd tell me that we didn't have the conversation."

"You're not making sense."

"*I'm* not making sense. *You're* the one who started the conversation telling me we didn't have the conversation."

"Let's start over. Hi, Shelly. I'm not calling to tell you I'm pregnant because I'm not, but I am calling to stick my nose in where it doesn't belong, so maybe we could sweep the dust of the conversation under the rug and pretend we didn't have it."

"That makes a little more sense."

"What I want to talk about isn't really any of my business, but I do have a reason and I can't tell you what it is … so that's another reason we're not having the conversation."

"This conversation we're not having is becoming more complicated than any other conversation I didn't have in a long time."

Shelly had been in Rileigh's unit in Afghanistan on her first tour. She was one hard-ass soldier, determined to prove that she was as good as any of the men in the unit even when nobody doubted her — which most of the time set her at odds with Rileigh, who didn't have anything to prove.

It had come to a head right after a firefight when Shelly had lambasted Rileigh for not being more aggressive. And Rileigh'd had enough of the constant goading and nasty remarks. She turned around and decked Shelly, knocked her flat, then stood over her and told her that if she ever accused Rileigh of not being aggressive enough again, Rileigh would mop up the camp with her sorry ass.

And they were friends after that. Shelly only served one tour and then went to work on her lifelong dream of being an FBI agent. They'd only spoken a couple of times since Shelly had joined the Bureau.

"What are you sticking your nose into that's none of your business?"

"The FBI."

"Yup, that's none of your business, alright."

"I would just like to know how likely it would be that someone in an FBI safe house had not been safe."

"Not very damned often," Shelly spat, but then paused. "Come on Rileigh, shit happens, you know that as well as I do. And right now, we're doing a sight better than the DEA or Homeland — but that's all scuttlebutt. I only know because one of the guys was a friend of mine."

"*Was?* I don't like the past tense of that verb."

"The DEA has lost four agents in the past eight, ten months. And those are just the ones I know about personally."

"Lost as in misplaced?"

"Lost as in vanished."

"Vanished?"

"I swear I'm not exaggerating. One of them literally disappeared out of the stands while he was watching his son in a Little League game. He's the one who was my friend — Blake Hollister. We weren't close, but we knew each other pretty well, we worked together. His is the only body they've found, but they're not holding out any hope for the others, at least as far as I know." She took a breath. "And he'd been tortured."

"Tortured?"

"There's not any other thing that would explain the wounds on that body. Somebody had wanted to send a message, and given that it's the Drug Enforcement Agency, it's not hard to figure out at least a generic who, but what the message was supposed to be, nobody knows."

"Didn't know Baltimore was that dangerous."

"As a matter of fact, Blake's last big assignment was somewhere out in the boonies. Down in your neck of the woods, as I recall, somewhere in Tennessee."

"Do you know where?"

"No, but I can find out if you need to know, and if you're working on something involving missing agents, I also heard that Homeland has lost some. Drug cartels get around."

Rileigh added sarcastically, "It's a good thing our southern border is *secure.*"

"You got *that* right!"

Rileigh sat in silence for a while after she ended the call with Shelly. Three different agencies … but how in the world did any of that have anything to do with Lamar Devereaux?

She couldn't stop thinking about the agent who had been snatched away from his son's Little League game. How was that possible?

Chapter Eleven

MITCH STOOD ON THE LOGGING ROAD, THE HILLSIDE stretched up above him covered in big old trees that cast such shade around them the undergrowth beneath them was sparse. On the other side of the logging road was an incline down to a creek, and that's where the body lay. It had been discarded there like a rag doll, a young man lying on his back, the creek detouring around the contours of his body. Mitch stood on the logging road for a moment longer before he went down, just soaking up the good before he had to look into the face of evil.

Going squirrel hunting with Rileigh and Gus had reinforced Mitch's determination to spend more time in the woods. The beautiful mountains, the place that tourists drove across the country to get to, the great Smoky Mountains, weren't *in* Mitch's backyard, they *were* his backyard.

He took deep breaths of the forest's smell, the damp earth, honeysuckle, wildflowers he couldn't name but he was sure Rileigh could, and heard the sounds of birds crying out to each other in half a dozen different voices. It was so still, not a breath of wind, just the green leaves and the blue sky visible through the lacy pattern of them above. Then he let out the breath he had pulled in and headed down the embankment to the creek.

Deputy Mullins was creekside with a state trooper who had been summoned by the hysterical woman who had found the corpse face up in the creek. The state police had summoned an ambulance, not for the clearly dead young man, but for the woman who had found him and had gotten hysterical. It wasn't surprising given the condition of that body. The woman had found it earlier this morning when she'd come upon it as she tramped up the creek, her ginseng bag attached to her belt, looking for the plant that sold for hundreds and hundreds of dollars. The elusive, wild ginseng that actually seemed to hide from those seeking it out, hunkering down into shady places behind rocks and out of sight. The woman said that this was a new place that she'd never looked before and certainly would never return to again.

Mitch knelt down on one knee beside the body to get a better look at it. It was hard to look into that face, not so much because the face itself had been brutalized. It had been, but Mitch had seen worse. No, it was hard to look into that face because he couldn't do it without imagining the looks that must have been on it when brutal killers had not been satisfied with just murdering him, but had to beat him almost literally to a pulp in the process.

All of the fingers on both of his hands had been crushed, smashed, pulverized. Mitch had never seen anything like it. Like somebody had used a sledgehammer on an anvil.

Mitch thought about Rileigh's hand that her Aunt Daisy had crushed, shattering the bones with just one blow from a sledgehammer, how unbelievably painful that had been. Someone had used a sledgehammer *repeatedly* on this young man's hands, maybe even crushing each finger individually. But it didn't stop there. His knees were crushed, his legs broken, and Mitch could see blood in his crotch area and decided he would let Gus be the one to determine what kind of horror had been inflicted on him there.

Deputy Mullins looked down at the body and then up to the logging road. It wasn't hard to see what had happened.

"Somebody come down that road and parked up there, dragged this poor kid's body out of whatever they were driving, plopped him on the ground and gave him a shove, and he rolled down here until he stopped."

"This isn't a very well-traveled road, is it?" Mitch asked.

Of course, he knew that the vast majority of the small roads that only locals knew about were not well used because there weren't that many people running up and down the mountainsides on them. Rileigh probably knew hundreds just like this one.

"No, sir, I doubt that there's more than a couple of vehicles a month come up or down this road. Whoever it was that dumped that body didn't expect it to be found for a long time, maybe not ever. After scavengers had had at it, it'd be impossible to tell what the killers had done to him. If it hadn't been for that ginseng hunter, that body had been here for no telling how long, you can't even see it from the road."

The EMS had been summoned but hadn't yet arrived to take the body out of the creek and to Gus's office for him to perform an autopsy. As Mitch thought about that, he shook his head. Gus would be examining this dead body in the room next to the live body that he wasn't exactly hiding. It wasn't like he had Anne Frank stashed away to keep her safe from the Nazis. He wasn't *hiding* the FBI agent. He just wasn't disclosing to the world the agent's presence in the little guest room right down the hall.

Gus and Mitch and Rileigh had agreed to meet there later this afternoon to talk to the FBI agent. Gus had assured Mitch that by then the fellow would no longer be adversely reacting to his pain meds and would be rational. And then maybe they would find out the story of how he had ended up in the woods holding a gun on Jeremiah Johnson.

Mitch shook his head as he heard the sound of the siren on the ambulance dying as it turned off the main road at the logging road. He hadn't told Gus or Rileigh about this murder. But he needed to call Gus now to notify him that the body was on the way in case he needed to do anything to prepare to perform the autopsy on it and to ensure that his private guest remained out of sight.

Mitch looked up at the logging road as the reflections of the ambulance's flashing red light danced among the trees and took his cell phone out to call Gus. He'd call Rileigh after that, *not* to invite her to some fancy restaurant so that they could enjoy their long-awaited big date. Nope. They'd had that one *on the calendar* … but it had been put on the back burner. It didn't seem like he and Rileigh could ever catch a break. Just when they thought … He stopped himself before he said, "It was safe to go back in the water," because that had become such a tired phrase between them. But it was true. Just when they thought it was safe to go back in the water, they wound up with an AWOL FBI agent and an unrelated murder at the same time. Of course, that was the nature of law enforcement. Nobody needed you until something bad happened.

Chapter Twelve

MITCH FOLLOWED IN HIS CRUISER BEHIND THE AMBULANCE that was carrying the body of the unidentified murder victim they had found in the creek to Gus for an autopsy. Mitch wasn't looking for the cause of death — the man had a bullet hole in his forehead. What he needed was an ID of the victim and for Gus to tell him what'd happened to him.

It was slow going. They got stuck behind some terrified tourist who was certain that if he went any faster than fifteen miles an hour, he would go flying off one of the cliffs and crash down the side of the mountain.

It didn't do any good that the ambulance had its red lights on, not its siren but the lights, because there was nowhere to pull off to allow it to pass. And even if there had been, the tourist probably would have been too frightened to pull his car over onto the edge of the road.

During the slow ride to Gus's office, Mitch called Rileigh and told her about the murder.

"Holy shit, Batman," Rileigh said. "It never rains, but it pours."

"This one's really ugly."

"Aren't they all?"

"This one is ugly on a much greater scale than most of the bodies we take to Gus."

"I had a talk with my friend in the FBI," Rileigh said.

"I talked to my friend in the FBI too," Mitch said. "Let's compare notes when we get to Gus's."

Mitch disconnected the call and crept along behind the ambulance toward Gus's office, thinking about the odd turn of events that had dumped him personally hip deep in shit. He was at the very least *morally* obligated to inform the FBI that he'd found their agent injured. And he hadn't done that. And Gus had been legally obligated to inform authorities that he had treated the victim of a gunshot. And he'd done exactly that. He'd informed Mitch. Now Mitch knew officially about that gunshot. And still had kept his lip zipped about Agent Devereaux. But Mitch's silence had a limit. He was fast reaching it. He certainly hoped Devereaux had answers and could clear up all the mysteries.

He pulled in beside the ambulance at Gus's office and saw Rileigh's car already there. She'd gotten there faster than he had because his office wasn't terribly far from her house — at least as the crow flies. Even taking the road *around* the mountain was faster than being behind a terrified tourist.

The ambulance crew pulled the gurney out the back of the ambulance with the black body bag on top of it and rolled it into Gus's examining room.

"Haven't seen you in a while," Gus said, looking at Mitch.

"Absence makes the heart grow fonder. Rileigh here?"

Gus raised his eyebrows and cut his eyes toward the

door to the hallway that led to the guest room where Agent Devereaux was resting.

The two EMTs moved the body bag from the gurney to Gus's examining table.

"It's times like right now that I'm glad I'm not a coroner," said one of the EMTs.

"Most days I wouldn't want your jobs either," Gus said.

"Wait till you see *this* guy." And the EMT nodded to the body bag. Then he and the other EMT left, got back into the ambulance and drove away.

"Coast is clear," Gus hollered out. And moments later, Rileigh came into the examining room from the hallway.

"How is he?" Mitch asked.

"He's making sense. And that's certainly an improvement over the last time we saw him. He's still dopey and groggy, but he's up to being examined."

Gus unzipped the bag and revealed the body inside. And Mitch saw Rileigh involuntarily recoil.

"I haven't seen one of these in a long time."

"One of these?" Rileigh asked.

Mitch picked up the young man's smashed hand. "Missing fingernails, crushed fingers. This is Mexican drug cartel work. I've seen it before."

"So what is a Mexican drug cartel doing in Yarmouth County, Tennessee?" Rileigh wondered aloud.

"Killing people, apparently," Gus said. "It would appear to me that somebody wanted to know something that this young man knew, and they would go to any lengths to get him to talk. And apparently, he did."

"Why do you say that?"

Gus indicated the bullet hole in the forehead of the body lying on the table. "They killed him. If he hadn't told them what they wanted to know, they would have tortured him until the torture killed him. They put this guy out of his misery. So either he didn't know what they wanted to know, or he spilled the beans."

"Where did you find the body?"

Mitch told them about the woman looking for ginseng and how the body would not have been found for weeks, months maybe, if she hadn't stumbled upon it.

Gus reached over and zipped the body bag up to the top. "This young man was killed less than twenty-four hours ago." The unspoken message was: it isn't "ripe," no harm in waiting awhile to examine it. "I'm itching to have a heart-to-heart conversation with that FBI agent in my guest room."

"Aren't we all," Mitch said.

Without another word, Gus led the trio down the hallway and knocked on the door of the little room where he had put a bed to sleep in when he had to work late

"Come on in," said a voice from inside — weak, but Devereaux didn't sound deranged, and that was improvement over the last time they spoke.

Chapter Thirteen

THE FBI AGENT WAS SITTING UP IN BED, PROPPED UP ON some pillows, sipping from a straw in a glass of water that he was holding in his one good hand. The shoulder that had been dislocated, Gus had put into a sling, explaining that Devereaux could use his arm and fingers, but it would be painful, and he needed to curtail as much movement as possible because the dislocated shoulder had stretched ligaments and tendons, and it would take time for those to heal. And until they did heal, the shoulder could snap back out of its socket.

Rileigh thought the man looked in some ways worse now than he had when they had brought him into Gus's office, because the bruising and swelling had all spread out.

"Good afternoon," Mitch said as they filed into the room.

"Three against one?" the agent said. "Not fair."

"Hey, I thought we were all on the same side," Mitch said.

"True that." The agent made a gesture with his good

hand holding the cup. "Have a seat. It's not much, but I call it home."

Mitch and Gus and Rileigh pulled up chairs around Devereaux's bed. Mitch opened his mouth to speak but the agent cut him off.

"Thank you, all of you, for what you've done," he said with great sincerity. "You saved my sorry ass. I should be dead. I would be, if not for you. I owe you my life."

"That part's debatable," Mitch said, "but you do owe us one thing — an explanation. Tell us what the hell is going on."

"I'll do the best I can." The man let out a sigh and carefully set the glass of water down on the table beside the bed. "Ask me whatever you want to know."

"Who shot you?" Mitch asked.

"That part doesn't matter. Bullets were flying everywhere, and that's starting the story in the middle." The agent leaned back. "You need to hear the whole thing."

"Humor me," Mitch said. "Who shot you?"

"Fine, I'll start there. I finished the kidnapping case here. It was my first case as the lead agent again after I got out of rehab, but that's getting ahead of the story. So I was champing at the bit to go looking for that little girl, Shiloh's parents, when suddenly, I got yanked off the street and parked behind a desk shuffling reports. Then, they decided to put me in a safe house.

"Two nights ago, the shit hit the fan. There were four agents stationed with me on guard duty around the clock — three outside, one inside. Agent Greg Rogers and I were playing cards. I'd just gotten up to go to the bathroom when they came at the house from all directions and opened fire on the agents outside. A ricochet flew through the bathroom window and got me in the shoulder. There was a huge chest of drawers in the bathroom, and I toppled it over on its side in front of the door. With it jammed between the door and the bathtub like that, you'd have to take off the door to get in. There was an attic opening in the ceiling of the bathroom, so I crawled up into the attic to fire at them from above through the vent slats.

"By the time I could see the yard, two agents were already down and Greg was firing at them from a down-stairs window. I fired from above, took one out and hit another. Apparently, they didn't see where the bullets were coming from, though, because they didn't return fire. Then I ran out of bullets. And when Greg … stopped firing … I figured it was time to boogie." He stopped, took a breath. "I took out some of the vent slats on the back attic wall and crawled out onto the limb of a big yellow birch."

For the first time since he started talking, Agent Devereaux smiled, weak but genuine. A smile that made it all the way to his eyes.

"When I was a little kid, I spent every waking hour climbing trees. We lived outside Montrose, Louisiana, right up next to the Kisatchie Hills Wilderness Area. And I wanted to be a park ranger just because of the trees. I got to know them all, wandered the woods searching among the fir, pine, and spruce trees for climbing trees, hardwoods — red oak, white and blackjack oak — climbed every one I found. So I was in my element up in that old yellow birch. Pulled a Tarzan — which wasn't easy with a bullet hole in my shoulder — and climbed from the birch to a white oak, then down it to the ground behind the oak. I knew it would take them awhile to break into that bathroom and see I was gone, so I had a little head start. I ran, came out on the other side of the woods at a convenience store, hot-wired an old pickup truck parked out back—"

"You didn't just go into the store and call the police?" Gus asked.

"Are you serious? You know who would have shown up — the FBI! They'd already flunked the can-you-keep-Lamar-Devereaux-safe exam." The outburst took a lot out of him, but he settled back on the pillows and kept talking. "Parked the truck in a Walmart lot. Waited for some woman in a hurry to get out of her car and leave the keys in it. Stole a Prius and was on my way."

"On your way where?" Mitch asked.

He paused then and fixed his eyes on Mitch. "To you."

"Why me?"

"When you're on the run, the only really safe place to hide is somewhere you've never been before where nobody knows you and there's no possible way to trace you there. That has its downsides though. If you know nobody, you have to interact with the world personally, and eventually you wind up on a surveillance camera somewhere."

He paused again. He was getting very tired.

"Ideally you need a place where somebody will help you, a place that nobody else in your life knows about. And that's when I thought of you, Sheriff Webster." He grimaced from pain somewhere and his face looked drawn. "I almost made it. Damn mountain roads. I missed a curve and..."

He took a long breath.

"Obviously, I didn't intend to show up on your porch looking like this," he gestured down at his injured body. "I didn't just come to you hoping you'd agree to hide me, stick me in a hole in the ground like Osama bin Laden. When they parked me behind a desk as a report jockey, I stumbled on something I think's important — that nobody else has figured out. It started with a murder that mentioned a particular MO — near Yarmouth County. I nosed around quietly and found two similar cases. I'd already decided to give you a call, see if we could meet and talk about it, when I was suddenly shipped off to a safe house. I had planned to tell you my story AND how my story might actually be *your* story. The plan was that the two of us would work *together* to figure this out because I thought you and yours *might* have a dog in this fight. Now, I'm sure of it."

"Why is that?"

"The unidentified body on the exam table I so recently vacated." He cocked his thumb toward the exam room. "He fits the profile, too. That makes four."

That surprised them all.

"How do you know——?" Rileigh began.

"I heard you talking about it."

Heard them talking about it? Was his hearing *that* good? Must be, because the only other explanation was he had gotten out of bed to eavesdrop as they discussed the murder and the condition of the body. He didn't look strong enough to stand up on his own. There was a lot more to this guy than Rileigh had supposed.

"The young man I brought to Gus for an autopsy — you know something about who killed him?" Mitch asked.

"Maybe. I'll let you be the judge of that once you've heard my story." The agent looked at Gus, and Rileigh could see him sizing the man up. "Before I start this tale, I'm thirsty, you think you could…"

Gus got to his feet. "Sure, I'll get you some more water."

"I was hoping for something a little stronger than that."

"Such as?"

"This is Tennessee, isn't it? How about some Jack Daniels?"

Chapter Fourteen

Gus allowed Devereaux a single shot of bourbon — and the agent groaned audibly when Gus tipped it up and poured it into the small pitcher of water beside Devereaux's bed.

"What a terrible thing to do to good whisky," the agent lamented.

"Be grateful I let you have any at all," Gus said. "Just for medicinal purposes."

Rileigh poured Devereaux a glass of water from the pitcher, started to put ice into it, but he held up his hand.

"It's diluted enough without melting ice in it."

Gus looked from Rileigh to Mitch. "When I say we're done, we're done. I haven't had a live patient in years, and I'll be damned if I'll lose this one."

Devereaux took two big swallows of the water, wrinkled his nose, and began his tale.

"It started with a joint operation — DEA and FBI. And then damned if they didn't haul in Homeland Security."

FBI, DEA, and Homeland — those were the three

agencies Rileigh's friend had mentioned. She'd said all three had lost agents in the past year — brutal murders

Devereaux shook his head. "It was a dumpster fire from conception, and it only got worse after that. Its purpose was to capture on American soil and arrest one Guillermo Castilla."

"*The* Guillermo Castilla," Mitch said, his eyebrows up.

"The one and only Guillermo Castilla?" Rileigh asked.

"Okay, I am clearly not impressed enough by that man's name to be able to participate in this discussion," Gus said. "Who is Guillermo Castilla?"

"They call him El Nuevo Escobar," Mitch said.

The new Escobar. Gus whistled. Even he had heard of Pablo Escobar, the meanest dog in the drug lord junkyard, the guy who started as the pilot of his own plane smuggling cocaine into Florida, and eventually had a fleet of fifteen airplanes and six helicopters. The billionaire could afford to buy government officials and weapons on the same scale. He owned his own Caribbean island with landing strips and hangars for the jets bringing drugs in from Colombia to be loaded on smaller planes for distribution in Florida, Georgia, and the Carolinas.

"'Little Pablo' Castilla is just as rich … and they say 'Pablito' is twice as ruthless as his namesake," Mitch said. "So how did the DEA plan to catch the guy on American soil and arrest him?"

"That was the original purpose of the operation. But like everything else run by the government, it just got bigger and bigger. They decided to try to catch *two* fish with one net, two big ones. Guillermo's Castilla and … one Barrington Griffin Davidson, III."

"Davidson!" Mitch leaned forward and put his elbows on his knees. "This gets more interesting by the minute."

"I hate to be Nanny Know Nothing again," Gus said,

"but what does the guy who owns that Walking Horse farm in Pendleton County have to do with Guillermo Castilla?"

"According to him, absolutely nothing," Devereaux said.

"Just like Davidson has nothing to do with Damien Afanazyev and the Russian mafia, or Tony Gregoria, who runs the Sicilians on the Upper East Side in New York, or —" Mitch began.

"Has his toe in the water with half a dozen other reeeeeally bad dudes in all manner of other illegal enterprises," Rileigh finished for him. She grimaced. "Of course, to the home folks he's just that nice guy who donated fifty thousand dollars to build a senior citizen center and was the grand marshal of last year's Christmas parade."

"You don't have to scratch Griff Davidson very deep to find rot," Mitch said.

Rileigh held up her finger. "At least that's what the rumor mill says."

Devereaux shook his head. "It's more than rumor. His business associates call him Mr. D."

"For Davidson?" Gus asked.

Devereaux shook his head. "Mr. D. is for Mr. *Detergent.* He's a money launderer. And if you're doing something illegal on a really big scale, he's your go-to guy to clean up the proceeds so you can fill out a W-2 form."

"So how does he figure into all of this?" Mitch asked.

"Seems he's branching out beyond scrubbing other people's money into buying and selling stolen merchandise. The higher-ups decided to take him down with Castilla, charge him with racketeering."

Devereaux sighed. "One sting, one target. Move light and fast, get in and get out ... that would have worked. But three agencies, none of whom are noted for playing well with others — with the DEA in charge."

Mitch rolled his eyes. "Well, that explains a lot."

Devereaux nodded.

"Not to me it doesn't," Gus said.

"The DEA is by reputation the ... clumsiest of all the federal law enforcement agencies," Mitch said. He looked at Devereaux. "Would you say that's an accurate characterization?"

Devereaux cocked his head. "Clumsy. Okay, I'll buy clumsy. Or inept. Or just plain incompetent. We always said the DEA was unfixable because you can't cure stupid."

"So how did the DEA plan to lure Castilla out of Central America?"

"Didn't have to. Through some kind of network of informants, the DEA discovered that Castilla was going to meet personally with Mr. Davidson. *Here,* in Tennessee. And they found out *when.*"

"You're joking." Rileigh said, almost choking, but Devereaux shook his head. She went on in a mocking voice, "So I'm the biggest, baddest drug lord south of the border, the guy every American law enforcement agency — local, state and federal — would crawl over three miles of broken glass and rusty Spam lids to arrest ... and I decide to go to a slumber party in Tennessee?"

Devereaux shrugged. "Makes absolutely no sense, I know. There's a whole lot about this operation that I don't understand. I wasn't in charge. I was just one of the troops. Those higher on the food chain might have known the reason, but they didn't share it with the front lines. All I ever heard was that it had something to do with horses."

"Tennessee Walking Horses?" Gus asked.

Devereaux shrugged again.

"Maybe. Castilla has horse ranches in Venezuela and Argentina, for thoroughbreds, I think."

"Davidson has another Tennessee Walker ranch in Belgium," Rileigh said. "It'd have been a helluva lot safer to meet there than…" She let the rest trail off.

"We were set to spring the trap as soon as Castilla was inside Davidson's house, had it surrounded. But he didn't show — I found out all this after the fact — and suddenly four unidentified choppers came roaring over the mountain and landed at the same time at different places on the farm … *not* up by the house, but next to the woods and down at the barns where the horses were kept."

"He got wind of something?" Mitch asked.

"Or you had bad intel," Rileigh said.

"Obviously, they were running decoys, which meant our intel was at best flawed. If I'd been in charge, I would have moved in as soon as I knew he made us, but I wasn't running the show."

Devereaux described how he and two other agents had been stationed in and near the barns — just as backup, and suddenly their positions became the dance floor.

"I don't know what all went wrong, and I'm not sure I even got the straight story on what I do know. Davidson and Castilla were in the horse barn. We saw them, and the three of us could have taken them down. Right then and there, both of them! But we were under strict orders to wait for the signal to move in and nobody gave it, so we stood down. When the signal finally came, Castilla's men had flanked us, caught us in a crossfire," he paused and took a deep breath, "and Castilla slipped through our fingers."

Devereaux paused. Stumbled in the telling, lost concentration, and looked confused. When he continued, he sounded exhausted.

"The next thing I knew, I woke up in the hospital, and they told me I'd been in a coma for almost a month from a skull fracture that should have killed me."

"I remember hearing about some kind of raid at Davidson's Willow Creek Farm," Rileigh said. "But the press made it sound like poor Griff Davidson was a victim of mistaken identity, not that a bunch of federal officers came in with guns blazing and found absolutely nothing illegal going on … and some of them ended up shooting each other."

"Shooting each other?" Gus asked.

Rileigh held up her hand.

"I was going through my own personal nightmare in Memphis at the time at the time and barely listened to the garbled version from Mama. But I figure she was right on one point — Davidson came out the other end smelling like a rose." Rileigh paused and shook her head.

"What I learned in bits and pieces later was that when Castilla got away and vanished, Davidson called all of his friends in high places, hired every pricey lawyer between New York and Chicago, and threatened to sue every government agency that was there for harassment, because they'd come up with a handful of nothing. I don't think he ever did anything but threaten. Just saber rattling."

"No … gloating. But none of that was my concern. I was in rehab, then light duty. It wasn't my concern until the bodies started dropping."

"Bodies?" Mitch asked. Rileigh leaned in. It wasn't the first time today she'd heard of bodies dropping.

"Nobody put it together at first — three agencies, with a total of … I don't know, close to thirty thousand agents altogether? It was a while before anybody connected the dots. Then a DEA agent vanished out of the stands at his son's Little League game and—"

"His name was Blake Hollister," Rileigh said.

Devereaux gawked at her. "How do you know that?"

"A friend told me about it."

"Did your friend say they found his body — very dead and very messed up?"

"Messed up?" Gus asked. "In what way? It's a professional question."

"All his fingernails had been pulled out. Both of his knees were broken. And he had been beaten so severely that he was totally unrecognizable."

"My friend said that Homeland Security had missing agents, too," Rileigh said.

"And the FBI," Mitch added.

"How many murders are we talking about here?" Gus asked.

"There were twenty-one agents on the raid altogether — six from the FBI, eight from the DEA, and seven from Homeland Security. "

Devereaux took a shaky breath.

"As far as we can determine … I'm the last man standing."

That knocked the breath out of Mitch, Rileigh, and Gus.

"My partner, Chad Gregory, was killed before I even came out of the coma. The two of us were in a horse stall together in the barn. He wasn't tortured though. Car bomb."

"That's … odd," Mitch said.

"Out of nowhere. Just boom. C-4 under the seat. Red mist."

Rileigh remembered red mist from Afghanistan. Red mist was when a body was blown up with such powerful explosives that there was literally nothing left of it but a red mist.

"We didn't connect the car bomb to this operation until other agents started getting hit. Once we figured out the common denominator, we knew who had targets on their backs. We just didn't know why."

"That doesn't make any sense," Gus said. "Why would Castilla start killing off the agents who were a part of a botched sting operation? A vendetta is for sore losers who go after the winners. But Castilla won. He got away."

"That question has been the topic of discussion in the FBI, the DEA, and Homeland for months." Devereaux sighed. "As agents kept going missing, one after another, it got where the rest of us were looking over our shoulders all the time. Checking every room before we went into it. When the original twenty-one was down to four — one FBI, two DEA, and a Homeland guy — they pulled me off the street, stuck me behind a desk shuffling paper. That came as close to killing me as a bullet would have. But it was when I was shuffling paper that I noticed something."

He turned to Mitch.

"It was what I wanted to talk to you about. They're murders with the same MO as the agents, but the victims were civilians. And all of them had some connection to Willow Creek Farm. I thought maybe you and I could work on the local angle … and then suddenly I was called into the captain's office. He didn't say anything at all, just handed me two reports. One of the DEA officers had gone missing. Another's mutilated body had been found. And the Homeland guy…" He paused, shook his head. "He ate his gun."

Rileigh saw Gus look from one to the other, uncomprehending.

"He killed himself," she told him.

"And then there was one. Since I was the final chip in the game, they decided to put me into protective custody."

The agent had been growing progressively paler as he talked, his voice weaker.

Gus finally stood. "I think it's time we let Agent Devereaux get some rest."

"AW, come on Gus. We're just getting to the good part — the local murders," Mitch said.

"I had planned to bring you all the reports," Devereaux said. "But they moved me into the safe house before I could gather it all up. I can give you names, places, and when they were killed, but you're going to have to dig out the rest of it on your end."

"Why local people?" Rileigh mused.

That's what I was wondering," Devereaux said, his voice weak. "It's an aberration. I'm thinking if we could figure *that* out..." His voice failed.

"Okay, boys and girls. Party's over," Gus said, making shooing motions with his hands. "He's not going anywhere. You can ask him more questions later."

Chapter Fifteen

Gus shooed Rileigh and Mitch out of Agent Devereaux's room and down the hall into the examination room, where the black body bag containing the unknown victim still lay on the examining table. Rileigh was anxious to hear what Mitch had learned from talking to his contact in the FBI and to share her story.

Gus tossed them the ball. "When you left here, you said you were going to shake some trees in the FBI and see what fell out. Sounds like you both found ripe fruit."

"I talked to my friend in the FBI in Chicago before we got the call about the body in the creek," Mitch said. "First thing I asked was about safe houses and whether or not the location of a safe house could have been outed. He said it wasn't possible. But he admitted in the end that maybe…"

Mitch paused, deep in thought.

"According to Devereaux, when his safe house was breached, the other agents were killed. Right?"

"What's your point?" Gus asked.

"Just that Bill … surely he would have heard if other agents were killed."

"What do you think that means?" Rileigh asked. "That Devereaux's making it all up? Or isn't coherent enough to know what really did happen?"

"Or your friend isn't in the loop because he's all the way up there in Chicago," Gus suggested.

"Yeah, but when an agent goes down, word of it gets out fast," Rileigh said.

"So that leaves us with option number three," Gus said.

"And that is?" Mitch asked.

"The FBI is keeping it quiet even in their own ranks."

"Whoa," Mitch said. "It would take some serious clout to do a thing like that."

"Which would mean whatever Devereaux's involved in is some serious shit."

Mitch turned to Rileigh. "You talked to your friend Shelly who's in the FBI, didn't you?"

"Yeah. And I got something like the same story, except not about the FBI. According to Shelly, the DEA has lost four agents in the past six months who simply vanished."

"Do you hear an echo in here anywhere?" Gus said.

"And, of course, Shelly told the same story Devereaux did, about the agent snatched out of the stands at his son's Little League game."

Rileigh paused.

"I saved the best for last," she said, and the two men perked up. "Shelly said that her friend who was snatched away from the baseball game had worked a case down in 'my neck of the woods,' in Tennessee."

"Well, we're getting at least some verification of the authenticity of what Devereaux saying."

"I don't want to sound like a parrot, but it's hard not to keep asking the same question," Rileigh said. "Where does that leave us?" Both men looked at her. "Come on, we've got an injured FBI agent in there who has gone completely

AWOL from the FBI, and we haven't said hi, bye, or kiss my foot to any of the authorities about it."

"Because he asked us not to," Gus said.

"Because if they found him, they would kill him," Mitch said. "And from what information we've been able to substantiate, sounds like he's right — that somebody's killing off FBI agents and DEA agents and Homeland Security agents connected to the raid on Davidson's Willow Creek Farm."

Rileigh furrowed her brow. "And with all the money and resources the FBI and the DEA have to throw at investigations, I'm assuming they still didn't find out anything?"

"You know, in at least one respect, what's happening now is reminiscent of the one occasion that I worked with Agent Devereaux — on that kidnapping case. They set up a complete headquarters in the Sheriff's Department with equipment and resources and people. They had access to all kinds of information. And they expected to bring that to bear in little Yarmouth County to find those children. Now, as it worked out, that's not how the children were found. But even at the time, I thought—" Mitch paused. "If you've got a fly on the wall you want to get rid of, you've got lots of options. And true, *one* of them is shoot it with a shotgun. I think the big agencies shoot a lot of holes in a lot of walls when a flyswatter would get the job done."

Rileigh nodded at Mitch.

"We need to find out who killed the young man in the body bag. I'm betting locals know more about that than they would tell any federal agent."

"And this guy in the body bag isn't the first local who has been killed with this MO. Agent Devereaux knew about others—"

"I didn't perform the autopsies," Gus said.

"He said they were in surrounding counties, and I can

find out where as soon as he gives me the names of the victims. And perhaps those sheriffs already have information that would help us find out who killed the guy on the table." Mitch rose slowly to his feet. "I think I know the answer to this question, but I need to ask anyway. Are we still good on this — hiding Devereaux? Do we still believe we're doing the right thing? "

The other two nodded.

"I think we're saving this guy's life," Gus said. "We can't just throw him to the wolves now."

"Which begs the question," Mitch said. "What are we going to do with him? He can't just stay here."

"I think I have a plan," Rileigh said.

Chapter Sixteen

MAMA COULDN'T WAIT TO TRY OUT THE WAFFLE IRON THAT she and Jillian had bought at Walmart on Saturday. She got it out of the box the night before, cleaned it all up, and had it ready for waffle batter for Sunday morning breakfast. Rileigh and Mama would be going to church after breakfast. Jillian, probably not. She still wasn't up to going to places where people hung out and talked to each other. She told Rileigh she thought she had forgotten how to do that. And Rileigh and Mama didn't push her to do anything she didn't want to.

"Come on down here, girls. I'm making waffles. They might be good hot, but they taste like placemats when they're cold."

Rileigh went downstairs into the kitchen, where Jillian was already prying the first waffle off the waffle iron.

"Be careful, don't break it," Mama said.

"It tastes the same, broken or solid," Jillian said. "That's what you always told me about a piece of cake."

"I never said no such thing."

"Yes, you did," Rileigh said. "You'd cut a piece of cake,

and your cakes were always so soft and flaky and good that they piece just fell apart on your plate. And when we'd whine about it—"

Jillian took up the story. "You would tell us it tastes the same in pieces as it does whole."

Mama grumbled something under her breath, then she handed the plate with the solitary waffle on it to Rileigh and poured batter back into the iron and closed the lid on the batter. "You just turn this little thing right here. It's just so easy," she said.

Rileigh had been considering how best to bring up the subject she needed to talk about. But as it turned out, she didn't have to.

"So you said you'd tell us where you were all night Friday night," Jillian said. "And I believe there's more to this story than how many squirrels you bagged."

Mama's eyes lit up at that. "Oh Sugar, I've been meaning to tell you how thrilled I was that you got enough squirrels for me to make stew."

Rileigh had come home exhausted after spending all night dragging Agent Devereaux down the mountainside. But she had stretched to the outside limits the length of time she could wait after shooting a squirrel before cleaning it. She had to clean them as soon as she got home. Mitch squirmed out of it. And he would pay dearly for having done that.

"Sit down, Mama, let me get you some coffee," Rileigh said. "Actually the adventure didn't start until after we had already shot all the squirrels."

Jillian lifted an eyebrow. "Oh, I was hoping you were going to tell us how some of the squirrels decided to fight back, you know, built a little fort out of nuts."

Rileigh smiled at the remark. Every time Jillian made some silly joke like that, it warmed Rileigh's heart to the core because … Jillian, *her* Jillian, was coming back to who she used to be before the 30-year nightmare that stole so many years of her life.

"We ran into Jeremiah Johnson in the woods."

Mama's face lit up. "Jeremiah Johnson. I haven't seen him in the longest time."

"He told me to tell you hello," Rileigh said. A bright smile wreathed Mama's face at that. Rileigh cut her eyes to Jillian, who shrugged.

"Jeremiah had come looking for us. Well, not for us, but for Mitch. He had found an injured man in the woods, and the man sent him to find Mitch."

"If he was injured, the rescue squad would probably have been better qualified to go get him out than Mitch," Mama said.

"The man didn't want anybody to know that Jeremiah had found him."

"Why not?"

"Because he's on the run."

"On the run? From whom?"

"That's a good question."

Then Rileigh told them the whole story. Mama cackled when Rileigh described how Agent Devereaux had identified himself as the man Mitch met "and didn't have to unzip his pants."

"So it was that FBI agent who was here when Chloe and Mason got took?" Mama said.

"Yes."

"And why didn't he want to give his name to Jeremiah Johnson?"

"I'll get to that."

"So you and Mitch and Gus carried that man out of the woods by yourselves?" Jillian asked.

"Gus had a collapsible stretcher. The rescue squad

wouldn't have had better equipment than that. They'd have had to haul him out on a stretcher too."

"Yeah, but there are more of them."

"And I don't mean no offense, but Gus don't strike me as very strong — needs more meat on his bones."

"Gus, Mitch, and Jeremiah Johnson switched off carrying the stretcher down the mountainside, and they did fine."

Rileigh took a breath.

"And when Gus started treating him, he realized that he'd been shot."

"Shot?" Mama and Jillian's heads both popped up at the same time

"He had a bullet hole in his shoulder … which Gus did not report as is required by Tennessee law."

"Why not — who shot him?" Mama asked.

"And why was he hiding?" Jillian asked.

Rileigh recounted that part of the story.

"He ain't like his daddy," Mama said.

"Did you know the senior Griffin Davidson?"

"We didn't exactly travel in the same circles, if that's what you mean," Mama said. "But I knew him. Everybody did. He was a good guy who cared about only one thing in life — them horses. He spent every waking moment with them. But in the process, his wife left him because he never paid any attention to her. And his son might as well have grown up an orphan. And from what I hear, he is a man who really could have used a strong father figure, if you know what I mean."

"What do you hear, Mama?"

"The guy is crooked as a dog's hind leg. In all kind of illegal enterprises. But it's all real hush-hush and won't nobody talk about it. So apparently, he's as good at doing things illegally as his father was at horses. Because he's become so successful, everybody's scared of him now."

Then Rileigh told them the last piece of the story. How after that joint operation on Davidson's farm, FBI agents and DEA agents and Homeland Security agents began to disappear.

"One of them literally was snatched out of the stands at his boy's little League game."

"How could anybody do that?"

Rileigh shrugged.

"But after a while, somebody managed to put it together that the only thing all of these agents from all over the country in three different organizations had in common was that they'd all worked that one case in Pendleton County. They pulled Agent Devereaux off the street, parked him behind the desk for his own safety, and finally decided to put him in a safe house."

"Is that anything like witness protection?" Mama asked.

"Not the same thing. It's basically a house that nobody's supposed to know the location of, where FBI agents can guard somebody who needs guarding. But Agent Devereaux's experience with the safe house was that it wasn't safe. They came after him, shot him, he managed to get away, hot-wired a car, and came looking for Mitch."

"Why Mitch?"

"Gus and Mitch and I talked about that. In the beginning, we thought it was just because this guy needed a place to hide from somebody who was out to get him, and he figured wherever Mitch was a good place because nobody knew that he knew Mitch. That's what we thought until he told us that he'd been on his way to Mitch because he had uncovered an interesting fact that nobody else had noticed yet, which was there were people in local counties around Davidson's Willow Creek Farm who had also been murdered and tortured like those agents. He was on his way to talk to Mitch about the two of them working together on that case, but he missed a corner, wrecked his car, and wound up with a dislocated shoulder and a broken leg … on top of the bullet hole, of course."

"And you carried him out of there … you never fail to amaze me, girl," Mama said.

"I didn't chuck him over my shoulder in a fireman carry and haul him down the mountain, Mama. All I carried was the lantern. It wasn't until late yesterday afternoon that we found out the whole story from Devereaux."

Jillian had grown progressively quieter during the conversation, pulling back, pulling away.

"You said that the agents and some local people had all been killed in the same way." Jillian lifted her eyes and looked directly into Rileigh's. "What way?"

Rileigh paused then said, "Torture."

Mama looked shocked. Jillian responded by freezing in place, clamping down on any response that Rileigh could see.

"I'm not going into details, I don't want to describe the kinds of horror perpetrated by Mexican drug cartels. But that's how these people were killed."

"And this Devereaux believes those same people are after him, right?" Jillian said.

"Right."

"And that if they catch him, they'll kill him that way, right?"

Rileigh nodded.

There was a silence around the table then. Rileigh got up, refilled her cup of coffee, and sat back down. "Mitch now believes that the young man whose body was found in the creek and maybe some other local people agent

Devereaux told us about were killed because they had something to do with that raid at Davidson's farm."

Rileigh paused and then went on, her voice strong.

"He thinks the two of us can get somewhere with an investigation on a local level. People will talk to us. Agent Devereaux's life is in danger every moment until somebody figures out who's behind all these killings and what possible motive they could have."

"How is this Agent Devereaux doing?" Jillian asked.

"He lost a lot of blood, not so much that he needed a transfusion, Gus said, but enough that it left him in a very weakened condition. His broken leg, the bone is not displaced, meaning it didn't shift out of place, so the splint that Gus put on it should hold it firm until he can get some kind of walking cast on it. And his shoulder is weak. When you pop a shoulder out of socket, it messes up all the hinges inside. They're pulled apart wrong and it makes it easier for it to dislocate a second time. So he's got that in a sling."

Jillian looked at Rileigh. "He can't stay at Mitch's office."

Rileigh was surprised that Jillian had gotten there so fast.

"No, he can't. It's too public a place. And Gus can't take care of him 24-7, look after him, cook meals and all."

"But he has to stay hidden because his life is in danger. Right?" Jillian said. Rileigh nodded.

Mama looked up then from her waffle. She hadn't even appeared to be paying attention to the conversation. But Mama could fool you. You might think she didn't hear a word you said, and three days later she repeats it back to you verbatim. This was one of those times. She looked up, her eyes alert.

"Well, if that young fellow needs a place to stay, he can

stay with us," she said. "Me and Jillian will take care of him. Won't we, Jillian?"

Jillian nodded, clearly only because Mama had asked it of her. Rileigh exhaled the tension that she hadn't even realized she was holding up tight in her chest. She knew Mama would volunteer to help, because that's the kind of person Mama was and she was grateful that she didn't even have to ask.

"Well, you need to wait to bring him over here until after church," Mama said. Then her face broke out into a beatific smile. "I think I'll fix squirrel stew for supper."

Chapter Seventeen

"As I understand it, you're going to be on the receiving end of Lily Bishop's famous squirrel stew for supper tonight," Gus said to Devereaux.

He could tell the FBI agent was in a lot of pain, but he refused pain meds. Nothing but Tylenol. He said he didn't like his mind all cloudy.

"So tell me about this woman who is willing to take in a stranger, an AWOL FBI agent, and hide him in her chicken coop," Devereaux said.

"Lily does have a chicken coop, but I'm sure she plans to put you in one of the huge four-poster beds in her house, all of them with feather mattresses."

"My grandma had feather mattresses on all the beds when I was a kid. To this day, I don't think anything man-made has come close to being as soft and comfortable as they were. So a feather mattress rather than feathers on the hoof in a chicken coop. I like that. Who is this woman?"

"Rileigh's mother." Gus smiled again. "When you meet her, she will probably remind you of someone."

"Who?"

"Aunt Bee on *The Andy Griffith Show*. But maybe not. Lily Bishop has always reminded me of Aunt Bee, but every time I bring it up to Rileigh or Mitch, they look at me like I'm crazy, but I swear … judge for yourself and let me know."

"I had a teacher once who reminded me of Tweety Bird's grandmother."

Gus smiled again. This guy was coming around. His sharp edges were showing.

"Lily Bishop has dementia. It's never been diagnosed specifically which of several different kinds she has, but it doesn't matter what name is on it. The symptoms are pretty much the same. There was a while last winter when she believed she was dating Elvis."

Gus paused and started over.

"No, it wasn't Elvis. It was Rhett Butler. She believed that Rhett Butler came and visited. Often. Was sweet on her. That's the way she put it. And she said Scarlett O'Hara did not like her."

"And she believed all that?"

Gus nodded.

"No wonder she invited an AWOL FBI agent she didn't know to come live in her house."

"I know it sounds like she is profoundly impaired," Gus said, "but she really isn't. There's still a whole lot of there there. She's a widow. Her husband died when Rileigh was a little girl. There's a story, but you really don't want to hear it."

Devereaux just nodded.

"And also living there is Rileigh's older sister Jillian. She's mid to late 40s and has her own baggage … lots of it. Steamer trunks full."

The agent lifted one eyebrow.

"Jillian disappeared when she was 18 years old on the

night before her wedding. Rileigh was seven at the time and no one knew what happened to Jillian or where she was for about 30 years."

"Seriously?"

"When she came back, the family discovered that she had been kidnapped and sold into the sex trade. She had literally been a slave in the Middle East for decades."

"Holy shit," Devereaux said.

"I'm telling you that because Jillian is a little fragile."

"She's earned fragile."

"Yeah, but—"

Before Gus could continue, he heard a commotion out front. A car pulled up, skidded to a stop. Then another one pulled up and then a third. He heard car doors slamming.

"I'll see to this." Gus stood and went out of Devereaux's room and down the hall. He was going through the waiting room when the front door opened and the room filled with a frantic family.

"Where is he? Where's my Cody? They said he was here. Where's my Cody?"

The woman speaking was absolutely wild-eyed. Gus noted that she only was wearing only one flip-flop, so apparently the other one had come off and she hadn't noticed. She was a round-faced woman in her late forties with big blue eyes that were now open way too wide.

Two young men came in behind her, a teenage girl and an older man.

"We tried to hold on to her," said the teenage boy. He was about 17, had bright red hair and freckles mingled with a bad case of acne. "As soon as she heard, we couldn't stop her."

"I want to see my Cody," the woman said and tried to push past Gus, but he stood his ground. The boys came up beside their mother and took her arms, not restraining her, just holding on.

"Why do you think—?" Gus started.

"Jimbo said," the woman interrupted. "Jimbo said he'd seen the tattoo on Cody's head. He knows, he knows it's my Cody and he told me."

"Who is Jimbo?"

"He's an emergency medical technician and he works for the ambulance service," said the other teenage boy.

Gus vaguely remembered that one of the two young men who'd brought the black body bag on the gurney into his office had been called Jimbo and he knew instantly what the woman meant by the tattoo on his head. Gus had noticed it immediately but hadn't been certain until he got it under bright light and examined it exactly what it was supposed to be. It was a horse. The young man had shaved his head and had a tattoo of a horse on the bare skull. It wasn't just odd, though, it was bizarre, because whoever did the tattoo was either drunk or on drugs. The animal only bore a slight resemblance to a horse. Gus wouldn't have figured it out at all except the front legs were held up high in the air like a Tennessee Walking Horse. Gus was sure that the young man lying in there on the exam table was this woman's son, but that body was such a mess. He'd been hoping to release it directly to the mortuary where perhaps they could do something, or better yet, just have the body cremated. It was not a sight any mother should see.

"Ma'am, it's possible that the young man in there is your son, but—"

"It's my Cody. I know it's my Cody. Get out of my way." The woman tried to shove past Gus.

"You really don't want to see him in his current state."

The woman let out a wail, a shrieking wail, and would

have collapsed on the floor if her two sons hadn't held her up, but when she stopped screaming, her eyes cleared and she made to get past Gus again. "My Cody needs me. Get out of my way."

"Ma'am, excuse me."

Everyone in the room turned and looked at the door leading into the hallway, and there stood Agent Lamar Devereaux. There had been a crutch leaned up against the wall in the storage room, and he'd gotten to it. Now he stood there in a white t-shirt over scrubs — borrowed from Gus.

"Please, Mrs. Whitlock, please listen to me."

The woman stared silent in shock and surprise.

"I'm a police officer, and I worked a really terrible wreck years ago. There were three teenagers in a car, and it caught fire."

The woman shrank back from the image.

"I was in the coroner's office when the parents of those children came in to identify their bodies."

The woman gasped and couldn't speak.

"Ma'am, do you have a picture of Cody?" Devereaux asked.

"Sure I do. My phone... I got one, I do..." She fumbled around for her phone as one of her sons pulled out his, opened it to pictures, and held out the image of a smiling young man to Agent Devereaux.

"This is him. This is my brother Cody," the boy said. Agent Devereaux pointed to the picture.

"Ma'am, that's your son Cody. That is the image of him you want to carry with you for the rest of your life. That smiling young man right there with that kind of crooked grin. That's your boy."

Devereaux paused before he continued quietly. "Please, *please* don't destroy that image in your mind by seeing the shape your son's body is in right now. It's just his body. He's gone. He's not in any pain, but you will be if you look at him, and you will be in pain for the rest of your life. Years ago, that wreck, two of those mothers listened to my advice and didn't go in to identify their children's bodies, but one of the mothers was determined to see her baby girl. I met that woman years later and she was still tortured by that sight. Please ma'am, don't do that to yourself. It will accomplish nothing but hurting you."

The old man stepped forward then.

"I'm Cora's brother. Take me in and I'll identify him. I'll make sure it's Cody."

All the steam had drained out of the woman then. All her energy was gone. She sagged in the boy's arms, and they sat her down on one of the chairs in the waiting room. Gus turned and took the old man back to the examining room.

When he lifted the sheet off the young man on the table, the older man gasped and turned away. "Oh dear God. Dear God. Oh God."

"Is that Cody? Is that your nephew?" Gus asked.

"That's him. What happened to him?"

"Someone murdered him, and we don't know who or why."

Gus did not pull the sheet down far enough to reveal the boy's crushed hands and other broken bones.

Gus took the man's elbow and escorted him back to the waiting room, where he took his sister in his arms and told her.

"It's Cody. It is, Cora, and you don't want to see it."

She collapsed in his arms, sobbing. One of the teenage boys burst into tears then, too. The other one was holding together but just barely, and Gus pulled him aside while the others were crying.

"What's your brother's name, son?"

"Cody Ernest Whitlock."

"How old is he?"

"He's twenty. I mean, he'll be next month. He's really nineteen, but he'll be twenty next month."

"May I have his address, please?"

A smile skittered across the boy's face but he couldn't hang on it.

"He just moved out into his own place for the first time, ain't been gone from home but three months." The boy leaned close. "Had a girlfriend. Annalise Henderson lives over in Weatherford County and he wanted a place where…" He didn't finish, just said, "I don't even know what the address of the new place is."

The young man had to stop talking because he was afraid he was going to burst into tears.

"Son," Gus said, leaning close, "have your brother cremated. Don't have a casket funeral. Have your brother cremated. Your uncle will agree."

The boy stood, gawking. Found his voice.

"What happened to—?" He couldn't finish the sentence.

"We don't know."

It was a few minutes before the family got themselves together enough to leave. When they were gone, Gus turned and looked at Agent Devereaux.

"You did that family a huge favor," he said.

Chapter Eighteen

THEY WAITED UNTIL AFTER DARK TO TAKE AGENT Devereaux to Rileigh's mother's house. He had demonstrated that he could walk using the crutch he had found in the storage room, but Gus cautioned against it. He didn't want him inadvertently putting weight on that leg. The broken bone was not displaced, but the wrong move could displace it, and then it would be ugly.

Devereaux was unwilling to be carried into Rileigh's house on a stretcher by Gus and Mitch. When they got to the house, he got out of Gus's jeep and hobbled, with Gus under one arm and Mitch under the other, up the walk and up the steps onto the porch, where Mama, Rileigh, and Jillian were waiting to greet him.

Mama was never one to stand on ceremony, and as soon as the young man hit the top of the porch, she enveloped him in a huge, loving hug and told him how glad she was for him to come and be her guest for a little while. She was looking forward to it.

"I'm making special squirrel stew just for you tonight, Agent Delacroix." she said.

"His name is Agent Lamar Devereaux, Mama," Rileigh said, but Mama smiled in the vacant way that meant she either hadn't heard what you said or it didn't matter if she did, she wouldn't remember it.

"I got fresh squirrels," Mama said.

"Yeah, about those squirrels…" Mitch began.

Rileigh resisted the urge to tell him that he was getting all squirrely on her or that he had squirreled out of helping her clean the little critters that they had shot. She'd leave that ammunition for another time.

Jillian reached out her hand. "I'm Jillian Bishop, Agent Devereaux."

"Would you like to sit out here on the swing for a bit?" Mama asked. "It's sure pretty tonight. You can hear the tree frogs and the crickets. Just like they was in your shirt pocket."

"The squirrel stew is simmering on the stove," Jillian told him. "We can have it whenever you want."

Gus took over then, *Doctor* Gus. "How about we get him settled in bed somewhere? Maybe let him rest for a while before supper. Would that be okay?"

"I don't need to rest, I'm fine," Devereaux said.

"Like I said before, you're the first live patient I've had in twenty years of practice, and I'm not losing you."

"We fixed up the downstairs bedroom at the end of the hall for Agent Devereaux," Jillian said. "We didn't figure with a broken leg, he'd want to be tromping up and down the stairs."

"The bedroom has its own bathroom," Rileigh said. "You go get cleaned up, and we'll sit out here on the porch, and you can join us whenever you feel like it."

While Jillian ushered Devereaux, with Gus assisting, down the hall to the room, Rileigh stood with Mitch, and Mama went back into the kitchen to check on the stew.

"That man looks pale and weak," Rileigh said quietly to Mitch.

"I thought so, too. I think Gus is kicking himself for not sending him off to an emergency room somewhere, not because Gus couldn't treat his wounds, but because Devereaux lost so much blood. They'd have given him a transfusion, standard operating procedure. As it is, he's just weak."

Gus came back out of the bedroom a few minutes later and found Mitch and Rileigh sitting on the porch, Rileigh in the swing, and Mitch in the rocker. Gus sat down opposite them.

"Cora Whitlock came by Gus's office this afternoon to identify her son, Cody," Mitch said. "He told me about it on the way here."

"How did she know Cody was there?"

"An EMT said something about the patient that he had delivered to the morgue."

Gus ground his teeth. "The head of emergency services needs to have a talk with those young men. They don't realize that the little things they mention in passing are being picked up by other people. The medical information about any one of the patients treated by the emergency services is privileged medical information, even their names. They're divulging information they're not supposed to."

"Duly noted," Mitch said. "I'll have a talk with them."

While Gus was telling Rileigh and Mitch about his visit from Cora Whitlock, Jillian joined them.

"The woman barged into the office semi-hysterical," Gus said. "She'd heard her boy was there, and nothing would do but that she had to go see him. I tried to keep her from going in there. I didn't want her to see the kid in that shape. I wasn't having any luck until Agent Devereaux showed up."

"Devereaux?" Jillian said.

"Yep, he hobbled down the hallway on a crutch and talked to the woman. He asked her if she had a picture of Cody, and when one of Cody's brothers produced it, Devereaux told her, 'That is your son, Cody. That's the boy you want to remember for the rest of your life. Don't go into that room and see the body that he's not in anymore. It will haunt you.'"

"Did she listen?"

"The rest of the family got her under control and got her out of there."

"I talked him into lying down for a little while," Jillian said, "told him he didn't have to go to sleep, just lay down and close his eyes. As soon as he did, he was out like a rock."

Jillian looked at Mitch. "Rileigh tells me this man is in danger. That several other agents have been killed and there's reason to believe he's been targeted, too. Is that right?"

"He says it is, and I believe it."

"No offense, Mitch." She paused before going on, "Is there any reason to be concerned about his safety?" She paused again and then finished, "Or *ours*."

"I would never have put him here if I thought there was any risk, but the only people on the planet who know that Agent Devereaux is at Lily Bishop's house are the four of us, and if the killers can't find him, he's not in danger, and neither are you."

"Agent Devereaux gave Mitch the names of some people who live in surrounding counties who were killed in … like Cody Whitlock."

"Tortured, you mean," Jillian said. Rileigh nodded.

"We're going out tomorrow and talk to the sheriffs and see what we can find out about them. Devereaux thinks that finding out who killed the local people will be a lot easier than trying to find out who killed federal agents."

"Do you agree with him?"

"Yeah … maybe easy-*er*, but definitely not easy. I don't know how much Rileigh and I are going to be able to find out about those murders."

"If you strike out and come up with nothing, what are we going to do with Agent Devereaux?"

Rileigh and Mitch looked at each other and shrugged.

Chapter Nineteen

RILEIGH AND MITCH MET EARLY THE NEXT MORNING TO GO pay a visit to Sheriff Simon Tackett of Pendleton County to find out what he might or might not know about the murder of Alex Spaulding. That was one of the names Devereaux gave to Mitch that he'd gleaned when he was riding a desk in Nashville, searching through anything and everything, trying to come up with a motive for the murders of so many federal agents. In that search, he had stumbled upon a similar MO in the murders of three people who lived near Davidson's Willow Creek Farm in Pendleton County. The most recent of those murder victims was a man named Alex Spaulding — he'd lived in Pendleton County, and his body had been discovered there, so it seemed the best place to start.

"So, how did it go last night?" Mitch asked.

Rileigh took a few seconds to answer. "There are a couple of layers to that answer," she finally said. "Mama was tickled to death to have a house guest. She couldn't do enough for him. I finally had to force her to leave him alone and let him get some rest, convinced her that he didn't need any cookies or lemonade, and that he didn't want to come sit on the porch in the swing."

"That sounds about right."

"Then there's Jillian."

Mitch glanced over at her. There was a tone in her voice that raised a red flag. "What about Jillian?" he asked.

"I don't think she wants him there. No, let me correct that. I'm *sure* she doesn't want him there."

"Why not?"

"Well, duh. It's dangerous. Agent Devereaux has a target on his back. People out there trying to find him so they can murder him, and he's parked in the bedroom downstairs from us."

Rileigh held up her hand before he could respond.

"I know, I know, and she knows *intellectually* that there's no danger to us since nobody on the planet knows he's there except us." Rileigh paused. "And nobody except us can find out, and that has caused a bit of a burr under Jillian's saddle."

"How so?"

"She can't tell David about him."

"How does she feel about that?"

"She didn't say how she felt about it, but I know she doesn't want to play some cat and mouse game with David, their relationship being as tenuous as it is."

Mitch looked at Rileigh questioningly. "Tenuous?"

"Oh, I don't mean there's anything wrong. It's just … come on … they're walking on eggshells. They didn't see each other for 30 years, and that leaves a lot of catching up to do. And Jillian is not exactly in the greatest mental health to be entering into a relationship in the first place." Rileigh sighed. "And in my humble opinion, neither is David. I'm not sure how to feel about a man who didn't get married for thirty years because he was still in love with the woman who walked out on him. There's gotta be bats in that belfry somewhere."

Mitch had never been to Cochran, the little town that was the county seat of Pendleton County. He'd met the sheriff, Simon Tackett, though, at Mum's going-away party several months ago. Every sheriff for a hundred miles in every direction had attended, and Mum had dragged Mitch from one to the other, like introducing his favorite son, or, as Mitch thought of at the time, his obedient dog.

They crossed into Pendleton County and descended into a hollow and drove along beside the white fences of Willow Creek Farm for what seemed like miles.

"You sure this farm's only 400 acres?"

Rileigh nodded. "Seems like a lot more, doesn't it?"

"What do you know about Sheriff Tackett," he asked.

"He's been sheriff since God was a corporal, and that's always suspect to me. Anybody who can get elected every four years consistently, no matter who the competition is, has their finger on the scale somewhere. At least that's how it always seemed to me. That was certainly the case with..." She paused and made eye contact with Mitch. "Mum."

Mum was the saintly old sheriff of Yarmouth County, who in reality had murdered Rileigh's father thirty years ago.

They pulled into the parking lot in front of the newish building that held the sheriff's office and the Cochran Police Department as well.

Simon Tackett was a man in his early sixties with a mane of salt and pepper hair and eyebrows that looked like two woolly worms crawling across the top of his face.

Mitch and Rileigh were shown immediately into his office.

"Would you like some coffee?" he asked as he sat down

behind a desk that was roughly the size of a pool table. "How can help you, Sheriff Webster?"

"I'd like some information about a case that you worked here, a murder case. The victim's name was Alex Spaulding."

Tackett leaned back in his chair. "I remember that one." He rolled his eyes. "What that poor young man went through before he died … oh my."

"Tell me about it," Mitch said.

"Well, it looked like he'd been attacked with a hammer, all kind of broken bones. Not broke from some accident — crushed, on purpose, fingers and knees and...."

"Where was the body discovered?"

"At the landfill. It would have vanished out of all remembrance if the fellow driving the dump truck hadn't noticed what looked like a human shoe sticking out of the trash — with a foot still in it."

"What do you know about this Alex Spaulding?"

Tackett punched a button on the telephone on his desk and asked the receptionist to go to the files and dig out the report on Alex Spaulding. A few minutes later, she brought it in and put it on the sheriff's desk. He scooted it across the pool table to Mitch.

Mitch picked it up and thumbed through it. "Says here he was employed at Willow Creek Farm."

"He was a mechanic, I think. Maybe not a vehicle mechanic, but he was one of those kids who could fix anything, whatever it was. If it was broke, if you had a vacuum cleaner or a toaster that didn't work, he was the go-to. His father ran a fix-it shop out of his garage on Huxter Lane. And he and the boy made all kinds of machines serviceable again. When he died, Alex went to work for Mr. D at the farm."

"When was he reported missing, and who reported it?"

"He lived at home with his mama and two sisters, and he just didn't come home from work one day."

"Meaning he disappeared from the farm."

"We assume. I talked to everybody who worked with him out there and the foreman. He said Alex came to work that morning, but beyond that, nobody saw him. He didn't leave that afternoon. His truck was still parked in the parking lot. After a day or two, his mama called and said he still hadn't come home."

"Any leads? Suspects? Motive?"

"That would be no, no, and no. He was a likable young fellow, didn't have any enemies. Certainly not anybody who would have done that to him. As far as I could tell, he wasn't involved in drugs, but with that kind of mutilation, you got to think drugs had something to do with it. I can't find anybody who saw him after 9 o'clock that morning at the farm. And there's lots of folks who worked there. Grooms and stable hands and trainers and such spread out all over the place. The foreman said Alex was sent up to the workshop outside Zephyr."

The sheriff paused. "The barns out there are names for famous Tennessee Walking horses, but you don't recognize Zephyr, do you?"

"Nope."

He smiled. "Allen's Gold Zephyr was—"

Rileigh interrupted. "Trigger, as in Roy Rogers' horse."

"Seriously?" Mitch asked.

"Seriously," Rileigh said. "Roy Rogers' horse was a Tennessee Walker."

Mitch brought the conversation back to the topic. "So Alex Spaulding went up to the workshop outside one of the horse barns and…"

"And nobody saw him after that," the sheriff said. He paused. "Can I ask you something, Sheriff Webster?"

"Shoot."

"Why are you so interested in the case of Alex Spaulding? The way I hear it, there's so much mayhem going on in Yarmouth County, surely you're not out looking for something to do."

"I became curious about this case because I've learned there are a couple of other cases like it nearby."

"You mean the one over in Buchanan County and the one in Whitley County?"

"Yeah, that's what I'm talking about. You know about those?"

"Alex was the last of three. I talked to both Sheriff Huxley and Sheriff Barker. And they came up with as much motive and as many suspects as I did. Now, the boy in Buchanan County was running with a rough crowd and wasn't nobody surprised that he eventually come up on the short end of the stick."

"Did you find any connection between these victims, anything they all had in common?"

"Well, sure, all three of them worked at Willow Creek Farm."

"So three employees of Davidson's farm were brutally murdered in the past six or eight months — obviously by the same killer — that's what I'm hearing?"

"Uh-huh. And I had a talk with Mr. Davidson about that very subject, but he couldn't shine any light on the motive or suspects either."

"How many murders do you typically have in Pendleton County in a year?"

"A handful. Domestic violence. Laurie Avery got beat to death by her husband about four weeks ago. Things like that. Certainly not as much murder and mayhem as you got going on in Yarmouth County."

Then Rileigh noticed a picture on the shelf behind the

sheriff's desk. It was a picture of the sheriff and Griff Davidson shaking hands, holding onto one of those "made into a poster size" checks to advertise a donation. Apparently, Mr. Davidson had contributed $40,000 toward the building of a new senior citizen center in Cochran.

"Tell me about that picture," Rileigh said.

Sheriff Tackett turned around and looked at it, then turned back, smiling. "Oh, that's just the latest donation. Mr. D gives a lot of money to support various things in Pendleton County. The animal shelter, the senior citizen center. He pays for school trips, school assemblies, and he's a pretty soft touch if there's been some disaster, somebody's house burned down or something."

Rileigh spoke then with a touch of sarcasm in her voice. "You telling me Griff Davidson is a philanthropic pillar of the community? Because that's not the reputation he has."

The sheriff bristled at that. "I know what his reputation is, and all I can tell you is he's been good to the people in this county. Don't nobody scratch any deeper than that."

When they got back out to the car, Rileigh said, "I bet if you bothered to look up the records in the Pendleton County courthouse, you would find out that the single largest contributor to the election campaigns of Sheriff Simon Tackett is Griff Davidson."

"You think so?"

"I bet the rent."

"You think he runs interference for him?"

"I'm sure he does if Mr. D needs interference. I've always figured the guy had enough money and has had it long enough that he knows how to cover his own tracks, and he doesn't need much interference."

"The FBI has been trying to catch him for years as a money launderer, yet he loses three employees to brutal murders — all with the same MO — and nobody on a federal level notices? Doesn't that strike you as out of the ordinary?"

Rileigh shrugged. "How would they know? Agent Devereaux tripped over the reports from different counties and different jurisdictions because he noticed they'd been killed with the same MO as all those agents. Sheriff Tackett should have taken the lead with the most recent victim, since the common denominator was here in Pendleton County, and clearly there was a serial killer on the loose. But it would appear he swept it under the rug."

"When you add Cody Whitlock ... just like Devereaux said, that makes *four* murders," Mitch said. He looked thoughtful. "Sounds like Willow Creek Farm is a dangerous place to work."

Chapter Twenty

"You know, you really shouldn't be putting any weight on that leg," Jillian said to Devereaux. "It is broken, after all."

"Have you ever had a broken leg?"

"No."

"Neither have I, until this one. And I'm here to tell you it hurts like a son of a bitch. But I'm not about to sit on my ass in bed just because it's painful to get up."

"I'm not talking about pain. I'm talking about injuring it. Making it worse."

Gus had made it clear he didn't want the FBI agent to get out of bed at all. But here he was, sitting in the kitchen, having a cup of coffee with Jillian. Mama was outside feeding the chickens. Jillian sighed. If he wanted to risk a compound fracture, who was she to deny him the privilege?

"Would you like another cup of coffee, Agent Devereaux?"

"Ah, come on, call me Lamar."

"Alright, Lamar, would you like another cup of coffee?"

"No. What I'd like is for you to sit down and let's talk about this."

"Talk about what?"

"About the fact that you don't want me here."

Jillian was not used to someone reading her reaction that accurately. She'd spent years learning how to crawl into a bubble inside herself, close the door, and not let anyone in. And she'd been trying desperately through therapy to dismantle all that defensive paraphernalia, because it was keeping everybody out. She was doing a pretty good job of it, but this was a brand new one.

Jillian opened her mouth to argue with him — *no, no, that's not true. I don't mind you being here.* But she closed it before the words made it all the way across her tongue. That was foolishness. For starters, obviously he could tell she didn't want him here. But more than that, it was just so much trouble to keep up some kind of wall, some kind of facade, to pretend to be what you're not. She let out a sigh. Being transparent was a whole lot simpler.

"What's to talk about?" she said. "I don't want you here."

"Then there's nothing to talk about except that I don't blame you."

She said nothing to that.

"If I were you, I would have said no. I'm surprised you didn't talk your mother out of it."

"You don't know my mother very well. You don't talk my mother out of anything she's got her mind set on doing."

"Yeah, but if you just raised some kind of alarm..." He didn't finish the sentence, just closed his mouth, took another drink of coffee, and then continued. "I've never been in a situation like this, not in my whole life. I've never been so vulnerable and fragile, and I'm here to tell you it totally, one hundred percent, sucks."

Well, Lamar Devereaux certainly got points for transparency.

"So, you don't want me here," he continued, "and I don't want to be here, and I don't know a fix except to tell you I'm sorry, I didn't plan it this way, I didn't want it this way, and if there were any way in the world I could get the hell out of here, trust me, I would." He looked down at his broken leg. "But what with a broken leg and all…"

"Look, it's okay."

"No, don't do that. Don't explain away your legitimate concern. You have every right in the world not to want me here. If I were you, I wouldn't. Although I have to admit, if I were you, I would have pitched a green fit at the time, and I wouldn't have let it happen."

"And where would that have left you?"

"Well, that wouldn't have been your concern, would it? I guess I'm interested to know why you didn't say anything."

He held up his hand. "And don't tell me it's because you couldn't talk your mother out of it. None of us can talk our mothers out of anything. But we all still try, constantly, all the time. You didn't even try."

"I don't want you here because it's dangerous, duh."

"I get that. Five by five. There are people out there who want me dead. But that's not your concern either."

"What is my concern is the safety and welfare of my mother and my sister, and you're putting that in danger."

"Well said. Point taken. Is that it?"

"Is what it?"

"Is that all of it? The whole reason you don't want me here?"

Before she could speak, he held up his hand again. "And don't tell me it is, because I can tell that it isn't."

"How can you tell that it isn't?"

"Let's just say I'm good at reading people." He smiled. "Even people as locked up tight as you are — with the windows shut and the shutters drawn and the big bar across the door… and, well, also, a chifforobe scooted up against it."

Jillian almost smiled at that. "Is that what I look like?"

"Not to anybody but me. I'm sure most people don't see that at all."

"I'm damn good at putting up a front."

"You're still skirting around the question. What's the real reason you don't want me here?"

"I don't have another reason."

"Yeah, you do."

"No, I don't. I—" She stopped, forcing herself to look inside and see her real motivations. She drew a breath. "Okay, I don't want you here because we can't tell anybody that you're here. And I'm going out with a man, and I don't know how to do this with him. He's just… it's kind of a delicate situation."

"How so?"

Jillian found herself just blurting it out. "Because I walked out on him thirty years ago on the night before we got married."

"That'll leave a mark."

She couldn't help but smile. And somehow that lightened up the conversation in a way she couldn't have defined.

"Mitch told me about that," Devereaux said. "That you were kidnapped by a trafficking ring. That's ugly. I've seen it. I know."

Jillian liked the way he looked at her when he said that.

Whenever Rileigh or her mother or even her shrink broached the subject of where she'd been and what had happened to her, their brows always knitted together, and there was such a look of concern on their faces that it made her feel uncomfortable. He just said it as plainly as "pass the salt."

"I worked the Special Victims Unit in Baton Rouge before I transferred to Nashville. I saw what happened to some of those girls. That you made it out alive after being there that long is an absolute miracle. I gotta hand it to you, Jillian. You are tough."

Nobody else in her life had said that to Jillian. They'd all been so concerned by what happened, so upset by what happened, so terrified that they would bring up something that would upset her that they walked around on eggshells, and this guy saw her escape as something she should be proud of.

"The last place I was," she said, "I was a house servant to an Arab family and a bedmate for the man in the house whenever he wanted it."

"An Arab family? Where?"

"Sudan."

"And if there were any little boys in that family, they treated you like shit, didn't they?"

She nodded.

"But you took it. You made it out. Damn." She could hear real admiration in that expletive. "And that makes it even harder for you that I'm here, because you've seen real violence."

"I'm not the only member of the family who's seen real violence," she said. "Rileigh was a soldier. She's been in combat. Two tours in Afghanistan."

His eyebrows shot up. "I did not know that. Wow, your mama raised some tough girls. And that's kind of surprising given that your mother is about as sweet an old lady as I've ever been around."

He paused. "I used to watch the old reruns of *The Andy Griffith Show*. And your mother reminds me of Aunt Bee."

Jillian had never thought about it before, but as soon as she did, it fit perfectly. "You're right. She reminds me of Aunt Bee too."

"That part had to be hard, wasn't it?" he said.

"What part?"

"Coming back home and they're all changed. When you left, your sister was, what, a first grader? And your mother, a young mother trying to scratch out a life for herself and her child. You come back, and your mother is an old woman who clearly isn't dragging a full string of fish, but delightfully so. Your sister was a soldier, and now she's a cop."

He sat back in the chair. "You are a piece of work, Jillian Bishop."

"What are you talking about?"

"Just what you've been through, how you've negotiated your life, dealing with the cards you were dealt. I don't believe I ever met anybody who had a harder hand to play. I'm sure you don't need to hear it from me, but you've done one hell of a job."

She didn't need to hear it from him. But she liked it.

Chapter Twenty-One

THE FIRST PHONE CALL MITCH GOT ON TUESDAY MORNING
was from a man who turned out to be the un-Simon
Tackett.

"This is Weatherford County Sheriff Collier Atkinson," the voice said and got instantly to the point. "I'm
calling you because of the email you sent out where you
said you were looking for murder cases that had a particular MO. I just came from a crime scene that would have
been the picture beside that MO in the dictionary."

That got Mitch's attention, and he sat up straighter in
his chair.

"Obviously," Atkinson continued, "you have worked a
similar case, and I'd like to pick your brain and find out
what you know."

"Brain picking is one of my very favorite activities,"
Mitch replied. "We have a diner here in Yarmouth County
that should be famous all over Tennessee, but isn't … yet.
It's called Red-Eyed Gravy, and you can get the best milkshake you've ever had there, but it also serves a pretty
decent cup of coffee. How about we get together at, say,

ten o'clock for a game of you-show-me-yours-and-I'll-show-you-mine."

"Done," the man said, and Mitch could hear a smile in his voice. Then he hung up.

Armed with the crime report and the autopsy results on Cody Whitlock, along with what little information he had been able to ferret out about the other victims on Devereaux's local people hit list, Mitch was seated at the counter talking to Big John when Sheriff Atkinson came in. One look at the man told Mitch he was former military — erect posture, hair cut high and tight, and you could have cut a piece of steak with crease in the pants of his uniform.

"Sheriff Webster," the man said and stuck out his hand.

"Call me Mitch."

"I'm Collier."

Mitch nodded goodbye to Big John and led the way to the back table that he was coming to think of as his "other office." The waitress followed them there to take Atkinson's order.

"What can I get you, sir?"

"I'll have whatever he's having." He pointed to the drink Mitch had carried with him from the bar to the table. "Is that a vanilla milkshake?"

Mitch grinned. "They make me a special brew."

"It's bananas and vanilla, but we mix in little pieces of pineapple and blackberries ... just because it's you, Sheriff," the waitress said.

"Like I said, I'll take what he's having."

When they were alone, Atkinson pulled out a file and laid it on the tabletop, and Mitch matched his file with one of his own. When Atkinson opened the file, Mitch was surprised to see that the victim was a woman. Though all the others had been male, it was clear from the brutality that they were dealing with the same killers. He opened his file to the pictures of Cody Whitlock and could tell that Atkinson instantly came to the same conclusion.

"This is a pretty specific MO," Mitch said. "Don't see Mexican drug cartel violence every day."

"Not just violence. This is torture." Atkinson pointed to the hand of the young woman whose body lay on the side of a ditch. "Yesterday morning the mailman who delivers to houses along Sycamore Lane found a shoe by the side of the road beneath a mailbox. He thought it must belong to the people who owned the house, so he got out to pick it up and put it in the box, happened to glance down into the ditch and thought he saw somebody down there, just dialed 911. It was obvious the victim had been beaten to death. I don't have the autopsy report yet, but just from physical observation, it appears that the bones in her hands, both hands, had all been smashed, and her knees. She was naked from the waist down, looked like she had been sexually assaulted."

He paused. "If I had to guess, I'd say somebody used garden snips on Annalise's toes and pulled her fingernails out by the roots. And—"

Mitch stiffened.

"*Annalise* — is that what you said?"

"Yes, her name is Annalise." He flipped over to the first page of the report. "Annalise Henderson, twenty, 342 Rock Hill Road — her parents' address. She still lives at home."

"I believe I know the connection between these two victims," Mitch said. "The county coroner, Dr. Gus Hazelton, spoke briefly with Cody's family. He was dating a Weatherford County girl. Her first name was Annalise."

"So these two young people were a couple?"

Mitch nodded. "Cody Whitlock went missing from his

work last Friday morning. He was a stable hand at Willow Creek Farm."

"Davidson's farm," Sheriff Atkinson said. Just the two words.

"How long have you been on the job, Collier?"

"A little over three months. The county held a special election after the sheriff died."

"Well, if the raised eyebrow I saw when I mentioned Willow Creek indicates that you have heard something about the place, and more than rave reviews for it being the finest Walking Horse farm in the state, then you won't be surprised to learn that there have been three other murders — same MO — of farm employees."

"Griffin Davidson comes off as something of a Robin Hood in Pendleton County, always there with a smile and a handshake and a check. But as I understand it, the source of the funds he's handing out is shady at best. I hear he's a money launderer for" — he pointed to the pictures of the brutalized bodies — "Mexican drug cartels."

"You get around for a man who hasn't been on the job but three months."

"I have a deputy who's an old hand, and he gave me a heads up. Then I did a little digging on my own. If you scratch Barrington Griffin Davidson the third very deep, the stink of the rot will spoil your lunch."

Mitch sat back in his chair. "You didn't hear this from me, okay?" Atkinson nodded. "I know someone who did a little nosing around and discovered that there have been a number of federal agents who have been murdered recently with the same MO."

"Federal agents?"

"FBI, DEA, Homeland Security."

Atkinson's eyebrow went up again. "How many agents are we talking about here?"

"Maybe as many as twenty."

"Twenty federal agents! You can't be serious. I haven't heard anything about a federal investigation."

"And you won't, because there isn't one. Not yet, anyway."

"So why didn't I hear this from you?"

"Because I didn't hear it from the person I heard it from … or he'd be dead, too. Right now, we need to leave it at that."

Mitch looked directly into Sheriff Atkinson's eyes, and the man read the message loud and clear.

"So … will you keep me in the loop?" He nodded with his chin at the pictures of the young woman beside the ditch. "I had to deliver the death notification to her parents. And I don't want to have to deliver any more of them."

"Copy that," Mitch said.

Chapter Twenty-Two

When the two suit-and-tie men came walking up the road toward Jeremiah Johnson's cabin, he cursed himself for a fool and determined to do one of two things before the rooster crowed tomorrow morning. One was buy himself the damned hearing aids he needed. He could hock one of his rifles to pay for 'em. Or second, get a dog.

Cleaning that raccoon he'd been stalking for a week, he was so intent on what he was doing that he flat-ass didn't hear 'em coming. Didn't notice the movement out of the corner of his eye until it was too late. He could have dropped the coon carcass and made off into the woods, but he didn't like running from these sons of bitches. They didn't have no right to be on his property anyway.

"I don't know who you are, and I don't care what you want," he said without looking up. "You're on private property and you ain't welcome here. Get the hell off my land."

"You're just about as friendly as everybody said you'd be," said the older blond man with a paunch. He was wearing a blue suit and a red tie, and for that, though for no other reason, he reminded Jeremiah Johnson of Donald Trump.

"I know *I* need hearing aids. I done been to the audiologist about it, but you boys need to get *your* hearing checked if you didn't hear what I just said — get off my property."

Neither one of them made any move to do as he'd instructed. The Donald Trump one reached into his side pocket and pulled out a badge and flipped it open … like Jeremiah didn't know the guy was FBI. The younger man, tall and skinny, followed suit. He didn't bother to read the names on the badges. He could have if he'd wanted to. There wasn't nothing wrong with his eyesight. It was his hearing that'd got his ass in trouble.

"I'm Agent Hank Gilbert," said the older guy, "and this is Agent Bill Conroe. We work out of the Nashville field office of the Federal Bureau of Investigation, and we just got a couple of questions for you, and then we'll leave you alone."

"Write 'em down and mail 'em to me. Now get off my land."

"All right. Just one question then. Answer it, and we'll leave. How did you come by the leather briefcase you hocked in Kirby's Pawn Shop in Gatlinburg? It belongs to the owner of a 2024 Prius reported stolen."

"I don't have no idea what you're talking about."

But he did.

And if he could have managed it, could somehow have contorted his body so he could, he'd have kicked himself in his own ass!

What had he been thinking? It was them damned hearing aids. He was so determined to make enough money to get them so he could hear that he'd given in to the urge. After they got that FBI agent down to that doctor's office outside Black Bear Forge, Jeremiah had got up the next morning thinking about that fellow's car. He'd wrecked it somewhere, and apparently the wreckage hadn't been found 'cause nobody had raised any stink about it. There might be something in that car that Jeremiah could sell. He'd at least ought to look.

Jeremiah went back to the place where he'd found the man behind the rocks, then backtracked the fella up the hill and through the woods. It wasn't hard, hadn't rained since he came through there. The little drops of blood that had dried to brown spots all along the way woulda washed off in the rain. He found it and wondered how anybody'd walked away from a wreck like that. He managed to pry open the back driver's side door to get into the vehicle, and on the floorboard there, he found the briefcase. It was expensive, made of that soft kind of brown leather that cost an arm and a leg. He knew he could get a couple of hundred for it easy from the fella he dealt with on Crossing Street, who gave him a good price for things and never tried to cheat him. What a fool Jeremiah had been. He'd ought to have known that that car was stolen.

"Yeah, you do. The pawn shop owner knows you. Now, I can take you in and let him pick you out of a lineup, or—"

"I found it in a car that was wrecked in the woods. Didn't figure nobody wanted it, so I took it. Surely to God you got better things to do with your time that hauling me into jail."

"We're not here to arrest you for stealing, Mr. Johnson." That was the younger fellow, had a surprisingly deep voice you wouldn't expect to come outta somebody so skinny. "We just need your help."

"How so?"

"The man who was driving that car, what happened to him? Where'd he go?"

Jeremiah shrugged. "How the hell would I know? I'd just come on the wreck, dug around in it and found that briefcase. How would I know what happened to the fella driving it?"

"So you're telling us that you were out in the woods and just stumbled upon a wrecked car?"

"Yep, that's exactly what I'm telling you."

"So you didn't make any effort at all to find out who was driving that car?"

"What would I do a thing like that for?"

"The car was wrecked. The driver could have been wandering around in the woods injured."

"No skin off my nose."

The older blond man, the Donald Trump man, Jeremiah had already forgot what his real name was, stepped forward with his phone and showed Jeremiah a picture. It was a picture of that FBI agent he'd found in the woods. He was a nice-looking fella when he wasn't all tore up and beat up.

"Do you recognize this man, sir?"

"Nope. Never seen him in my life."

"This is Senior Special Agent Lamar Devereaux with the FBI, and we believe he was driving the car that you found in the woods."

"An FBI agent and he stole a car? Sounds like you got bigger fish to fry than coming all the way out here to pester me with questions about it."

"He's still missing, and we're trying to find him."

"Well, don't look at me. How would I know where the hell he is?" The two agents looked at each other, perhaps some kind of nonverbal communication going on between them about whether or not they'd ought to believe him. He didn't care whether they did or not. There wasn't nothing they could do about it either way.

"We need you to tell us where you found that wrecked car," said the younger agent.

"You think I remember a thing like that?"

"I'm sure a mountain man like you remembers *exactly* where he found it." There was a sharpness to his tone that revealed some of the metal beneath the pleasant facade.

Jeremiah backed off a little then, wasn't no sense in telling them he didn't know. He just needed to misdirect them.

He let out a sigh. "I was coon hunting on the other side of Sycamore Knoll, and I went down into a ravine, chasing this fella." He nodded to the half-skinned raccoon. "There was a car down there all tore up. Airbags all went off. It was a mess. But there wasn't nobody anywhere around it."

"Did you see any sign of the person who'd been in the wreck, blood maybe?" asked the Donald Trump man.

"No telling how long that wreck'd been there. Why would I go looking for the driver now? I didn't see nobody — that FBI agent or anybody else."

"How would that car have gotten into that ravine?"

Jeremiah fixed the younger man with the condescending stare.

"How in the hell do I know how it got there? Ain't that your job to figure out?"

He could tell that pissed him off. So he relented a little. Getting FBI agents pissed at you was like shaking up wasps in a mason jar. They ever get out of that jar, they'll sting you good.

"If I was to guess ... the state road going into Black Bear Forge is uphill from there. I didn't go investigate, didn't have no reason to, but maybe the car knocked down a bunch of trees when it run off the road into the woods."

He had their interest now — giving them the wrong information was just as effective as giving them no information at all, and it went down smoother.

"So orient me to where that road is in relation to where you found the wreck."

"Orient you?" Jeremiah couldn't help playing the dumb hillbilly. "Now what in the name of God's blue heaven does orient mean?"

The agent started to explain, but Jeremiah held up his hand. He needed to get these guys gone from here.

"If it means where on the road is close to where I found that car, then like I said it's uphill. If I was to draw a line in my head from where the car was to where on the road it might have come off, probably somewhere between the 11- and 12-mile markers. But I didn't go look and see if there was trees knocked down. I dug around in the wreck, found that briefcase, and I went on my way."

The younger fellow reached into his pocket, drew out his wallet, and picked out a card and held it out toward Jeremiah. He didn't reach to get it and then figured that was needlessly rubbing their noses in his contempt, so he took the card.

"My number's on that card," the agent said. "If you think of anything else or you find anything else that might help us find Agent Devereaux, give me a call."

Jeremiah didn't say nay, he didn't say aye. He just stood looking at him. Then he spit into the dirt beside his feet and went back to cleaning that coon. Soon's their backs was turned, he tossed the card into the bucket with the coon's guts.

Chapter Twenty-Three

MITCH DIDN'T RECOGNIZE THE NUMBER ON CALLER ID, BUT it was a local area code. Not that many people had the number of his cell phone, so he took the call.

"Had me some company come visiting yesterday morning."

It took Mitch a moment to realize who it was. Jeremiah Johnson.

"Anybody I know?"

"I doubt it. They was FBI agents. One of them was a fella named Hank Gilbert. The other's last name was Conroe — Phil or Will or Bill. Something like that."

Mitch felt a rock land smack in the middle of his belly.

"The FBI came to see you." It wasn't a question.

"Yep."

"And they were looking for Agent Devereaux." That wasn't a question, either.

"Yep."

"And how in the world did they come to be calling on you?"

"My own damn fault," Jeremiah said, "See, I need me

some hearing aids. Needed 'em real bad 'fore I get me a coon dog." Mitch wasn't tracking, but he just let the old man talk. "I been saving up to buy the damned things, and I thought maybe I might find something I could hawk in that car that FBI agent was driving."

Mitch shook his head, "Oh, no."

"I was a damn fool. I dug around in that car and found a fancy leather briefcase. It was found property. I didn't steal it from nobody. I figured I could pawn it in Gatlinburg, put the money in my little cookie jar where I'm saving for them hearing aids."

"You didn't think about the briefcase being traced."

"Well, if I'd thought about that, I probably wouldn't have taken it, would I?" Jeremiah snapped, then he quieted. "It ain't nobody's fault but mine."

"What did you tell them?"

"What do you think I told them? I said I hadn't seen nobody, and if I had seen somebody, I sure as shit wouldn't a'tole them about it."

"Do you think they believed you?"

"Yeah, I think so. They was just fishing around, wasn't interested in what I took. They was interested in where I took it from. They showed me a picture of Devereaux, wanted to know if I'd seen him, and I said no. So they got him traced this far, but they'll be chasing their own tails around for six months trying to find that wreck where I told them I *thought* I saw it. The younger fella gave me his business card and told me if I thought of anything that I had somehow not come to mind when they was questioning me, would I give them a call. I chucked the card in a bucket of coon guts."

"Thanks for the heads up, Jeremiah." He paused. "You watch your back now, hear?"

The old man made some kind of clucking sound and hung up.

Rileigh came into Mitch's office when he was still talking to Jeremiah Johnson. He had asked her to go with him to talk to Griffin Davidson at Willow Creek Farm.

And her eyes were doing that thing again. That thing where the hazel color darkened to jade green. Just an illusion. Had to be.

He found he couldn't look directly into them or he would totally lose his train of thought and stand there babbling nonsense.

"The FBI has chased down that car and connected it to Jeremiah Johnson," he said, looking down at the papers he was needlessly shuffling on his desk.

"But Jeremiah didn't tell anything," Rileigh said. "Of course, he didn't."

"I'm not really worried about these guys, the ones who questioned Jeremiah. I'm worried about where else the information about that car might go. Lamar said he was in a safe house that wasn't safe. And Bill told me that the locations of safe houses are very closely guarded secrets. So if somebody breached a 'safely guarded secret' and found out where he was, then…" Mitch let the sentence dangle.

"You're afraid that they could find out the FBI went to question Jeremiah Johnson, too."

He nodded and sighed. "Let's go."

"Don't be so glum. The guy running the place may be slime, but Willow Creek farm is … well, you'll see."

She smiled at him, and the blow it struck made it hard to draw a breath. Oh, he was sure the horse farm would be beautiful, but he was equally certain it wouldn't take his breath away the way Rileigh's nearness sometimes did. He had to keep a tight grip on his emotions all the time, or…

Yeah, or *what?*

When they crested a hill and went around a bend and suddenly Willow Creek Farm was laid out before him, Mitch had to admit Rileigh hadn't been exaggerating its beauty.

"The proper response is 'Wow!'" she said. "Maybe throw in a 'Holy Shit!' or two."

"Is that…?" he sputtered.

"Yep, that's Willow Creek Farm."

"How big is that thing?"

"I think it's about 400 acres. It looks bigger here because it takes up all of Mill Pond Hollow, which is the largest piece of flat real estate in Pendleton County, and probably you could include Yarmouth County."

The view stretching out below them was something you'd put on a calendar or a postcard. It was that perfect. It was early morning, so there was still Smoky Mountain mist in all the hollows and rising up off the creeks. Below them, outlined in white fences, was a fairy tale. There were beautiful horses in the fields separated by the fences. What Mitch assumed must be horse barns with steeples on the top reminded him of the spires at Churchill Downs in Kentucky and looked fancier than any house he'd ever lived in his life.

There was a house set back from the road. The driveway leading to it was lined by stately oak trees, and the house itself was a big brick Colonial, or at least that's what Mitch thought that architecture style was. His first thought was it looked like Tara in *Gone with the Wind*.

"While you're busy being impressed and astounded by Willow Creek Farm, keep in mind that he has another one like this in Belgium."

"Belgium?"

"I don't know why Belgium. I just know that there's a European Tennessee Walking Horse Association. Davidson is always shipping horses back and forth across the Atlantic to show and stud — horses from here to improve the lines of the horses there. His farm is right outside Antwerp." She paused. "Who names a city Antwerp?"

"I know less than zero about Belgium."

Rileigh smiled. "I had to memorize 'four important facts' about every country we studied in geography class in high school." She wrinkled her brow, then parroted, "Belgium has more castles per square mile than any country in Europe. There are more than 450 varieties of Belgium beer. Antwerp is the world diamond capital because it imports more raw diamonds and exports more gemstones than any other country. And — I saved the best for last — a unique chocolate called *cuberdon* is exclusively produced in Belgium by a few craftsmen who have the secret recipe."

"Like Kentucky Fried Chicken's eleven herbs and spices?"

"How can KFC's recipe be a secret when every restaurant has to know the recipe to cook it?"

She had him there.

Mitch parked in the circular drive out front, and they went up onto the wide porch and knocked on the door. A butler answered and said that Mr. Davidson was expecting them.

Mitch had seen Griff Davidson's picture on a shelf in the office of Pendleton County Sheriff in Cochran a couple of days ago. Mr. Davidson was shown holding a poster-sized check for $40,000, demonstrating his contribution to the Senior Citizen's Center. And Mitch had thought then that Davidson must have gotten his fashion cues from *Cat on a Hot Tin Roof*, because he looked just like the character who had played Big Daddy in the Nashville stage production of it. Big Daddy was big and broad, white shirt, white coat, white pants, black string tie, and black patent leather shoes.

The butler showed them into Davidson's office. Davidson rose and extended his hand to Mitch.

"I'm glad to meet you, Sheriff Webster. Griffin Davidson. I've heard all about you," he said, smiling.

That smile never reached his eyes, which were cold and calculating and wary, Mitch thought. The eyes of a predator.

Chapter Twenty-Four

THE NEXT MORNING, JILLIAN WAS IN THE KITCHEN FIXING A breakfast tray to take to Agent Devereaux when she looked up and saw him standing in the doorway of the kitchen. He leaned against the door frame on one side and had a crutch under his arm on the other.

"You don't take orders very well, do you?" Jillian said.

He ignored the question. "I knew I would find you doing this."

"Doing what?"

"Making a tray to bring to me in the bedroom. Not happenin'."

"Your leg's broken. Why shouldn't I make a breakfast tray to bring to you?"

He hobbled precariously to the table, pulled out a chair and eased himself into it. "Because I don't need it."

"That is your opinion, and it is not shared by your doctor."

"He's a worrier. He'll get over it."

Jillian stepped back and studied the FBI agent. He still looked rough. He had bruises all over his face, plus the cut

143

on his forehead that Gus had stitched up. She winced at that. He was going to have a nasty scar for the rest of his life. She figured Gus was accustomed to cutting open and then stitching back up dead people who didn't complain if his handiwork wasn't neat and tidy.

Agent Devereaux was weak and pale, and Jillian knew that some of that was due to losing so much blood, but she suspected that his hollow-eyed look had come before the accident. She figured that a man who was being hunted by vicious killers for no reason that he could determine and who had watched one comrade after another be killed by them probably hadn't been sleeping too well.

"You got plans for what you're going to do when you accidentally put weight on that leg and the bone snaps?"

"Nah, I figure I'll just wing it."

He grinned. His was the kind of grin that was infectious, slightly mischievous, a little boy grin. She managed somehow not to return it, but it did take an effort.

"All right, I've made you some breakfast and I was about to bring it to you on a tray, but since you're sitting right here…" She started unloading the tray onto the table.

"Where is everybody?" he asked, picking up his cup of coffee and downing it in three long swallows.

"Rileigh went into town to Mitch's office … and I think they're going to go have a talk with Griffin Davidson at Willow Creek Farm."

Devereaux lifted an eyebrow. "That should be an interesting conversation."

"Or maybe not. Rileigh usually doesn't say exactly what she and Mitch are going to be doing. And Mama is at her friend Mildred's house helping her scrapbook."

"I didn't know that was a verb anywhere outside of Louisiana," Devereaux said. "My aunts had scrapbooks piled on top of scrapbooks. I was always afraid a birthday candle would set fire to one of them and the whole house would have gone up."

"Did you sleep well last night?" Jillian moved his plate of scrambled eggs and bacon off the tray and set them on the placemat in front of him and did the same with the silverware.

"Better than you did."

"How would you know a thing like that? If you slept better than I did, you would have been asleep. To know that I slept poorly, you'd have had to have been awake."

"You're quick." He paused. "I'm sorry. No, I didn't sleep well. This is not a particularly comfortable situation for any of us. And I know that you didn't sleep well either because I heard you upstairs in your studio."

Jillian's studio was directly above the bedroom on the first floor where they had put Lamar Devereaux.

"I'm sorry. I didn't know I was stomping." She got up, poured him a second cup of steaming black coffee, and then sat back down.

"You weren't stomping. I could just hear you up there. I knew you were awake, painting."

"That's the studio Rileigh made for me so that I would have something to do with my hands — sort of occupational therapy. I was really surprised at how much I enjoyed painting. Never did it before, but I like it now."

"Your sister loves you very much," he said.

His words were jarring. Everything about him was jarring. He didn't say what you expected him to say. He wasn't predictable. And that was one of her favorite traits about David. He was predictable. You knew how he would respond to a particular situation. You knew what he would think about what you were about to say. He was reliable and safe.

And as she thought both of those words, she thought that neither one of them sounded very interesting.

"Yes, she does and I … wasn't expecting you to say that. Most people don't notice such things, and if they do, they don't mention them."

"Your sister is precious to you, and you are to her. And she's worried to death about you, and you're worried to death about her." He forestalled her objection by holding up his hand. "It's as plain to see as if it were written on your forehead in red magic marker. It makes sense that she's worried about you. I don't quite understand why you're worried about her, though."

"What she does is dangerous."

"Dangerous?"

"Well, law enforcement is dangerous. I never dreamed my little sister would choose to go out and chase criminals. It's just hard."

She sat down.

"Aren't you going to eat breakfast?" he asked.

"I had breakfast earlier with Mama before she left."

"So how will you spend the day while she's scrap-booking and Rileigh's gone. Will you be painting?"

Jillian poured herself another cup of coffee, added a couple of teaspoons of sugar, got creamer from the refrigerator to turn the black liquid brown, then put the creamer back in the refrigerator — he'd already established he took his coffee straight up.

"o   Might try a little coffee with that cream and sugar," he pointed out as he eyed the mixture in her cup.

She sat down across from him and stirred the concoction. Truth was, she'd been up last night painting because she'd been thinking about Agent Devereaux. His presence was making her realize that she didn't know how to relate to normal men. She spent her whole life closing herself up from men. Building walls. Barricades to hide behind to escape their brutality.

Dr. Al-Masri was helping her to realize that what she'd experienced would leave huge scars ... but there were things she could do to mitigate the awful. And one of those things was learning how to be in a conversation with a man and not feel threatened, not withdraw behind some barricade to keep from being hurt.

She had to admit that she wasn't happy with the realization that she was able to return to some kind of relationship with David Hicks mostly because he carried all the weight of the relationship. He wanted to be with her, and he would do anything to make it easier on her to be around him. She was aware of him orchestrating their interactions and their conversations, steered them away from the rapids and the rocks into very smooth water where it was safe.

That was the right description. David Hicks was *safe*.

Lamar Devereaux, on the other hand, was not safe. He was relating to her the way any man would relate to any woman. He was not going through mental and emotional gymnastics to make sure that everything was pleasant and calm for her so she wouldn't be upset. So she would enjoy herself. So she would like what they were doing. Agent Devereaux just ... *was*. Which was disconcerting but also refreshing. She noticed it yesterday when he mentioned what had happened to her, told her she had "done good" without being affected by it, without becoming enmeshed. He just acknowledged that what had happened to her would have lasting effects. He wasn't ... invested in it. That's what it was! He wasn't invested in her past and how it had intersected with the lives of the people she left behind and how much pain and angst and agony they had all gone through all these years. Lamar Devereaux was outside all of that. He was just a casual observer. And Jillian found that very relaxing. She found him easy to talk to because she wasn't guarding what she said. Wasn't trying to keep from blurting out some terrible memory that would hurt her mother and her sister to hear. Devereaux was easy.

"What did you paint in the middle of the night last night?"

"Blobs of swirling color ... your basic two monkeys and a cat in a paint fight. It doesn't look like anything. I don't know how to make it look like anything. It's just sort of me vomiting my feelings out onto the canvas."

"I'm sure that your paintings give an insight into who you are in ways nothing else does."

"That's pretty much what my shrink said. That painting was my subconscious speaking truth my conscious mind did not want to know. That sounds suitably academic, doesn't it? She also said that painting was likely to trigger memories and dig up really ugly shit and make me look at it."

"Maybe I ought to take up painting."

"What for?"

"Maybe painting would help me uncover some memories. Not things I'm trying to forget, but things I'm trying to remember."

"What things?"

He stared past her out the window into the beauty of the mountains for a few moments before he seemed to come back to himself. "Nothing. I don't mean anything specific."

"You know, you're not a very good liar, and that surprises me. I would think an FBI agent would have honed the craft."

He said nothing and she pushed it.

"You wish you could paint to remember something. What?"

He put his half-empty cup down on the table. "If I knew what it was I wanted painting to help me remember, I wouldn't need painting to remember it, now would I?"

"I'm sorry. I didn't mean to pry."

"No, I'm sorry. I didn't mean to be so prickly."

She picked up the coffee pot to pour herself another cup. If he didn't want to talk about it, she certainly had no right to ask.

"What I can't remember might be the answer to the question we've all been asking."

"What question is that?"

"Who's trying to kill me?"

Chapter Twenty-Five

"You mean you have forgotten who wants to kill you?"

"No, that's not what I said. I've … lost a chunk of time. I have retrograde amnesia from a blow to the head. And I'm becoming more and more suspicious that whatever happened during the time I can't remember is what sent somebody on a killing spree."

Jillian opened her mouth to reply and then closed it in shock. Out the kitchen window, she could see David Hicks's 4X4 pulling up behind the house, hauling a trailer loaded with a four-wheeler and a dirt bike.

"Shit!" she said.

"What?"

She pointed out the window. "That's David. We talked about going four-wheeling today. I said sure, that sounded like fun. But that was four days ago, and I forgot all about it. He usually texts before he shows up, but this time he didn't."

"I need to get out of sight."

Devereaux rose to his feet and picked up his crutch.

But he was moving way too slow to get out of the room down the hall and into his bedroom with the door closed before David came into the house. Jillian went to him, grabbed his arm, wrapped it around her shoulder, and became a crutch on that side, and they hurried down the hallway with him crutching and leaning on her. She got him into the bedroom just as she heard David's voice.

"Hello all, where is everybody?"

Jillian rushed into the kitchen, trying not to look flustered.

"Oh, everybody is … well, Mama went to Mildred's to scrapbook, and she'll probably be there until suppertime. And Rileigh is doing … whatever it is Rileigh does when she goes running off with Mitch and you don't see her for hours, sometimes days."

He looked her up and down, and she realized she wasn't dressed to go four-wheeling. She was going to have to own it.

"David, I forgot all about us going four-wheeling today. Just a lot of things happened … I'm sorry."

That was her opportunity to bug out of it all together, but she didn't. She didn't want to disappoint him. "It won't take me but a minute to change."

"That's okay. I got the whole day."

She rushed up the stairs to her room, tore off the pair of shorts she was wearing, grabbed a pair of jeans off the back of the chair, pulled them on quickly, and added high socks and hiking boots. Grabbing a heavy denim shirt off a hanger in the closet to throw on over her t-shirt, she ran down the stairs and found David sitting at the kitchen table. He had helped himself to a cup of coffee.

"You have company this morning?"

Jillian almost choked. "Why would you think we had company?"

"Nobody in this house drinks black coffee," he said, indicating the cup of half-drunk, still warm, black coffee sitting beside the plate of equally half-eaten breakfast. She could claim the breakfast plate was hers, but…

"We ran out of creamer." She prayed he wouldn't open the refrigerator door and see that she was lying. "I decided to drink it black. Or at least to try. Other people drink black coffee. So I thought I'd give it a shot." She knew she was babbling and forced herself to stop talking.

She could see doubt on his face.

"How did you like it?"

"It's awful, tastes like road tar."

David got to his feet, smiling. "Drink a lot of road tar, do you?"

"Only when I can't get black coffee."

She turned and hurried out the back door. David followed, and she helped him unload a dirt bike that was red, but so beat up it was hard to tell the color, and what looked like a brand-new black four-wheeler. And maybe it was brand new. Maybe David had bought it just so she could use it to go biking in the woods with him. It wouldn't really surprise her if he had.

She boarded the four-wheeler, turned the key, and started it. David jumped a couple of times on the dirt bike's kick starter before it roared to life, then he led the way out onto the trail into the woods. Jillian cast a glance over her shoulder but could see no one standing at the window in the bedroom where Agent Lamar Devereaux had been stashed.

David had brought over the four-wheeler and the dirt bike on several occasions. Jillian had gotten very good at driving the four-wheeler. She could go just about anywhere, understood how to turn, how to shift her weight from one side of the four-wheeler to the other, how to shift, slow, and stop. They rode now on trails that were merely cow trails over the mountains. Sometimes they drove for a while on a logging road, sometimes up a dry creek bed. Gratefully, it hadn't rained in a few days. There wasn't a lot of mud, but what there was flew up off the tires and splattered on the back of Jillian's shirt.

They finally stopped at the crest of Eagle's Nest Peak, a very grandiose name for a small mountain. All the other mountains towered above it.

"I brought lunch," David said, opening the cooler that he had used bungee straps to attach to the rack on the back of the four-wheeler. He thought of everything. He always did.

Jillian scratched back through her mind, trying to remember if he had always been that thoughtful, always anticipated what she wanted and had it before she even had a chance to ask, or if that was merely a product of three decades of separation and what was clearly a desire on his part to keep her near and dear. She wouldn't allow herself to go past that they were seeing each other, that's it. She drew the line firmly in the sand, and he never tried to get across it. He reached and took her hand once just to help her climb up onto a rock, and then he let go of it. She couldn't even fathom what a physical relationship with a man might be like, what it would mean, how it would make her feel. There was nowhere in her that could even go there, and David intuited her need for physical privacy and was very careful not to touch her. And that struck her as both very kind and very sad.

He had packed the picnic basket with sandwiches and drinks and chips, a container of potato salad, and of course pickles. Jillian loved sour pickles. He spread the feast out before her under the limbs of a majestic oak tree that towered into the sky.

"So tell me about your week," she said as she settled back with her choice of peanut butter and jelly from the selection of PB&J, ham and cheese, chicken salad, or tuna salad.

"Well, I can't seem to manage to retire."

She smiled at that. They had talked about the fact that he wanted to step back from management of his businesses, enterprises which she suspected were even larger and more complex than he told her. But he kept getting sucked back in by the younger members of the company who clearly didn't have his expertise or his charm or his connections and were terrified that when he finally hung up his sword and they were in charge, the company was going to fall apart. He had taken the younger members of the team around, introduced them to the key players in their industry, people with whom they would have to conduct commerce and make deals. But Rileigh suspected that none of his proteges were particularly impressive. They were good guys, and they knew their jobs. They just didn't show well. And David, with his hulking chest and bulging arms and shoulders, was a walking advertisement for a gym.

She let her mind wander as he told her about his conversation with the younger men in his office, thinking about what Agent Devereaux — no, the man's name was *Lamar* — what Lamar could have meant by his suggestion that he might know why everyone was trying to kill him but he had just forgotten it.

Chapter Twenty-Six

Barrington Griffin Davidson III was a Southern gentleman, charming and cordial and slick. After the pleasantries — no, they wouldn't care for a cup of coffee, or lemonade or iced tea made Southern style with lots of sugar — Davidson said, "I can't imagine how I could be of any assistance to you, Sheriff Webster, but I'd be glad to help any way I can. I understand that some fella died, was one of my employees."

He smiled broadly and shrugged. "But I got three hundred or so people working for me in the stables here on the farm. I have a farm in Belgium too and we ship horses back and forth, so we got an army of transport people. As you might suppose, it requires a very specific skill set to take care of a horse on an airplane."

"I suppose you've been informed that one of your stable boys, a young man named, Cody Whitlock, has been brutally murdered, right?"

"I have been so informed, yes."

"An investigation revealed that he is the fourth murder

victim from among your employees. A Pendleton County boy named Alex Spaulding was killed—"

"As were young men from Buchanan and Whitley Counties. I talked to Sheriff Tackett about their deaths some time ago, but I could shed no light on his investigation."

"They were all killed in the same manner — they were tortured, bones smashed, fingernails torn out, that kind of thing," Rileigh said, in a soft steady voice that made her words all the more shocking.

Mitch saw a muscle beside Davidson's left eye twitch, but his voice carried no emotion at all.

"So I was told."

"Cody Whitlock isn't the only murder victim whose body we've found in the last 48 hours," Mitch said, seeing Davidson's jaw clench as he went on. "The other was Annalise Henderson. She was his girlfriend."

"I did not know *that*," he said. "My, my, that young man must lead a dangerous life if whoever tortured him to death tortured her, too."

"I didn't say she was tortured."

Mitch saw anger flash in Davidson's eyes as bright as lightning, but his voice was even.

"I just assumed. She was, wasn't she? *Tortured*, I mean."

"Yes, she was, and you don't think the brutal murders of *five* people associated with this farm — all killed in the same manner — has anything to do with their employment here?"

"Well, of course not. What in the world could any of them have done here that would make somebody want to kill them? I didn't have any direct contact. No do I think I ever even met any of them, but you are as welcome as the flowers in May to talk to the people who did know them. They've been instructed to cooperate one hundred percent with your investigation, tell you anything you want to know."

Mitch said nothing about the murders of the federal agents. He couldn't do that without implicating Devereaux.

Davidson signaled that he wouldn't answer any more questions about the murders by changing the subject. He turned to Mitch.

"Do you know what a Tennessee Walking Horse is, Sheriff?"

"Sure, they're the horses that prance, lift their feet up really high."

"Have you ever seen one up close?"

"No sir, I have not."

"Well, we shall not allow that gaping hole in your cultural heritage to remain unfilled. Will you join me in a walk down to the barn and I'll show you some?"

He somehow made the polite request sound like "an offer he couldn't refuse."

So the three of them set out down the walkway toward the barns. The roads between the barn and the outbuilding and the main house and that ran between the rows of white fences were not asphalt or concrete or even gravel. They were covered with wood chips, softer on the horses' hooves, Davidson explained.

Mitch caught the unmistakable tone of Mr. Davidson's speech coloring his words, the self-deprecating, "Yeah, I'm a rich guy but I'm just good people at heart, put my pants on one leg at a time like everybody else."

He cultivated that tone in an effort to disguise his thinly veiled belief that he was a cut above the rest of humanity, singularly blessed with intelligence and every virtue — including humility. Oh, my yes, Griff Davidson was humble. And proud of it, too.

They entered the cool of one of the barns. Mitch was

impressed by the measures taken to create a horse-friendly environment. Nothing stuck out that could scratch a horse when it walked by. Any necessary protrusion was covered in a thick pad. They walked through double doors at the end of the building with a center aisle stretching out in front and horse stalls on either side. The horse stalls were enclosed except for the area above a half door, and as soon as the horses heard the sounds outside, several of them came to that half door and stuck their heads out.

"Isn't this a beautiful animal? Just look at how sleek and fine he is." The warmth in Davidson's voice was genuine.

Davidson reached into his pocket and pulled out a sugar cube, and the horse picked it up as gently off his palm as a mother's touch.

"Do you know that Shelbyville, Tennessee is the Walking Horse capital of the world? Our farm in Belgium is considered to be the Walking Horse capital of Europe. Roy Rogers' horse, Trigger, was a Tennessee Walker."

"Not until a few days ago."

"Oh, indeed he was. He was a full-blooded Tennessee Walking Horse named Allen's Gold Zephyr, bred right out of Readyville, Tennessee. I named one of my barns after him."

A young man was leading one of the horses out of the barn through the central walkway. Davidson called a halt and displayed the animal for Mitch. It was indeed beautiful, its coat slick and shiny.

"You see, what's special about Walking Horses is they're gaited horses, but they have a unique four-beat kind of running walk, this real flashy movement. And it was originally developed because of how comfortable it is to ride one of them. They're the easiest riding horses in the whole world."

When he spoke about his beloved horses, Davidson sounded like a proud father, not a ruthless killer.

"And if it wasn't for all the nastiness having to do with scoring, that gave them all a bad name…"

Mitch knew what scoring was, but he asked anyway to keep Davidson talking, hoping he might reveal more than he intended to share.

"What's scoring?"

"There are breeders and trainers who are unethical, and they'd do anything to win, including hurting an animal." Davidson's eyes glinted and he dropped the Southern facade briefly. "If I ever see anybody — trainer, breeder, groom — touch a horse in any harmful way, I will kick their asses so far up between their shoulder blades they'll have to unbutton their shirt to take a shit. No offense, ma'am."

Davidson explained that unethical breeders put weights and other devices on a Walking Horse's front hooves to train them to lift their feet up higher.

"All that was banned by an actual act of Congress! The only thing allowed now is normal pads on a their hooves." He pointed to the front hooves of the horse standing beside them. "Those are called 'stacks'."

The stacks reminded Mitch of the shoes he'd seen on teenagers in the mall. They were built up at least two inches, more like three in the front, and he supposed it was a little like a woman walking in high heels for the horse to walk in shoes like that, which promoted an exaggeration of the Walker's natural gait of lifting their front feet high.

Mitch got down on one knee to examine the stacks, held on with a band over the top of the hoof. They were four or five inches wide and three deep, and raised the front of the horse's hoof three inches off the ground.

When he got to his feet, he thought to wonder if

perhaps they were in the barn where Agent Devereaux had been when Davidson brought Guillermo Castilla to the barn to show off the horse that had arrived that afternoon from his farm in Belgium.

When Griff Davidson had strutted his stuff enough that he was convinced Rileigh and Mitch were properly impressed, he handed them off to his foreman.

"Glenn, you take them anywhere they want to go and show them anything they want to see and let them talk to anybody they want to talk to." To Rileigh and Mitch, he said, "You folks enjoy the rest of your day now, hear," in proper Southern gentleman style, then turned and headed back up to the big house.

The foreman took Mitch and Rileigh around and introduced them to several of the farm hands who worked with Cody and Alex at the farm. None of them had anything particularly enlightening to say. The only one who sparked Mitch's interest was a young man named Ben Clark. He was squirming, didn't want to make eye contact, and looked nervous. With little prodding, he admitted that he'd been the one who told Cody they'd found Alex's mutilated body.

"Looked like that scared the shit out of him," he said. "'cause Cody seen them come and take Alex away."

Mitch leapt on the remark.

"Somebody came and took Alex away and Cody saw?"

"Uh huh."

"Did you see, too?"

"No sir."

"What did he say about the people?"

"Nothing.

"He didn't describe what they looked like, what they were wearing, what kind of car they drove — anything?"

"No, not a thing. Well, except that one of them had

keys in his pocket and he kept jangling them. But that was all."

The Clark boy shook his head sadly. "I told him about them finding Alex's body and it being all tore up so no telling what happened to him. And damned if Cody didn't disappear the very next day. I told him he hadn't be … hadn't ought to be fooling around with Annalise around here."

Before Mitch could ask, the young man leaned close and spoke quietly. "Now you didn't hear this from me, but Cody brung his girlfriend out here one time, Annalise Henderson."

Mitch thought of the battered body of a young woman he had seen just that morning, but he didn't mention it.

"She just wanted to see the horses. But there ain't much that'll get you fired quicker than letting somebody on the grounds here that ain't supposed to be here, so he was risking his job for that girl. It was the night all that commotion happened, and he come within a monkey's eyebrow hair of getting caught. I don't think she was worth it."

Rileigh and Mitch left Ben and headed back up the wood chipped path from the barn to the house.

"The night all that commotion happened," Rileigh said. "Both of those kids were here."

"Yeah, and now both of them are dead."

Chapter Twenty-Seven

"So you really didn't have company this morning?" David said out of the blue. Jillian jumped. When she did, her elbow caught her soft drink, spilled it onto the blanket, and it ran downhill onto her pants.

Leaping to her feet, she snatched the soft drink and set it back upright and began cleaning up the mess she had made.

"We didn't have company. Why do you think we had visitors?" she asked.

"Because I'm not sure that if I held your nose and tilted your head back and put a gun to your temple and told you if you didn't drink a cup of black coffee, you would be dead … your mother would right now be making funeral arrangements." He was smiling when he said it, but it was a cautious, guarded smile.

"Well, I don't know what to tell you, but I tried it and didn't like it." Jillian heard herself stumbling and bumbling, knew she didn't sound convincing, but was so flustered by the question and by the thought that he had stumbled into their great secret that she couldn't do any better.

"Okay," he said. "I just thought maybe somebody dropped by."

Then she realized that's what she should have said. She should have told him that somebody dropped by. She could have named anybody. Somebody had a cup of coffee and left, and he would never have thought another thing about it. It was her professing to drinking a cup of black coffee that has set his antenna spinning.

She found her heart pounding in her chest.

She was uncomfortable.

It was too hot here, even in the shade. Too hot to be outside at all.

Then things began to blur around the edges.

Her heart was pounding.

Someone was speaking.

Who was it? Who was talking to her?

"It's me, David, Jillian. Look at me." There was nobody there. She looked around, trying to see where the voice was coming from.

"Jillian, it's me, David. You're at home. You're not there in that place. Jillian, look at me. Look at my face."

And then the confusion rolled over her like thick fog off the sea, stirring her in a morass of uncertainty, fear, and confusion.

"Jillian. Jillian, it's me. It's David. I'm here beside you. You're sitting under an oak tree on Eagle's Nest Mountain."

The words came at her out of the confusion.

"Open your eyes, Jillian. Look around. Open your eyes."

Jillian didn't even realize that she had her eyes squeezed

tight shut until she heard those words. Then she opened them and looked around, and the world didn't match. And some part of her understood what was going on because it had happened before. The lack of matching, the way the worlds didn't fit, the elements in them, the way the young man talking to her was like a ghostly overlay on the backside of the palm tree ... she wasn't sure what was real and what was not.

"Jillian, look around you. Can you tell me what you see? Do you see an oak tree? Look, feel the oak tree. It's right here. Feel of it. How rough the bark is."

And as he spoke, reality slowly shifted. It was like a scene evaporating — there and then not. Substantial and real and then becoming translucent, then transparent so that she could see through it what was on the other side and then gone altogether.

Jillian shook her head and looked into David's eyes, and she watched him relax and settle back on his heels.

"Jillian, talk to me. Tell me where you are. It's me. David."

"David. I'm sorry. I don't know what hap — I'm sorry."

David stopped her before she could continue. "I thought we talked about this." He was right. They had made an agreement that she was not allowed to feel guilty or anxious or embarrassed about having a flashback, because they weren't her fault. And intellectually, she totally understood that. If she had been talking about someone she knew, she would have been so compassionate for them, suffering this malady that they didn't cause and couldn't control. But she wasn't looking from the outside in. She was looking from the inside out, and she felt waves of shame and guilt and embarrassment wash over her.

"Jillian, come on. We had an agreement, remember? Look at me."

She did. She looked into David's eyes. She knew where she was and what was happening. And in the swirl of emotions was a new one, one she hadn't experienced before. Anger.

Anger at David.

She leapt into instant denial. No, no, it wasn't anger. She wasn't angry. It was just irritation, just annoyance.

But it was many rungs up the ladder from there. She was angry, and she couldn't understand why.

"You're here with me and you're safe," he continued. "Look around. You'll see you're safe."

Jillian understood that David was "managing her." David was using "clinical techniques" to help her deal with the after-effects of the trauma that she had suffered. But at that moment, she did not want to be managed. She didn't want to be someone who *had* to be managed. She didn't want to be broken. She didn't want anyone to have to take care of her, and particularly not David. And the fact that he was so kind, so very thoughtful, so very loving … it made her mad.

Irrational? Sure, it was. But realizing it was irrational didn't make her feel any better.

She shook her head and smiled at him, managed to say a few of the right things, and the tension began to ease. But she was very aware of the new reaction, something she hadn't experienced before. It wasn't the flashback that made her angry. It was that David had had to take care of her because of the flashback that royally pissed her off.

The rest of the afternoon was pleasant. They had a good time. It was an uneventful trip back down the mountainside until David decided to give the rock face on the utility cut a try.

About half a mile from where the trail forked off toward Rileigh's house, the utility company had cut the trees and brush and cleared a huge swath of vegetation near their lines. After a couple of summer rains and winter snows, the exposed hillsides that Mother Nature hadn't intended to be bare were eroded down to rock, and it was one of those that David and other bikers liked to try to climb on their bikes.

Jillian and David stopped at the base of the rocky climb, and David cast a grin her way before he backed up as far as he could from the base. He needed as big a run at it as possible.

He revved the engine, popped the clutch, and the bike almost leapt out from under him, roaring across the small flat spot before he hit the bottom of the incline. Then he tried desperately to keep his bike on the rutted-out trail worn by countless other bikes, in the best path up through the rocks. There was almost no traction, and keeping up momentum without flipping the bike over was the challenge of the climb. She'd seen many bikers give that rock face their best, get halfway, maybe three quarters of the way up, and then dump the bike.

David made it about a third of the way up before he lost control. The bike got away from him, and he tumbled off onto the ground. The bike slid 10 feet or so down the hillside, and in the process, broke the front brake handle off the handlebars. He picked the bike up and carefully walked it back down to the trail, where Jillian sat watching on the four-wheeler.

"Well, I certainly crashed and burned," he said as he rolled the broken bike up beside the four-wheeler.

"Yeah, but it was entertaining to watch," Jillian said, smiling. David stuck out his thumb, and for a moment she didn't get the gesture.

"Give me a ride back to the house?" he asked.

"What, you're leaving the bike here?"

"I can't very well take it down that slope."

Jillian understood then. There was a particularly rough, rocky slope between them and the house. To make it down a steep slope on a dirt bike, you had to alternate between the front brake and the back brake to slow you down, never allowing either one of the brakes to lock up the tire, because if they did, it would slide. With only a back brake, it would be almost impossible to keep from locking up the back tire, which meant the bike would slide … and so would you.

"I'll leave the bike here. Go into Gatlinburg and get me a new brake handle, come back and fix it in a day or two."

David pushed the bike off the trail and into the woods behind a bush hidden from view, though there was no one likely to come this way and see it if he'd left it parked in the middle of the trail.

Then David climbed onto the four-wheeler in front of Jillian. She wrapped her arms around him as they rode back home.

She grew anxious the closer they got to the house. Surely Rileigh was home and had gotten Agent Devereaux out of sight. When they got to the house, she took her time getting off the four-wheeler and taking off her helmet, being sure to give Rileigh enough time to sweep the FBI agent under the rug if David decided to come inside. He didn't.

Looking at his watch, David cried out, "Damn, I didn't mean to get back so late." He turned to Jillian. "Would it be okay if I left the four-wheeler and trailer here overnight? I don't have time to get back home and drop them off before I have to be at a board meeting."

"Absolutely fine. Thank you for a wonderful afternoon. I had so much fun."

She didn't like the hint of phoniness she heard in her own words and hoped he didn't pick up on it.

David unhooked the trailer and left it parked in the barn with the four-wheeler sitting beside it, the keys in the ignition in case it needed to be moved before he got back.

Jillian didn't relax until she saw David's brake lights flash as he got to the bottom of the hill and turned onto the road. Then she hurried into the house, where Rileigh sat at the kitchen table.

"Did you have a good time?" Rileigh asked.

"Yeah, sure. It was great. Where's Lamar?"

"He's in the bedroom taking a nap. Why?"

"Because David got here while he was still in the kitchen this morning."

Rileigh's eyes got huge. "Did he see anything?"

"Hell yeah. Lamar drinks his coffee black. You know anybody else in this family who does? David noticed the cup of black coffee."

"Oh boy."

"And I had to manage to convince him that I decided to give black coffee a try."

"Did he buy it?"

"He acted like he did, but how could he? Come on."

"Which means he's suspicious."

Jillian shrugged. "I think he suspects something's going on that he doesn't know about. And he's upset about it."

"Well, isn't that peachy," Rileigh said.

Chapter Twenty-Eight

As he parked his cruiser in front of his dark house at the end of the day, Mitch was thinking about Jeremiah Johnson's phone call that had started his day. He was worried about Jeremiah. If the FBI had found him, that meant the whole FBI *system* had absorbed the information about Jeremiah selling that briefcase out of the car Agent Devereaux had stolen from the Walmart parking lot. And if the word was out in the system, then whoever outed Lamar at the safe house knew it, too, or soon would.

Mitch hadn't taken more than a step away from his cruiser when a voice out of the shadows called, "Freeze."

Mitch froze.

"No sudden movements. Don't make me shoot you."

"Who are you, and what do you want?"

"Turn around and put your hands on the car."

Mitch complied.

"Now scoot your feet back."

Mitch moved his feet back a few inches.

"Put your weight on your arms and move your feet *way* back."

This guy knew what he was doing. He wanted Mitch off balance.

Mitch did as he was directed, then asked again, "What do you want?"

"All I want is to talk."

"If that's all you want, let's talk. You don't have to pull a gun on me. Who are you?"

"Let's just say I'm a friend."

"You're no friend of mine."

"I didn't say I was a friend of yours. I'm a friend of Lamar Devereaux's."

The hairs on the back of Mitch's neck stood up.

"Who's Lamar Devereaux?"

"Don't give me that shit. You know who he is."

"No, I don't. I've never met — Oh. Are you talking about the FBI agent who worked that kidnapping case here?"

"Uh huh, that's who I'm talking about."

"Fine then. I do know him."

"Seen him lately?"

"The last time I saw Lamar Devereaux, he was driving out of Yarmouth County to go to Nashville and start the search for the parents of an eleven-year-old girl named Shiloh who'd been kidnapped out of a stroller when she was eighteen months old."

"You saying you haven't seen him since?"

"That's what I'm saying. Why would I have seen him?"

"Because I think he came to you wanting help."

"Help with what?"

"Look, we're both on the same side here, okay?"

"If we're on the same side, put that gun down."

The man ignored him.

"I believe that you have seen Lamar Devereaux. I believe you know where he is."

"And why would you think a thing like that?"

"Because I know Lamar. I know his opinion of you. I'm doing this on my own. Shaking trees to see what will fall out. Trying to find Lamar before he gets his ass killed."

"You still haven't answered my question. Why would I know where Lamar Devereaux is?"

"Because he disappeared out of a safe house less than a hundred fifty miles from here, and I've been trying to think outside the box where he might go for help. I thought of you."

"Well, you need to climb back into the box, because I don't know where Lamar Devereaux is. But I am interested to know why you want to find him so bad."

"Like I said, I want to talk to him before he gets his ass killed."

"And why would you think he's going to be killed?"

"For the same reason all those other agents were killed."

"What other agents?"

"You're pretty damn good at playing dumb."

"Takes practice."

"By my count, and I may have missed somebody, since last summer, four FBI agents, eight DEA agents, and seven agents from Homeland Security have been murdered."

"Holy shit."

"Lamar's the next one on the list."

"Why are they being killed, and who is killing them?"

"Have you ever heard of Guillermo Castilla?"

"Yeah, I've heard of him. He's a Mexican drug lord."

"Well, Castilla is looking for something belonging to him. And he has gone from one of those agents to the next trying to find it."

"Lost his cell phone, did he?"

"He wants it back *bad*."

"And you want to talk to Lamar about this because…?"

"Because Lamar's got it."

Mitch was glad it was dark so the man with the gun couldn't see his shocked response. He swallowed and asked calmly, "Got what?"

"The bubbles."

"Bubbles? What are you talking about?"

"That's how Mr. D referred to what he was delivering to Guillermo Castilla … before he got interrupted."

"Why do you think Lamar Devereaux has it?"

"Because he saw Castilla with it. We both did. And when we did, Lamar was off to the races. He said we should take it, said it was the opportunity of a lifetime and no one would ever know. He was crazy. I said, 'How are we going to walk out of here with a thing like that?' Lamar thinks fast on his feet, and he said we wouldn't walk out with it. We'd hide it there. Under the floorboards or in the rafters. All kinds of places to put it. Then we'd come back for it later. I said no, that he was nuts. I wouldn't go along with it. When he couldn't convince me, he shrugged and gave up. At least, I thought he did."

The man in the shadows paused.

"And then everything went to shit, and we got separated, and the next thing I knew he was in the hospital with a head injury and they said he'd never wake up. I never told anybody what he suggested, never even told the higher-ups what he and I saw. What was the point? That was his last raid, and I didn't see any reason to tarnish his record. Nobody needed to know that. But then … it started."

"What started?"

"The bodies started dropping. I knew then that he'd gone through with it, that he'd taken it, and Castilla was trying to get it back. And there was nothing *I* could do! I couldn't confess after the fact what we'd seen. Lamar stole it! — you think anybody'd have believed I wasn't an accomplice? Hell, I couldn't even give it back to Castilla myself because I didn't know what Lamar did with it. He was in a coma — the docs called it a PVS, a permanent vegetative state. There was nothing I could do to make it right. All I could do was run."

"So you left the agency?"

"In a manner of speaking."

"And now you want to find Lamar because…"

"To talk sense into him, talk him into giving it up. He can't *keep* it — they'll find him eventually and torture him into telling them where he stashed it. He certainly can't turn it in … and admit that he's responsible for the deaths of all those agents. The only shot he has is to give it up *before* they catch him. *Give it back to Castilla* — cut some kind of deal to exchange it for his life. I'll be the go-between, broker the deal. I'll contact Castilla, set it up, but Lamar's got to come across with the goods. If he doesn't, he's going to die."

"You were an agent, too. You were there. How come Castilla didn't track you down after you left?"

The voice barked out a laugh. "Where I went, Castilla wouldn't bother to look. I'm safe. At least I *was* … I'm risking my life trying to save Lamar's."

"So you came to see *me* because…"

"I heard him talk about you. He trusts you, thinks you're a cop's cop. When I started scratching my head trying to figure out where he could have run to … one look at the map and I saw Yarmouth County. He's too smart to go to somebody who would be connected to him. Nobody would connect him to you."

"Except you … and you're wrong."

"No I'm not." He paused again. "I tell you what,

Sheriff Webster. You won't be able to deliver this message, of course, because you haven't seen him. But if you happen to run into him somewhere — say, oh I don't know, in the canned meats aisle in the grocery store — would you deliver a message for me? Tell him his only chance is to give it back. He'll have a life if he does that … and maybe I can get my life back."

Before Mitch could say another word, the voice out of the shadows said, "I want you to count to fifty, slow, out loud so I can hear you."

"And if I refuse to be your trained monkey?"

"You won't. You understand that a man will do a thing he doesn't want to do if you back him into a corner."

Mitch complied, knowing full well what was going down. The man was listening to his voice as he slipped into the shadows and got away. Mitch stopped at thirty-five and called out, "Hey dude out there in the dark, you gone yet?"

The shadows didn't reply.

Chapter Twenty-Nine

Jeremiah Johnson leaned over and scratched the little coon hound puppy behind the ears, and the dog began to lick his own nose, his big old tongue coming out of his mouth. Then he yawned. Jeremiah figured that meant he liked to have his ears scratched.

Jeremiah'd had dogs unnumbered throughout his life, and the reason he didn't have one before right now was because his last, Maggie, had died about three years ago. It tore his heart out of his chest. She was thirteen years old and could barely see, and he had to pick her up to take her outside to go pee, but he did love that dog, and after she passed, he just couldn't make himself get another one.

Until now. Now, he didn't just want a dog, he *needed* one.

He hadn't picked out a name yet, had several in mind but hadn't settled on one. He brought the dog home last night, and Clarence warned him that the first night separated from his mama, the little dog was going to cry, and that Jeremiah best ignore it — "he'll get over it in a couple of days."

But Jeremiah had forgot how pitiful a little dog sounded when it cried. The crying about broke his heart when he put the dog in a box beside the front door of his cabin. He couldn't take it, got the puppy out of the box, and put it in bed with him, and it went right to sleep.

He leaned over, picked the puppy up, and set it in the box again, which was now outside on the front porch. He didn't want it to go wandering off while he went out into the woods for some kindling to start a fire in the cook stove, and it would sure as shit scare off any rabbits before Jeremiah could bag one or two for supper. The dog didn't start crying or nothing when he left it there, but as he was picking up sticks behind a windfall of limbs in the brush fifty yards or so from his cabin, the little dog started to bark — or make a sound that passed for a bark from a coon hound puppy that when it was full grown would *bay*, not bark. Right now, though, the little thing couldn't produce nothing more than what sounded like the squawk of a goose.

It was going to town barking, and Jeremiah knew he was gonna have to teach the dog not to bark at every damn squirrel it heard in the trees or every damn deer that come near. He just wanted it to bark when…

Suddenly, Jeremiah's gut tied up, quick as if he'd yanked a knot in a rope. He froze where he was and quietly sank down behind the windfall.

Wasn't long before he seen a fellow coming through the woods, moving quiet. Dark green tee shirt over combat fatigues, his black hair too long, hanging in his eyes. The man carried a rifle that rested in his hands calm and secure like he was a man used to holding it.

If there was one, there was more than one, and Jeremiah wasn't going to move from where he was until he knew where the rest of them was. He stayed hunkered down, peeking out between the leaves, and waited. The first man met up with a second one. If they was two, they was probably four, so where was the other two?

He stayed where he was, hunkered down behind that windfall for an hour, not moving a muscle. He never did see but them first two ones, and they went on through the woods and left him be. Finally, he crept quietly out from behind the landfall and started back to his house. He went from tree to tree, careful, looked around him, got back to the clearing where his cabin was, and stayed hidden in the bushes where he couldn't be seen for fifteen minutes before he stepped out into the open there.

The box with the puppy in it was still sitting where he'd left it, but the puppy wasn't making no noise. Jeremiah ran to the house, leapt up onto the porch, looked down into the box where the puppy lay, dead. Somebody'd broken its neck.

"Stay where yew are," a heavily accented voice called out to him from the woods. Jeremiah spun, lifted the rifle to his shoulder and fired all in one movement. He'd aimed for the chest and missed — caught the guy dead center in the face and his head exploded. Jeremiah bolted, got all the way to the edge of the porch before he felt the bullet rip into his leg, must have broke the bone on the way through. The pain was unbelievable. His rifle tumbled out of his numb fingers and Jeremiah folded up, fell off the side of the porch in agony, blood gushing out of his leg, gritting his teeth as hard as he could not to cry out.

As Jeremiah lay in the dirt beside the porch, he heard a sound.

Jangle. Jangle. Jangle.

Somebody was foolin' with a ring of keys, taking their time to get to him, slow and casual like.

There musta been four of them fellas, just like he

thought there was. Two of the remaining ones dragged him out into the dirt behind his cabin while the third stood watching, an older fella, and he kept jangling his keys in his pocket. Jeremiah wondered if he'd been jangling those keys when he was looking for Jeremiah in the woods, and if he had, then Jeremiah ought to have heard him, would have heard him, if he'd had them hearing aids. Maybe that's what the dog did hear.

Then they commenced to asking him questions, standing over him as he lay in the dirt, looking up at them in agony. They wanted to know what he'd done with the man he'd found in the woods.

Jeremiah knew that was a bluff, because nobody knew he'd found anybody, but they could have found out that he stole that thing from the car. So he done the same thing he'd done with the agents — told them he didn't see nobody, that he'd come upon a wrecked car and took the briefcase out of it because didn't nobody need it anymore, and he took it into Gatlinburg and hocked it. He spit the words out in bursts, between the groans of pain he couldn't swallow. And he thought to himself that stealing that briefcase was the single dumbest thing he had ever done in seventy-six years of living. He was now paying the "stupid tax" on the deed, and it was gonna be a bitch.

The man with the keys had a strawberry birthmark on his face — stuck out on his brown skin — cold, calculating eyes, and a smirk on his lips that made it clear he *enjoyed* hurting people. Jeremiah had seen that look before.

"You lying," the man said. "You found more than a wrecked car, you found the driver. I want to know where he is."

"I don't know—"

The man didn't let Jeremiah finish. He slammed his

combat boot into Jeremiah's face, mashing his lips and breaking most of his front teeth.

Here it comes, Jeremiah thought. And come it did.

They beat him, kicked him, and stomped him as he tried to curl into a ball in the dirt. The man with the keys grabbed him by the hair and lifted him up onto his knees. Another of the men lifted his right arm and broke it, snapped it over his knee like you'd break a stick of kindling.

Jeremiah had been a POW in Vietnam, spent seven months in the jungle in a bamboo cage like where you'd put a monkey, so small it was impossible to sit up or stretch out. There were nineteen American soldiers — in the beginning, only eleven survived. The guards came three or four times a week and took one of the prisoners out of his cage and dragged him away to be tortured — nearby, so the others could hear his screams. They'd bring him back later — if the torture didn't kill him — and a couple of days after that they'd come for somebody else. Jeremiah always thought that the worst part of it was not the torture. The worst part was sitting there in the mornings listening to the footsteps, knowing they were coming, and wondering if they was going to pick you.

As for the Cong trying to get Jeremiah to "talk" — the day he and the other newbies went boots down in 'Nam, his lieutenant gave a short, sweet lesson. "Don't get captured. Save the last bullet for yourself. If you do get captured, that whole 'name, rank and serial number' bullshit is for the movies, not real life. Tell them *something*, hold out for a couple of days, and then it'll all be changed before anything you say could do any harm. The mission of every captured soldier is *survival*, so you do whatever you have to do to accomplish that mission." A Marine grunt in the cage next to Jeremiah's did the name/rank/serial number routine, and the Cong decided he must be somebody important and they tortured him to death. When the Cong questioned Jeremiah, he babbled, said anything that came into his head, wore his captors out with blather. But he never said nothing that mattered, nothing real, it was all lies, every word. He was proud of that, but of course they tortured him anyway.

Jeremiah's Mexican captors beat on him all day, broke his hands, broke his legs. He retreated to that place in his head he'd gone to when they tortured him in Vietnam. He hadn't been to that place in a long time, but he found it, clawed his way into its sanctuary, and slammed the door behind him. And then what they done to him, he wouldn't let himself feel it. Jeremiah listened to that fella's jangling keys. Every time he hit Jeremiah, his keys jangled, and Jeremiah thought about that guard in Vietnam who limped and dragged his foot. He was the mean guard — had a smirk on his face and cold shark eyes like the Mexican. That guard attached electrodes to Jeremiah's privates, splashed water on him and tied him to a wire mattress. When the guard turned on the juice, Jeremiah screamed. He wasn't aware of screaming, but he knew he must have, because afterwards his throat was raw.

He swallowed and his throat was raw now, so maybe he had been screaming. He didn't know. He babbled to the Mexicans like he'd done the Cong, but the difference was that he really did know the answer to the questions they was asking, but he was determined not to tell. So he talked nonsense as long as he could, but after a while, he couldn't seem to form the words to babble anymore. He couldn't find his way back from that place he'd gone to, neither, and began responding to every question: "Johnson, Jeremiah Joseph, Private E1, 32414196."

It was getting dark, he thought, but maybe the darkness

was inside his head instead of outside, when he looked up and knew where he was, at least for a moment. The fella with the jangling keys put the pistol to his forehead and told him he had one second to live, either tell him where to find the **FBI** agent or die. Jeremiah somehow managed to summon the energy to spit in his face.

Then it was over.

Chapter Thirty

MITCH CALLED RILEIGH FIRST THING THURSDAY MORNING.

"I had a visitor last night."

"Anybody I know?"

"Nobody I knew either. But he knew Lamar Devereaux."

"Who was it?"

"He said he was a friend of Lamar Devereaux's. An agent, or at least used to be."

"What did he want? And why did he come to you?"

"What he wanted was to know where Lamar was. He came to me because he knew Lamar really well, had heard him talk about me, and the safe house Lamar bailed out of is pretty near here."

"So he knew about that? About the safe house, and where it was?"

"Apparently."

"Must not be as well-kept a secret as your friend thinks."

"Apparently not."

"What did you tell him?"

"I played dumb, told him I hadn't seen Lamar Devereaux since last spring. Why would he think I'd know where he was?"

"Do you think he bought it?"

"No."

"Well isn't that swell."

"That's not all we talked about. There's more."

"What more?"

"He said he was looking for Devereaux to try to convince him to give back what he stole."

"What?"

"To convince him to return to Guillermo Castilla. What he took from him."

"What did he take from him?"

"A ... bubble."

"Bubble?"

"That's what he said, a bubble. I'm assuming it's a new street name for an old drug. But maybe there's some new drug, a new wrinkle on crack or meth or ... or maybe even weed that I haven't heard. This guy was serious. He said that Griff Davidson was delivering this bubble to Castilla the night of the raid and apparently it went missing, and now Castilla is trying to get it back."

"Which would explain the torture."

"Right. He's been trying to get the victims to fess up to stealing whatever this thing is. He said if Devereaux would give it back, he might be able to walk away from all this alive, and he also might keep other people from getting killed, too."

"Do you believe him?"

"It makes sense to me that *something* happened during that raid on Willow Creek Farm and whatever it was, it set Guillermo Castilla on a rampage. If he's looking for something..."

"You still haven't answered my question — do you believe him?"

"There's usually a kernel of truth in the best lie. How about you invite me to breakfast, and I will have a come-to-Jesus conversation with Special Agent Lamar Devereaux."

~

RILEIGH TOLD Mama and Jillian that Mitch would be coming over for breakfast, that he wanted to talk to Agent Devereaux, but she didn't tell them what he wanted to talk about.

Mama whipped out her waffle iron as fast as a gunslinger with a .45 and began making up a batch of batter to put in it. By the time Mitch arrived, there was a stack of waffles waiting for him.

And Mama had improved upon her original recipe. She'd bought fresh fruit at the grocery store in town and had chopped up some strawberries to put in the batter, then served him pancakes with both maple and strawberry syrup.

Rileigh, Mitch, and Jillian were already seated at the kitchen table, with Mama hovering over them, when Lamar Devereaux made his way slowly down the hallway. Mitch stood to offer his arm, but Devereaux waved him away.

Rileigh had given up trying to keep Devereaux from moving around on that crutch. Mama added cream and sugar to her cup of coffee, then stood and announced. "You'll have to excuse me, Sheriff, but I have a date."

"You do?" Rileigh asked.

"Don't be silly. You know I do. You was sitting right there when he said he'd come over after breakfast and we'd talk. We've got a lot of catching up to do, haven't seen each other in years."

"'We' who, Mama?" Jillian asked.

"Neil Armstrong and me. He's so humble, won't talk about what he done, but he promised he'd tell me all about the moon." Mama stuffed her "knitting" — a lump of tangled yarn and two needles — into a basket, hooked it on her arm, and poured a second cup of coffee. "He takes his black. We'll go sit on the porch and leave you be." Juggling the basket and two cups of coffee sitting in saucers, she left the kitchen, went through the dining room, and used her butt to shove open the screen door that squawked in protest.

In the silence that followed, Mitch got right to the point.

"I had a visit last night from a friend of yours," he said to Lamar.

Rileigh could see fear wash across his face, and thought what it must be like for Devereaux, looking over his shoulder every second, knowing that when they came for him, he'd be outnumbered and outgunned and that the other men they had come for had been trained law enforcement agents too. And they'd died horrible deaths anyway. All of them.

"Who was it? How did he find me?"

"He called to me out of the dark, I never saw his face. He said he'd come to me because he knew you well and figured out you'd come to me for help after what happened at the safe house."

"If he knew about the safe house, he must have been an FBI agent."

"Maybe. Probably. But he said he was looking for you on his own, trying to save your life. He said all the agents were targeted because during that failed operation, somebody stole something from Guillermo Castilla — this guy called it a 'bubble' — and whatever it was, it was so valuable to Castilla that he's been systematically going through the ranks of every human being who was on the property at the time of that operation and torturing them in an effort to get it back."

Devereaux looked baffled.

"What did you say it was?"

"A bubble. I know, it didn't make any sense to me either, like it was code for something. Or maybe just some stupid nickname."

"And this guy was looking for me — why? To warn me?"

"No."

Mitch paused and spoke the rest in an even voice, no judgment or accusation. Rileigh studied Lamar, watching his reaction. "He said you were the one who took it, and he was looking for you in an effort to get you to give it back, so Castilla wouldn't kill you too."

"*I* took it?"

"That's what he said."

Devereaux's surprise was real, but he also seemed confused. And when Mitch said that the man who spoke to him out of the dark said that Devereaux had taken the "bubble" from Castilla, Devereaux had flinched and looked terrified.

"So what do you have to say to that?" Mitch asked.

"I don't have anything to say to that. I don't know what he's talking about. You don't have any idea who he was?"

"I picked up on a slight Yankee twang, Boston maybe. He said he knew you well. Could he have been your partner?"

"That'd be a neat trick if you had a conversation last night with my partner."

"And why is that?

"Because Chad Gregory is dead. Remember? I told you. He was killed by a car bomb while I was still in a coma."

"Killed by a car bomb…" Mitch said. "How sure are you he's dead?"

"How sure? What do you mean?"

"This guy told me he was with you in the barn that night but you two got separated. The next thing he knew, you were in the hospital. When the other agents started getting killed, he 'ran' — somewhere Castilla wouldn't bother to look for him. Car bomb's a good way to fake your own death. And nobody looks for a dead man."

"But … how?"

Devereaux seemed so confused he couldn't even form a sentence.

"You said you and your partner were in the barn when Castilla and Mr. D came down to the barn to see the horse — right?"

"Yes. We were."

Rileigh saw Jillian flinch and look anxious. Jillian knew something about this that she wasn't telling. Something Devereaux had shared with her.

"Nobody's accusing you of anything — except maybe your ex-partner, who is dead," Mitch said. "But if there's anything, anything at all that would shed some light on the bubble that this agent says you stole from Castilla, you need to share it."

Devereaux shot a questioning look at Jillian, and Rileigh knew instantly that he suspected she had shared something with Rileigh that he had told Jillian *not* to share.

"Okay, fine. I have a hole in my memory."

"And that means?"

"I have retrograde amnesia, not uncommon with head

injuries. There's a portion of time that's just missing from my mind, a chunk of what happened the night of that raid that I don't remember at all."

"So maybe you know more than you think."

"I don't know anything about any bubbles. I don't know what he's talking about."

"Well, if the guy I talked to wasn't your partner, then who was he?" Mitch leaned back in his chair, thoughtfully.

"And if he was your partner," Rileigh said, "how'd he manage to come back from the dead?"

Chapter Thirty-One

Agent Lamar Devereaux looked from face to face — Mitch, Rileigh, and Jillian. All questioning faces. Not accusing, not yet, but questioning. Confused.

They wanted him to tell them what happened the night of the botched raid at Willow Creek Farm. Trouble was, he didn't know what happened.

"FOR GOD so loved the world that he didn't send a committee," Gregory whispers, and Devereaux turns to look at him.

"What?"

"A committee. A coalition."

Coalition is the word that's being used to describe the merging of the forces of the Federal Bureau of Investigation, the Drug Enforcement Agency, and Homeland Security in this big multifaceted operation to capture both Guillermo Castilla and Griffin Davidson, Mr. Detergent.

"Coalition." Devereaux parrots the word, spits it out, because at that moment, it tastes really gross in his mouth. "I've been on some

screwed-up missions in my life … I've followed along behind men I'd have marched down the barrel of a cannon with…"

"And behind idiots who could screw up a one-car funeral," Gregory puts in. Devereaux can't help but smile.

"But I swear this one takes the cake!"

"What do you expect when everybody's in charge … which means nobody's in charge."

"Five by five on that. I—"

Gregory pokes his arm and he stops whispering.

Devereaux leans forward so he can get a better view through the space between the slats of the horse stall where he is hiding with his partner. But he sees nothing. They've been told they're purely backup, that the main assault, when it launches, will be centered on the big house on the hill where a money-launderer extraordinaire is scheduled to welcome the head of a Mexican drug cartel for tea and crumpets.

He and Gregory are stationed in a horse barn, strictly "also-ran." And that's just fine with the two of them, because there's no way this operation is going to run smooth.

"Did I mention … I've got a bad feeling about this, Luke … uh, I mean Lamar," Gregory whispers.

"Yes, you have. Four times by my count, and the line wasn't that clever the first time."

The operation was a lousy plan for a lot of reasons, not the least of which was that communication among the three different branches of service was not the best in the world. And when the signal to go came down, Devereaux only hoped everybody would get the message and be on the same page.

"Hey, look at that," Gregory says. Devereaux looks and can't believe his eyes. Two men are casually walking down a wood-chipped path from the big house on the hill to the barn where they are hiding — Guillermo Castilla and Griffin Davidson.

"Holy shit," he gasps in disbelief.

"I've got a bad feeling about this—"

"Shove it!"

This was definitely a great deviation from the scenario painted by those in charge of the operation.

The two men are congenial, smiling, glad-handing. Even from this distance, looking into the faces of men he had never seen up close, Devereaux is sure that none of the merriment ever makes it to their eyes, that it's all a show, just the way you play the game.

"What should we do?" Gregory whispers.

"Follow the plan."

Right. The plan that said the two of them were backup, wouldn't see the action.

As they draw closer to Devereaux and Gregory's position, they can hear the conversation between the two men. Unfortunately for Devereaux, most of it is in Spanish. Apparently, Davidson is bilingual. Gregory understands and for a few moments simultaneously translates, but they're too close and he falls silent.

The two watch as Davidson goes into one of the horse stalls and comes out leading a majestic black horse with a coat that glistens in the light from the halogen lights on posts all around. The horse's mane is brushed out. Its flowing tail could have graced the head of a pretty little girl who'd just gotten out of the bathtub.

The intel was correct on some fronts. The barn is absolutely deserted. The stable boys, the groomers, the trainers, they're are all gone. So are the bodyguards, which means the men are utterly alone, or at least they appear to be. But with some signal, they might be able to summon a dozen men armed with Uzis.

Devereaux struggles to understand what is going on. Davidson appears to be explaining something to Castilla. He catches the words "Antwerp, Belgium" and knows Davidson has a horse farm there. Perhaps this horse is going there, or just got back from there. Castilla peppers Davidson with questions until finally Davidson holds up his hand and makes a gesture like "I'll show you."

He kneels down on one knee beside the horse and lifts up the horse's hoof, to display the huge, raised shoe that Tennessee Walking Horses wore to exaggerate their graceful gait.

DEVEREAUX LOOKED at the people sitting around the table and wished for all the world he could answer all their questions.

"I have memories, but they stop, like at a washed-out bridge. Then everything is as dark as if someone flipped a switch and all the lights went off."

Devereaux looked into Mitch's eyes.

"The images after that are nonsensical. People and places, random smells — horse shit and alcohol. Pieces of something — straw or hay — and then nothing but white. The doctors weren't surprised, said I had what was called retrograde amnesia, very common after a blow to the head or a coma. They said I might never remember, or I might blink and the memories would download into my mind like a file off the internet. No way to know. And in the beginning, it was just idle curiosity, until…"

Chapter Thirty-Two

DEVEREAUX REACHED OUT AND PICKED UP HIS CUP OF coffee and took a sip. Mitch could tell by the way he wrinkled up his nose that the coffee was cold. He sat the cup back down carefully in the saucer, then looked up and met Mitch's gaze.

"I have gone over and over every single memory I have of that operation. I have taken them apart, bisected them, looked under them, over them, around them, and through them. And here's what I know. I know that Gregory and I watched Davidson and Castilla walk down the pathway from the big house to the barn. We saw Davidson lead a horse out into the light and Castilla reached up and ran his hand along the horse's neck in the kind of casual gesture that lets you know he was a man who was accustomed to horses. And then they started speaking Spanish."

"Spanish? Really?" Rileigh said.

"Gregory tried to translate. He's bilingual, but they got too close and they were talking too fast and he couldn't keep up. So I *watched* them talk about the horse. I heard a couple of references to Antwerp and Belgium. Then

Davidson got down on one knee and lifted up the horse's right front hoof so that Castilla could see how the horse was shod with the 'stacks' that Tennessee Walking Horses wear."

Then Devereaux let out a sigh. "And that's it. That's the last image I have of that operation. At some point after that, I was struck on the head. It was a concussion. The next clear image I have is lying in a hospital, looking up and seeing an IV bag with a drip going, and thinking to myself, I guess I made it. They told me I'd been in a coma from a skull fracture that should have killed me."

"Do you know what happened in the operation after the point where your memory stops?"

"The captain described it to me … but it had been months, and everybody had their story straight by then. I could tell by all that he wasn't saying that it had been a dumpster fire of the highest order. The signal to move in was only transmitted to a few of the agents, not all of them. So instead of a coordinated force moving in on the target, the lead agents went charging in, but only from one direction, with no backup, didn't take out Castilla's bodyguards, and they closed ranks around him. I remember the captain looking at me with tired eyes and saying, 'FBI, DEA, Homeland, everybody's playing CYA, trying to keep their own asses out of a crack.'"

Devereaux paused. "It was a circular firing squad, and all of them were shooting the man next to them."

"Did you ever see Gregory again?" Mitch asked.

"They told me Chad was dead, that he had died while I was in a coma. Car bomb. C4. When he turned on the ignition … red mist. But now … I can't figure out who you talked to last night that would have known what he knew except Chad. So I guess he's still alive and hiding from Castilla."

"So what was Gregory talking about — what was the 'bubble' Castilla had he said you took?"

"I have no idea. There was nothing … Castilla didn't have anything in his hand, had nothing near him. I don't know what I could have taken. I guess I could have leapt out of hiding, mugged him, grabbed his wallet out of his hip pocket. But other than that…"

Rileigh watched Mitch come at the agent's story from different angles, poking here, prodding there, either attempting to jog Devereaux's memory or trip him up, but neither was successful. She had noticed Jillian squirm as Mitch lobbed questions and finally, she couldn't hold still any longer.

"Nobody asked me," Jillian said, "and I'm not a nurse or a doctor, but it appears to me that Agent Devereaux needs some rest."

"No, I'm fine, I'm fine."

Mitch got to his feet, "I don't have any more questions."

"The hell you don't," Devereaux fired back. "You've got a thousand questions."

"I don't have any more questions *right now.*"

"You believe him, don't you? You think Chad's telling the truth."

Mitch didn't respond.

"You think there was something, a bubble of something that Castilla pulled out of his ass at some point, and I took it? That's what he said I did."

"Are you denying it?"

Agent Devereaux sort of folded up after that.

"No, I *can't* deny it."

Then he surprised everyone by rising slowly to his feet without saying a word. He turned and started crutching down the hall. When Jillian moved to help him along, he shook his head.

They all waited until he was in his room with the door closed before they continued the conversation.

"What do you think, Mitch?" Rileigh asked. "Who do you believe?"

Mitch let out a long breath. "Well, on the face of it, I'm dealing with one man who admits he doesn't know what happened, and another one who says he does."

"Surely you don't think Lamar would have stolen something," Jillian said. "Is that what you think?"

Rileigh picked up on the defensiveness in Jillian's voice. She was sure Mitch did, too.

"Well, the other source of information is suspect, too. It has to be some FBI agent — seems obvious that it's Agent Chad Gregory ... who is dead."

"If you wanted to pretend that you died, blowing your car up with C4 so there wouldn't be enough of you left for a DNA sample would be a damned fine way to do it."

"If Gregory is pretending to be dead, he's a criminal, he's committing fraud," Mitch said. "You can't do that without falsifying all kinds of ID, maybe even doctoring records."

Rileigh had an idea. "Maybe the two of them were in on some deal together. Stole something from Castilla, and now Gregory has come back because Devereaux double-crossed him."

"The only reason to believe that Lamar did anything wrong is the word of a man who's out there breaking the law right now," Jillian said. "There's more to that deception than he's letting on. You don't completely abandon your life quickly, without planning it for a long time. Trust me, I've done it. I've become a whole new person. It's not easy … and it's expensive. I think that totally cancels out the veracity of everything he said."

Rileigh and Mitch exchanged a look. Why was Jillian so invested in whether or not this man had committed a crime?

Mitch let out a long breath.

"This isn't just an academic discussion for me. I have to figure out which one of them is telling the truth. Because I'm either saving an innocent FBI agent, or I'm harboring a thief and a killer."

Chapter Thirty-Three

JILLIAN KEPT TO HERSELF FOR THE REST OF THE afternoon, painted in her studio. She came down for dinner, only to discover that Agent Devereaux had said he wasn't hungry. And Mama, of course, had insisted on taking him a glass of lemonade and a ham and cheese sandwich and chips. She just set them inside his door. If he didn't want to eat them, that was fine by her. But if he decided he was hungry, well, they were there.

Rileigh didn't appear to want to talk about Lamar Devereaux. Not even the innocuous conversation her mother tried to initiate about whether Rileigh thought he was doing better.

"He's looking better, getting some color back in his cheeks. Don't you think so, Rileigh?"

Rileigh had merely smiled and nodded.

"Well, I do," Mama said.

All evening, Jillian tried to get her head around the magnitude of a hole in your memory. A piece of time missing. Gone. And you didn't know what had happened during it. There were certainly times when Dr. Al-Masri was digging at Jillian's memories, prying them loose, purposefully foggy and vague memories she clutched tight to her chest, because to let go was to see them clearly. It would definitely be easier at times like that to *not* be able to remember, just to forget it all.

But Dr. Al-Masri was having none of it. She never bought in to Jillian's denial, was always determined to help her remember, help her to *learn to live* with the memories.

Jillian was almost asleep when a thought hit her and she sat upright in the bed.

Dr. Al-Masri!

She had been working with Jillian to recover memories that Jillian had buried and didn't want to deal with. True, Jillian's weren't really "lost" memories. They were repressed. That's part of what Dr. Al-Masri did — helped people recover repressed memories that were affecting their psychological health. Was it possible that she could help Lamar remember what had happened? Was it possible her techniques would help a person with retrograde amnesia? It was certainly worth trying, or at least Jillian thought it was. Maybe there was a way to prove that he hadn't done what she was certain he hadn't done.

Jillian launched the subject at Rileigh privately before breakfast. And Rileigh, though not as excited about the possibility as she was, said that maybe it was worth a shot.

"But you know this will be his decision to make," Rileigh said. "You can't go digging around in somebody's head unless they give you permission."

"Whose head is it we're going to go digging around in?" Lamar said and surprised them both. They usually heard him clomping noisily down the hall on his crutch. But he had and somehow managed to move so quietly they hadn't heard him.

"Actually, it's yours," Jillian said, then plunged into a

combination explanation/sell job. "I told you that I was going to a therapist who was helping me adjust to the reality of what happened to me and the reality that it's not happening anymore. Hard as it may be to believe, accepting the reality of how good life is now is sometimes harder than you'd think."

"I can understand that," he said.

"And it occurred to me in the middle of the night last night that maybe Dr. Al-Masri could help *you* remember what happened to you, could help you recover the memories that retrograde amnesia erased."

Lamar was instantly interested. "Could she do that? *Would* she do that? Is it that even possible?"

"I don't know, I don't know, and I don't know, but I think it's worth asking."

Rileigh put her fork down deliberately beside her plate and Jillian instantly recognized the "I'm about to say something you're not going to like" gesture.

"If she does help you recover those memories, you have to be willing to accept that you might remember things you don't want to remember."

Lamar looked surprised at that. He hadn't had time to think it all through or he would have figured that out on his own. "So you're saying I might find out that my dead partner who has returned from the grave might be right? That I took Guillermo Castilla's bubble, whatever the hell that is, and that's why he's trying to kill me?"

Rileigh nodded. "If she helps you remember what *really* happened, then all bets are off."

"Do you still want to do it?" Jillian asked, finding herself holding her breath.

"Yes, I do. Do you think you could get her to talk to me?"

Jillian was careful not to let the relief show in her face.

"Well as it turns out, I have an appointment scheduled with her tomorrow morning. If she's willing to talk to you, you could have that appointment. Your needs are certainly more urgent than mine."

"Jillian is always looking for a palatable excuse not to have to go to therapy," Rileigh said.

Jillian overheard Rileigh on the phone telling Mitch about their plan to see if Dr. Al-Masri could help Lamar remember what had happened during that hole in his memory, the piece of lost time during which his not-dead partner was saying he was a thief. She only heard Rileigh's part of the conversation, of course, but it was clear that he thought that was a good idea but wanted something else. With only half the conversation, it took a little while for Jillian to figured it out what it was.

She confronted Rileigh as soon as she hung up. "Did Mitch just tell you that he would like for Lamar to grant permission for Dr. Al-Masri to discuss his case with Mitch?"

"Yes, he did."

Jillian was offended by that on several levels. The intrusiveness of it. The almost presumption of guilt of it. And even as she suffered those reactions, she realized they were an indication that she'd gotten deeper into this water than she ever intended to get

"Well, nobody asked my opinion," she said. "But I think what Lamar remembers is private and it ought to stay private."

"And it would be private," Rileigh said, "if what he remembers weren't possibly the reason almost two dozen people are now dead. That moves out of the realm of private information, don't you think?"

Jillian didn't, but she didn't say that. She just bit her lip and said nothing at all.

Chapter Thirty-Four

MITCH'S CLOSED OFFICE DOOR OPENED FAR ENOUGH FOR the department's receptionist, Vivian, to stick her head through the crack. "Sir, there are two men here to see you," she said. "They're FBI agents."

He groaned silently. Goody.

"Well, show them in."

Vivian stepped aside and held the door open wide.

Mitch walked out around his desk as the two agents came into his office. One of them was a large older man, with blond hair, and the other one was as skinny as a rail. The older man stuck out his hand.

"Hello, Sheriff Webster. My name is Hank Gilbert. I'm a senior special agent with the FBI." He flipped open a badge. "And this is Special Agent Bill Conroe." Conroe did the same.

Mitch shook hands with both of them and offered them a chair. "Would you like some coffee? I'm sure Vivian could whip some up. I don't guarantee the quality of it, but it probably won't kill you. Probably."

"I'll pass on the coffee," said Gilbert.

"I'd like a cup," said Conroe in a surprisingly deep bass voice. "Just fill it up with cream and sugar halfway and pour a little coffee on top."

Vivian looked a question at Mitch, and he shook his head. She left to get the coffee. Then he sat down and leaned back in his chair.

"To what do I owe the honor of a visit from the Federal Bureau of Investigation?" he asked.

"We're looking for a missing agent," said the older agent, "from a safe house in eastern Tennessee."

"Why would you think he'd be in Yarmouth County?"

"Do you know a man named Jeremiah Johnson?"

The question didn't surprise Mitch, but he acted like it did.

"Well, sure, everybody knows Jeremiah."

"Is he for real?" Agent Conroe asked.

Mitch smiled. "You don't get any more real than Jeremiah Johnson."

The agent shrugged "Well, the movie—"

"Is what turned him into a mountain man," Mitch said. "A friend of mine told me he watched it and that's what inspired him to become his namesake. How do you know Jeremiah Johnson?"

"We talked to him about the missing agent," Gilbert said.

"Because?"

"Because the agent was in a stolen vehicle, and the owner of the vehicle left a briefcase in the back seat. Mr. Johnson hawked that briefcase at a pawn shop in Gatlinburg."

"Where did Jeremiah get the briefcase?"

"He told us that he found it in a wrecked car and didn't see anybody around, so he took it."

"Do you believe him?"

"The main reason we came here was to find out if we ought to," Agent Conroe said.

"As far as I know, Jeremiah Johnson is as honest as they come," Mitch said. "But as far as I know isn't very far."

"What did he tell you about the wrecked car? Do you think the agent was driving it when it was wrecked?"

"That would make sense," Agent Conroe said. "He left the safe house in a hurry. There was a shooting. It's possible that he was injured, and maybe that's why he wrecked the car."

"Well, I can't think of any other way Jeremiah could have come by something out of a stolen vehicle. Stealing cars is definitely not in Jeremiah Johnson's skill set."

The agents nodded glumly.

"Sorry to rain on your only lead. You said the agent was shot. Have you checked—"

"No local doctor has reported treating a gunshot wound," Conroe said.

Vivian came in then with coffee for Agent Conroe. And from what Mitch could see, she had fixed it the way he'd asked, with a little coffee on top of some cream and sugar. It was in a Styrofoam cup. That alone would make it taste like rhino piss, but that was the best they had to offer.

"You sure you don't want more coffee, Sheriff?" she asked.

"I'm good, thanks, Vivian."

Vivian left the room and closed the door.

"Okay," Mitch said, stretching back in his chair, "now let's talk about all the things you aren't telling me, such as why is the FBI agent missing and what was he doing at a safe house? And if there was a shooting at a safe house, that sets off all sorts of alarms. I thought safe houses were safe."

The two FBI agents looked at each other and then back at Mitch.

"We didn't have this conversation," Agent Gilbert said.

"What conversation?" Mitch said.

"The conversation we're about to not have about Agent Lamar Devereaux."

"He's the missing agent? Whoa, whoa, wait a minute," Mitch said. "Lamar Devereaux?"

"You know him?"

"Yes, well, I don't *know* him. We had a double kidnapping in Yarmouth County back in May and called in the FBI, and he was the lead officer. He brought maybe a dozen agents with him, but the only other one I remember is Agent Phillip Parsons — tall, skinny, red hair and freckles. He was Devereaux's partner."

The agents paused.

"No, Parsons isn't his partner. Chad Gregory was his partner."

"Did you put that in past tense because he isn't Devereaux's partner anymore? Or did you put that in past tense because something happened to Agent Gregory?"

"You pick up on grammar really well," Agent Gilbert said. "Chad Gregory died a few months ago."

"I'm sorry to hear that." Mitch had steered the conversation in this direction because he wanted to find out whatever he could about Chad Gregory and verify the information both agents had given to him. "A good guy, was he?"

Bill Conroe smiled then. "I don't believe Chad Gregory ever met a stranger." He looked at the other FBI agent, who nodded agreement, smiling. "One of those people who, you know, walks into a bar, and ten minutes later he's on a first-name basis with everybody in the place. He was a lovable bastard, with a knack for smart-ass remarks."

Mitch said nothing, hoping silence would encourage them to elaborate.

"Oh, he was as ugly as the butt end of a wart hog," Agent Gilbert said, matching Conroe's smile. "He made fun of himself over it, but he was so charming after a while that you forgot what he looked like, and I guess for the ladies, that was his attraction."

"And he always had a harem of them."

"I read once where somebody interviewed several couples who'd been married more than 50 years, and they asked the women what had attracted them to their husbands in the beginning," Mitch offered, to keep the conversation rolling. "They didn't give the answer you would expect — good looks, money. Almost universally they said, 'he made me laugh.'"

"Yep, that was Chad," Conroe said.

"How did he die? Line of duty?"

"Car bomb."

"What did he do to earn getting blown up?"

"We're not sure. He was working on a couple of drug cases at the time. None of them would have offered any motive to kill him as far as we can tell, but we don't have any better explanation."

Mitch saw Conroe shoot a look at Gilbert. "So tell me about Agent Devereaux. Why is he missing, and why are you looking for him?"

"He was in a safe house, and it got made."

"My friends in the FBI would say that's hard to do," Mitch said.

"I'd say the same thing. There was gunfire, one agent was killed, two were injured, and Devereaux was gone."

"Why was he in the safe house to begin with?"

"For protection."

Conroe held his hand up before Mitch could say

anything. "I know, I know, it didn't work. He'd have been safer somewhere else."

"I have to ask. I understand if you can't tell me, but who did he need protection from … and why?"

The younger agent looked at the senior agent for permission, and Agent Gilbert nodded.

"Remember, this is a conversation we're not having," Agent Gilbert said. "There was an operation that was jointly conducted by several different federal agencies at a horse farm in Pendleton County."

"That wouldn't be Griff Davidson's farm, would it?"

"It would," Conroe said.

"What do you know about Davidson?" the senior agent asked.

"Nothing more concrete than anybody else does, but it's about common knowledge that he's up to the armpits of his white suit in illegal activity. Mostly I think as a money launderer, but I've never had a reason to looked into it."

"You know about as much as we know, and we *have* looked into it," Gilbert said. "Agent Devereaux and Agent Gregory were a part of that operation." He paused, and said slowly, "It was … not successful."

"That's not surprising," Mitch said. "If it had been, everybody in both counties would have known, so apparently you came up with a handful of nothing, right?"

"Right."

"How did that land Lamar Devereaux in a safe house?"

"Because ever since that operation, agents from all three of the federal agencies involved have been turning up missing."

Mitch groaned. "Just missing?"

"We found some bodies, but some are just gone."

"Since we didn't have this conversation, you didn't hear me say that operation sounds like a dumpster fire."

Both agents nodded and seemed to relax a little.

"Neither of us was part of the operation, but from what we hear, that's exactly how it went down," Conroe said. "The idea was to bag two wanted birds with one stone, and as it was, they got no birds at all. A couple of agents were injured, and one of them was Lamar Devereaux."

"And afterwards, other agents disappeared?"

"It took longer than it should have to see the pattern, because the agents were in three different agencies. But once somebody spotted it and started checking, it wasn't hard to figure out what they all had in common."

"So somebody's killing all the agents who botched a raid on Davidson's Farm."

"I think killing is the result, not the intent," Conroe said.

"Okay, what's the intent?"

"The bodies we have found have been messed up, as in Mexican drug cartel messed up. Tortured."

"Tortured then killed, or tortured to death?" Mitch asked.

"We think tortured to death."

"By whom?"

"Suspicion is falling heavily on the wanted man we were trying to catch."

"And who was that?"

"Guillermo Castilla."

"Damn, all this went down next door, and I never heard a word."

The two agents looked at each other and then looked back at Mitch.

"The saga of what happened at Willow Creek Farm

that day is a really large lump under the federal government's rug."

"Oh," Mitch said. "So now you've put all the remaining agents in protective custody, and one of them was Devereaux."

"No … Agent Devereaux is the last man standing," Gilbert said.

"What? You mean somebody has killed every agent who was at that farm? How many people are we talking about here?"

"More than you got fingers and toes," Conroe said.

Mitch leaned back and whistled softly. "Do you have any idea what the motive could be for killing off all the participants in a failed operation?"

"No, but it would appear that the kind of torture they used was not just to inflict pain but to get information," Gilbert said.

"Got any idea what they're looking for?"

"The only thing that makes sense to us — and us being all the heads that have been put together since this started going down, and that's a lot of heads — is that Castilla or Davidson or both believe that one of those agents saw something or did something or took something during that raid."

"And Castilla wants … what? To find out what they know?"

"Right, or to get back what they took," Gilbert added.

"I wouldn't want to be Lamar Devereaux," Conroe said.

Mitch said, "Neither would I."

Chapter Thirty-Five

RILEIGH DIDN'T TELL JILLIAN THAT SHE WAS GOING TO drive to Knoxville that morning and have a one-on-one conversation with Dr. Al-Masri. Apparently, Agent Devereaux's mental state was becoming a sore spot between them, and Rileigh wasn't completely certain why Jillian was so touchy about everything having to do with the man.

Rileigh didn't have an appointment and certainly didn't expect to be ushered into Dr. Al-Masri's office when she got there, assumed she would have to wait. She stopped in the bathroom before she went into the office and was surprised to see Dr. Al-Masri there.

"Well, hello," Dr. Al-Masri said, looking up from washing her hands. "We meet in the strangest places."

"I swear I'm not stalking you."

"Well, if you turn up one more time, you need a picket sign. You have business in this building?"

"No, I just wanted to catch a few minutes to talk to you. I'm sure now isn't a great time."

"My next patient isn't due for..." Dr. Al-Masri looked at her watch. "Fifteen minutes? I got that long."

"What I want to say won't take long."

Rileigh did the best she could to condense the story of Lamar Devereaux into only the few minutes that she had to tell it in. But even just hitting the high points, it was quite a tale. And last part of the story, of course, was that Devereaux had admitted he didn't know what happened. And that was a good segue into why she had come.

"We're trying to think of what creative way there might be to help him remember what happened."

"And so you thought of me," Dr. Al-Masri said, "that maybe I could help?"

"That's right."

"Well, I hate to disappoint you, but I doubt very much that I could do anything at all that would be helpful."

Rileigh didn't like the response, but wasn't surprised.

"I use every tool I can find to help my patients get well. All of them have suffered some great trauma or lots of great traumas. And I have to dig the memories out of some of them because they have buried them so deeply. That's where I *sometimes* use what is commonly called regression therapy." She paused. "But I'm not sure how much faith I have in basic regression therapy."

"Really?"

"I use it — *sparingly* — along with a lot of other tools, but there are those who use it almost exclusively. They use it with children to uncover memories of abuse. But I think what often happens is that regression therapy itself is abused, and the adults in those children's lives are abused because of it." She looked at her watch again. "Well, I'm supposed to be in my office right now."

"I'm sorry. I didn't mean to interrupt."

"It's okay. Doctors are supposed to make you wait.

That's what you pay for." Rileigh smiled. "There are just a lot more effective, *safe* ways to determine whether or not children have been abused."

Al-Masri took a breath.

"There are two issues I see here — my box full of psychological tools are for use on damaged *minds,* but not damaged brains. If the reason you can't remember is because a blow to the head caused retrograde amnesia, I haven't seen any studies where a physician used regression therapy to retrieve memories. That's problem number one. Problem number two is, according to a Johns Hopkins study, hypnosis as a memory recall method isn't that effective, but it can be used to find out if there's still thinking ability in that part of the injured brain."

"Meaning?"

"This FBI agent's memory loss might be a result of the injury he suffered, or it might be a result of some other trauma."

"Such as?"

"Perhaps something else happened to him in addition to the blow to the head, and whatever that was is at least part of the reason he can't remember. If that's the case, if retrograde amnesia didn't *erase* his memories and he's just *repressing* them, I might be able to be helpful in retrieving those."

She smiled ruefully.

"The most important word in that sentence is *might.* It's a crapshoot, Rileigh. I really don't think I can do this man any good. I'm sorry."

"Are you at least willing to try?"

Dr. Al-Masri cocked her head to the side and smiled. "Yeah, I'd be willing to do a lot of things for you."

Rileigh couldn't resist a spontaneous hug.

"Jillian has an appointment Saturday morning. How about we give Agent Devereaux that time slot?"

"I bet that suggestion was Jillian's, wasn't it?"

Rileigh smiled. "Yes, actually it was."

"Not surprised that she's in avoidance mode about her therapy sessions. They're very painful for her."

"Thank you so much, Aaliyah. We'll bring him here on Saturday."

"I think that's probably a bad idea," Dr. Al-Masri said. "Didn't you say this man has a broken leg that's only splinted?"

"It's the best we could do."

"And he has a bullet wound?"

"Well, there is that."

"And there are people trying to find him to kill him?"

Rileigh nodded.

"He's not coming to me. I'll go to him."

"Oh, I couldn't ask you to do that."

"I didn't hear *you* ask me to do that. Did *you* hear you ask me to do that? If you did, I didn't hear you."

Rileigh smiled broader. "I tell you what," she said, "if you come to my house, you will meet Mama and, of course, Jillian will be there. But if you'll come earlier, Mama will treat you to a real Southern breakfast, pull out all the stops — waffles with fresh fruit, brown eggs yanked right out from under a chicken, homemade jam and jelly on homemade bread—"

"Stop, stop. I'm in. I'm so in."

"And there's more. No guarantees here, you never know, he's an elusive creature…" Rileigh leaned closer and whispered.

"You might catch sight of Neil Armstrong. He's been dropping by a lot lately."

"*The* Neil Armstrong?"

"Yep — Neil 'One Small Step For Man, One Giant Leap For Mankind' Armstrong. Maybe he'll tell you about walking on the moon. He's told Mama all about it."

"You couldn't drag me away now with a team of Clydesdales and the Budweiser beer wagon. Give me an address, and I will see you on Saturday."

"Thank you again, Aaliyah."

The psychiatrist pulled Rileigh into a hug, then looked at her watch and said, "I've kept them waiting long enough that they are sufficiently impressed that I'm an important person. I can go in now."

When Rileigh got into her car, she saw the sky overhead had turned dark and foreboding. Thunder cracked. A storm was coming.

Chapter Thirty-Six

ELMER RATCHET HADN'T BEEN UP TO JEREMIAH JOHNSON'S place in ... hell, he didn't even remember how long. Jeremiah wasn't the friendliest man Elmer ever met. Never had been. He had moved up into the mountains because he disliked people and didn't want no close neighbors, so Elmer cut a wide path around him and left him be. But over the years, they bumped up against each other now and again and they'd got along. Might even call them friends, though Elmer figured Jeremiah would probably argue that point.

Still and all, Elmer had been happy to oblige when Jeremiah come to him the other day and said he was looking for a coonhound puppy. Elmer's bitch had birthed puppies about seven weeks ago and he still had three of them.

He gave Jeremiah the pick of the three. And of course he picked the male, the big one with the oversized feet and long floppy ears. Elmer thought he was the best of the litter.

"What'll you take for him, Elmer?" Jeremiah asked. Elmer had thought about it.

"Run across many beaver, do ya?"

Jeremiah nodded. "They built a dam up Hog Snake Creek. Now the water's all backed up in that hollow, turned it into a bog you can't hardly get across."

"I'd fancy a pelt to make a hat to keep my head dry this winter." He gestured up at his bald skull. "Ain't got no natural insulation no more. And maybe a fat tom turkey. That sound fair to you?"

"It does," Jeremiah had said and they'd shook on it. Which was the reason Elmer had come uninvited up to Jeremiah Johnson's cabin — to check on that puppy, see how it was doing, and to let Jeremiah know that he'd have to go into town to the vet and get that dog's shots on his own 'cause Elmer hadn't done it yet. He'd meant to say that when Jeremiah dropped by, but it had plumb slipped his mind.

Might be he'd ought to have waited until tomorrow to come. A doozy of a storm had just blown through the mountains, knocking down trees and power lines, biggest storm he'd seen this year. He'd had to get out of his truck three times to move downed tree limbs off the road on the way here, was sure there was roads that washed plumb out 'cause there was standing water everywhere. He parked his truck down at the bottom of the hill, far as he could get from a big puddle and walked up the steep grade to Jeremiah's cabin — like everybody had to. Elmer was sure that Jeremiah planned it that way. He didn't want just anybody to come calling. And he made it as difficult as he could for them as decided to do it anyway.

"Yo, Jeremiah," he called out. It wasn't never a good idea to surprise Jeremiah Johnson. And Elmer was pretty sure he knew why it was Elmer decided to get this dog —

so it could bark and let him know when folks was around. Elmer had to repeat himself sometimes with Jeremiah and figured out that the man was getting hard of hearing.

Jeremiah didn't respond, so he called out again. "Yo, Jeremiah, it's me, Elmer."

Elmer wasn't particularly surprised that Jeremiah didn't respond, that he might not have heard him — but that dog should have heard. That dog should have set up a racket as soon as he parked his truck down at the bottom of the hill. He walked up in front of the house and hollered out. Didn't see nobody. Didn't hear nobody inside. So, apparently, Jeremiah wasn't home and wherever he'd gone, he'd took the dog with him. Elmer was about to turn and go back to his truck and come another day when he heard the buzz of flies around a cardboard box on the porch. He took a step up on the front step, leaned over the box, and nearly choked to death.

"Oh God, oh my God." He wanted to cry. He dropped down to his knees. There was that puppy, that poor little puppy, dead in the box. His head was all crooked, neck was broke, and wasn't no dog broke his own neck in a cardboard box. Somebody musta broke that dog's neck on purpose.

Elmer was beside himself. He did love dogs of all kinds and his own in particular. And that somebody would kill a little puppy was so far beyond any thought Elmer could imagine that all he could do was choke and gasp and try to get his breath. He staggered back off the porch, leaned over, put his hands on his knees, took big breaths until he could get his breath.

Who in the hell would have broke that dog's neck? And right there in the box just reached in and twisted his head sideways?

And that was when Elmer commenced to wonder

about Jeremiah. No way in hell had *he* killed that dog. So if somebody else did, why? And where was Jeremiah? Elmer hung around and called out a couple more times. Didn't expect to hear nobody. Didn't know what to do about it. How could he look for Jeremiah Johnson? That man could be anywhere in the mountains. Elmer turned slowly in a circle, was about to start back down to his truck when he noticed something above the trees behind the cabin. Vultures.

His belly dropped down into his boots. There was something dead up there, and them vultures were circling, round and round. He didn't like thinking what he was thinking. Absolutely did not want to go have a look. But there was nothing else for it. Elmer reluctantly went around the cabin to the back.

He seen what was dead that had attracted the vultures, didn't get a good look at it, but he didn't need one. It was something burned. Something that had a man's legs.

Elmer went running down the side of that hill, crying like a baby.

MITCH STOOD beside Gus in the late afternoon light, looking at the charred bodies where they lay before the EMTs loaded them up into body bags. The storm earlier had caused communication chaos, had knocked down two different cell phone repeater towers in addition to all the phone and power lines torn out by falling limbs, and even radioing for an ambulance to come for the bodies had been a challenge.

There were two of them. One body was undeniably Jeremiah Johnson. That Vietnam veteran tattoo was still visible on one of his hands that hadn't burned. What was also visible, plain to see, was that he'd been tortured — just like all those agents, Alex, Cody and Annalise.

It was the second man that interested Mitch, his first suspect. Even with him dead, Gus might be able to get an ID from prints or DNA, Mitch's first scraps of real evidence.

"It looks to me like they dragged the bodies here, poured gasoline on them, and set them on fire, intended to destroy them, but the fire went out," Mitch said.

"I've been afraid of something like this. When Jeremiah called me the other day and said the FBI had been there to talk to him, I told him to watch his back. Someone in the FBI leaked the location of the safe house and it was attacked. The FBI tracked Devereaux to Jeremiah because of the briefcase Jeremiah sold out of that car Devereaux sold, and—"

Gus finished what he was thinking. "Whoever leaked the information about the safe house could have leaked the information about Jeremiah, too."

"They tortured Jeremiah just like they did those other people, but I don't think they asked him the same questions. They wanted him to tell them how to find Devereaux. And the question is ... did he tell them? Because if he did..."

"Then the Dark Lord has heard the name of Baggins ... or Hazelton."

Gus's black humor fell flat, and neither of them laughed.

"From the condition of those bodies, I'd say they must have set the fire sometime Thursday. If he told them what they wanted to know, they've had that information for more than twenty-four hours. It's a half-hour drive from here to my place. Why haven't they shown up on my doorstep?"

"I don't think he told them.

"You saw what they did to him." Gus pointed at the charred body. "They skinned his back."

"He was a POW in Vietnam. Rileigh said he told her mother once that he'd been tortured but he didn't break, just babbled nonsense."

"Maybe he still had that kind of steel in his backbone."

Chapter Thirty-Seven

Rileigh had slept very little after Mitch came by last night and told her privately about the murder of Jeremiah Johnson. He hadn't been able call because of all the line damage from the storm.

Rileigh had been devastated by Mitch's news. She and Mitch were alone, and when she started to cry, he drew her into his arms. The warmth of his touch, her head resting against his broad chest… she was certainly not a woman who needed a man to keep her safe, but that's how she had felt at that moment — *safe*. She had never realized what a glorious feeling that was.

She hadn't wanted him to leave. She didn't think he wanted to, either. And that was a pretty damned good feeling, too.

Rileigh didn't tell Mama or Jillian the news. Certainly not Lamar. It would have upset them terribly — why do a thing like that right before Lamar's first therapy session?

And to pull off the mammoth breakfast her mother was right now whipping up in the kitchen, Mama needed her wits about her, what wits she still had that hadn't moved out of the neighborhood entirely,

Mama was as happy as a pig in mud. There was nothing the old woman liked better than "doing for people," as she called it, and to have a houseguest *and* a guest for breakfast had made her week.

The storm that had wreaked havoc on Yarmouth County yesterday had delayed Rileigh's arrival home until late afternoon, but when she told Jillian, Mama and Agent Devereaux that she'd gone personally to talk to Dr. Al-Masri about his case — and that Dr. Al-Masri would be coming to breakfast before conducting a therapy session *with Lamar* in the morning — they'd each greeted the news in a different way. Mama was ecstatic, Jillian was grateful, and Lamar was … she wasn't sure, scared maybe.

Mama had gotten up while the rooster was still snoring this morning to work her wonders in the kitchen. She fired up her not-so-new waffle iron and had it piping hot and ready by the time Dr. Al-Masri arrived. She greeted the young woman as if she were family.

"Name's Lily Bishop," she said, "but I'm just Mama." Opening her arms wide, she continued, "Now come on over here and give your Mama a hug."

Dr. Al-Masri did exactly that. Mama held on tight, patting her on the back. "I pray for you every night. I thank you so much for what you're doing for my sweet Jillian."

"It's an honor to be involved in helping your daughter get well."

Mama drew back and looked at Rileigh. "You hear that? Listenin' to her talk's like listenin' to some television show where everybody says everything right." Dr. Al-Masri's Arabic accent was not pronounced, but Mama loved it.

Agent Devereaux came crutching out of the bedroom, looking in some ways worse than he had when he'd arrived two days ago, but that was just because of the nature of bruises, how they turned yellow and green as they healed. He moved slowly, careful of the bandages on his chest where he'd been shot and the splint on his broken leg that he couldn't put any weight on.

"Lamar, I'd like you to meet Dr. Aaliyah Al-Masri," Rileigh said.

"I'm pleased to meet you." He had a wan smile and held out his hand.

Mama picked up the ball then and made for the end zone with it, seating everyone and offering coffee, tea, or orange juice as she flitted from one to the next like a butterfly among wildflowers. The table overflowed with fresh baked biscuits, home churned butter, hash browned potatoes, eggs — scrambled, fried, and poached — and a mountain of bacon, sausage, and country ham.

She explained the nature of the waffle selection — made with "strawberries right out of my garden where they was looking up at the sunrise this very mornin'." She laughed. "The eggs was still warm from the chickens' butts, too, when I cracked 'em into the skillet." She also offered jelly, jam, marmalade, and compote that she'd canned herself.

Dr. Al-Masri was totally overwhelmed.

"I don't know the difference between … what is …? I know compote is French for mixture, but mixture of what?"

Mama beamed.

"Well, jam is made from crushed or chopped fruit and sugar, and it's kinda chunky like." She held up a jar. "Jelly is made from fruit *juice* and sugar. It's smooth and it wiggles when you poke it with a fork. Marmalade is similar to jam, chunky like, but it's made from *citrus* fruits, and you grate up the peel into it to give it a tart flavor. And compote is made from whole fruits, or big pieces, that are cooked in a syrup made from sugar and water. It's thicker'n jelly." She opened a jar, stuck a spoon in, and withdrew a helping. "But see … it don't wiggle like jelly does."

It was a dizzying graduate level course in the jam-inary arts.

When Mama noticed that Dr. Al-Masri had taken no meat on her plate, she asked, "Don't you want no bacon, ham, or sausage?"

"No, thank you. I don't eat pork, but it sure does smell good."

"How can anybody not eat pork?"

"Mama, there are a lot of people in the world who don't eat pork," Jillian said.

Mama looked surprised, then sorrowful.

"Well, I am sorry to hear that," Mama said, genuinely distressed. "It's such a shame to miss out on one of life's best-tastin' blessings."

Lamar had very little to say on any subject, and Jillian was unnaturally quiet as well, but Mama's bubbling glossed it over, and Rileigh reminded herself to cherish her mother's sweet, simple spirit.

When breakfast was done, Jillian asked Dr. Al-Masri, "Where would be the best place for you and Lamar to have a conversation?"

"You know, I saw a porch swing out front. Do you like to sit on porch swings?" she asked Lamar.

"My grandmother had one," he said, "and it squeaked like every movement was stepping on a pissed-off chicken."

"My porch swing is mute," Rileigh said.

"Mute?" Dr. Al-Masri said.

"It doesn't make a sound, probably the only one in Tennessee and maybe in the whole South that's silent. A true miracle of nature."

"Would you like to sit out there with me and talk for a little while?" Dr. Al-Masri asked Lamar. He nodded, got up from the table, and crutched through the dining room and living room to the porch.

Mama and Jillian busied themselves in the kitchen while Dr. Al-Masri and Agent Devereaux sat on the porch. Rileigh was aware of Jillian's sidelong glances to the front door, concern stamped on her features. The psychiatrist spent almost two hours with Lamar. Mama had just come in from working in the backyard garden when Dr. Al-Masri returned to the kitchen. Rileigh saw Lamar crutch from the front porch directly down the hallway to his bedroom and close the door behind him.

"I just wanted to thank you again for the wonderful breakfast," Dr. Al-Masri told Mama. "I don't know when I tasted anything that good."

"You need to change your mind about bacon and ham and sausage," Mama said, earnestly.

"Uh … probably not going to happen."

"Well, that is a pure D shame for a fact." Mama shook her head. "You need to eat all kinda other good-tastin' things to make up for the loss."

Turning to Rileigh, Dr. Al-Masri said, "Do you have a minute?"

When they were alone, Rileigh asked, "How did it go?"

"I can't tell you."

Rileigh stopped her. "I'm not asking you what he said or anything about that, just how was it?"

"It was difficult for him. Overall, I believe we made some progress, but we didn't get there if the goal was recovery of the memories. I told him I would be glad to meet with him again as many times as he wanted to, and he thanked me. But he didn't offer a time that he'd like to get together."

Dr. Al-Masri reached out and took Rileigh's hand.

"This is awkward. You have to believe that I meant to say this to you before I ever met Agent Devereaux, that it has *nothing* to do with what he said. I always explain this to family members before the first appointment, but this one came up so suddenly and was somewhat…"

"Unorthodox?"

"Yes, that."

She took a deep breath.

"It has been my experience that there are no more skilled liars in the world than those who are trying to hide something. They can be totally believable. I have come across many patients who, for one reason or another, pretend to have forgotten something — fake amnesia about certain events, or for a specific time frame. I am absolutely not saying that Agent Devereaux is a fraud. I just want to prepare you for every eventuality. Duplicity is the nature of the human heart, and some people have perfected it into an art form."

Then she hugged Rileigh goodbye and left. Jillian came in a few minutes later. "I saw Dr. Al-Masri drive away. What did she say?"

"Nothing. There wasn't anything she could say."

But that wasn't true. Rolling around in Rileigh's head was the warning she'd issued right before she left. Of course, it occurred to Rileigh that Devereaux might not be telling the truth, though he was, indeed, convincing. She probably ought to tell Jillian what the psychiatrist had a said about people who faked amnesia. But she didn't. Jillian was far too invested in Devereaux as it was … which was a conversation she absolutely did need to have. So was the conversation about Jeremiah Johnson. Just not right now.

"Well, what do you think?"

"No new thoughts. It's all speculation unless Lamar chooses to share something with us."

Chapter Thirty-Eight

JILLIAN LOOKED UP FROM THE TOMATO SHE WAS CUTTING for salad for dinner tonight, and Lamar was standing in the kitchen doorway.

"Got any awful coffee?" he asked.

"Yup. Freshly brewed and robustly awful. Mama went into town and Rileigh's taking a nap, so you'll have to help me finish it."

Lamar eased himself into the kitchen, held onto the table, and sat down heavily in a chair. He was a black coffee man, she knew, so she didn't bother to get the creamer out of the refrigerator for him. She hadn't told him that David had picked up on a cup of black coffee in the household of women who took theirs varying shades of tan.

She doctored up a cup of awful coffee for herself and sat down opposite him.

"How you doing?" she asked.

"Not worth a damn."

"I feel your pain," she said. "I always walk out of

228

sessions with Dr. Al-Masri feeling like a piñata at a little kid's birthday party. Did it go well?"

"I didn't remember it all," he said.

Her chin snapped up. "It *all?* But you did remember *some?*"

"Enough."

"Enough to what?"

"I know what the bubbles are. And I remember how most of the operation went down."

Jillian held her breath, wondering if he'd continue, and finally he did.

"I remember squatting with Greg in the horse stall when Castilla and Davidson suddenly came walking down the path … I told you that part … that I remembered up to the point where Davidson got down on one knee and lifted up the horse's right front hoof so that Castilla could see how the horse was shod with the 'stacks' that Tennessee Walking Horses wear."

Lamar paused.

"Talking to Dr. Al-Masri … it wasn't like all my memories downloaded. But we talked about things … emotional things … and it was like a fog began to lift. I could see little bits of what happened, the images becoming sharper as the fog thinned."

Jillian held her breath in anticipation.

"Davidson began to fiddle with the strap that held the stacked horseshoe in place. From our angle, we couldn't see exactly what he was doing. And then Castilla knelt down beside him and completely blocked the view. They were talking quietly in Spanish, but when I asked Chad to translate, he hissed, 'Hush!'"

Lamar wasn't looking at Jillian. He was watching a movie play on an invisible screen in the air in front of him.

"When Davidson stood up, he was holding the stacked

horseshoe that had been on the horse's hoof. Apparently, he had unfastened the strap in some way and taken it off."

Lamar stopped talking, studied the invisible screen as if to be sure he was seeing what he thought he was. Then he looked at Jillian and told her what he'd seen.

"The horseshoe stack was hollowed out and there was something inside it. Castilla reached in and pulled out a black velvet bag with drawstrings, opened it up, and poured some of what was inside into his hand."

She couldn't help blurting out, "Bubbles?"

"*Diamonds.*"

Jillian gasped.

"The two talked then and Chad whispered a translation. Davidson has a horse farm right outside Antwerp in Belgium — the diamond capital of the world. Davidson had smuggled the diamonds into the country in the hollowed-out hoof of that Walking Horse, right through Customs, nobody'd give it a second glance. You'd have to know how to get that hoof off to examine it, and it doesn't come off the way it looks like it does."

"Were they stolen diamonds?" Jillian asked.

Lamar shrugged. "Maybe. Maybe they were just Mr. Detergent's way of washing Castilla's money. Dirty money in, *untraceable* diamonds out. But maybe they *were* stolen ... if they were, they had to be the accumulated haul from more than one theft, because..."

Lamar stopped, almost seemed to lose his breath.

"... because Castilla had paid *fifteen million dollars* for the diamonds in that pouch. Would sell them for twice, maybe three times as much. *That's* why he came personally to Willow Creek farm — to take possession of those diamonds."

Jillian felt Lamar's hand on her arm and realized he was lowering it to the table, because she was holding a cup of coffee … and her hand was shaking so violently the coffee was splashing over the side.

"I'm … sorry," she said. She left the cup sitting on the table.

But Lamar didn't seem to hear her, just went on telling his story.

"That's when the whole operation went south. I know *now* what happened — the signal to move in was given to only half the agents. Chad and I never got it. But all I knew then was that the shit had hit the fan. Davidson snatched the black bag out of Castilla's hand and shoved it back into the empty space inside the horseshoe. He knelt down, fastened the horseshoe in place, didn't take the time to fasten the strap on it, just grabbed the reins of the Tennessee Walker and put the horse back into its stall. Then he ran back up the path to the house. And Castilla … vanished. Chad and I never got a signal to move in. We *had them both* … and they both got away."

Lamar slumped back into his chair.

"Chad lied to Mitch. He said stealing the 'bubbles' was my idea. It wasn't. It was his. He said they were there for the taking. We could slip into the stall, get the bag out of that horse's hoof before anybody saw anything. Hide it somewhere and come back for it. Nobody would ever know it was us."

All the air and energy drained out of Lamar so suddenly it was like he somehow imploded. He looked into her eyes and spoke. His voice was weak and tired.

"And that's where the fog rolls back in. It's all gone after that. The memories are gone."

"You don't know what you did, what your partner did?"

"I don't have any idea. At some point after that — I don't know how — I got hit on the head."

"But you don't know what happened?"

Some energy returned and he sat back up.

"I don't *know*, but do the math, Jillian. Davidson went back for the diamonds, but they were gone. Obviously, *somebody* took them out of that horse's shoe. Now, both Davidson and Castilla both are looking for the diamonds, and they will stop at absolutely nothing to get them back. They'll track down, torture, and murder anybody who was anywhere near that farm on the night of the raid."

"I don't think it takes a rocket scientist to figure out it was your partner Chad. He took them and faked his own death to get away with it."

"Then why'd he come back?"

Jillian's mind stumbled over the question. She had no response.

"If he had the diamonds and he was safely dead, why did he risk it all to come looking for me?"

"I … don't know."

"Maybe it's just like he told Mitch. I took them and hid them somewhere. But I wasn't supposed to wake up from that coma, so he had to run. He figures if I give the diamonds back now, he can come home to his old life."

"There's more holes in that theory than a wino's raincoat. Why didn't he come to you as soon as you woke up? Why didn't he go to his superiors and tell them what was going on, save the lives of some of those agents? Why'd he lie to Mitch? Why'd—"

"Maybe we were partners and I double-crossed him."

"Maybe he double-crossed you. Or here's an even better explanation — maybe you didn't have anything to do with the theft at all."

"Then why is he looking for me?"

Suddenly, Jillian's phone rang. It was doubly startling

because she thought cell service had been knocked out all over the county.

She pulled it out of her pocket and looked at caller ID, then groaned inwardly. David. David Hicks was the last person on earth Jillian wanted to talk to right now.

The phone rang again, and Lamar looked at her questioningly. She couldn't explain to him why she didn't want to take the call … so she got to her feet and went into the dining room and answered.

"Hi David."

"Hey, can you believe it — the call went through. But we better talk fast. I hear calls are blinking on and off everywhere."

"So, how are you?"

"That depends."

"On?"

"On whether or not I can take you to dinner tonight. The brake handle for my bike came in, and I thought I'd come over this afternoon and put it on, then maybe we could go out. What do you say?"

Shit! What could she say?

"Today's not a good day, David. Maybe sometime next week."

She heard her own voice, and she sounded cold and formal and standoffish. She hadn't meant it that way at all.

"Next week." It wasn't a question, it was a response, flat and toneless.

"Yeah, I'll … give you a call."

"Right. Don't call us, we'll call you."

Jillian wanted to backpedal but didn't quite know how.

"I didn't mean it that way … how about Tuesday? Or Wednesday."

"Or week after next maybe?"

"Sure, the week after next would—" She was halfway

into a response when she realized he was being sarcastic, and she'd reinforced it.

"Just let me know when you're free. I'll—"

Silence.

"David?"

No response.

"David, are you there?"

Dead air.

The call had dropped.

She put the phone on the sideboard and hurried back into the kitchen. Lamar was gone.

Sinking down into the chair where she'd been sitting, she tried to get her wits about her. She was so rattled that she'd hurt David's feelings. She hadn't meant to. That annoyed her. And she didn't like that it annoyed her. She should feel bad about it.

But dammit, he couldn't just show up anytime he wanted, he didn't own her.

Jillian froze.

The words "*own her*" banged around in her head like a bowling ball in an oil drum. Was that it? Was Jillian unconsciously responding to David's solicitousness as possessiveness? Is that why the closer he wanted to get, the more she pulled back.

That was definitely a thought to explore with Dr. Al-Masri, but she didn't have time to think about that right now. Didn't have time to think about David at all right now. She had to help Lamar.

Chapter Thirty-Nine

Lily Bishop felt a little like she used to when she and her sisters would sneak out behind the barn with some of Daddy's moonshine, pass the jar around, giggling, excited to be doing something so forbidden and so dangerous. While what Lily was about to do wasn't dangerous, it was forbidden, at least implicitly forbidden. Rileigh had insisted that when Mama went somewhere in town, she went directly there and directly home. She wasn't allowed to go wandering around because she might get lost.

But today she was planning on breaking that rule. She needed to go to the grocery store. She'd come up with an idea, a really good one. She was going to make Lamar shrimp creole. She'd never made nothing like that before, but she'd seen it every now and then in her cookbook, the one with the pages falling out. Lily didn't look at a cookbook very often. She had recipes in her head, and most of them wasn't something you could write down. It was just something you knew how to do, but this one was in her cookbook, on the page across from beef stew, one of those splattered pages.

She grinned. She remembered once Rileigh telling Georgia that if you wanted to know what the family liked to eat, just open up mama's cookbook and look for the pages that were splattered with something. She chuckled out loud.

Lily planned to surprise Lamar with the dish at Sunday dinner tomorrow, but trouble was, she'd got out that recipe book and she didn't have all the ingredients that was in it. Oh sure, she had most of 'em — things like butter and green peppers, onions, celery, and spices like bay leaves, oregano, parsley, and thyme. Those was herbs she grew in her herb garden. But she didn't happen to have no fresh shrimp lying around handy. And she didn't have no Cajun or creole seasoning — which was two entirely different things, according to the cookbook. She'd have to go to the grocery store and buy her some, and she'd planned to do that on her way to church tonight.

Her sewing circle met the last Saturday of every month. That's where she and women she had known most of her life got together and made quilts that they sent to orphanages and gave to poor families at Christmas. They'd been doing that for forty, maybe fifty years. Nobody remembered anymore who came up with the name for the group — Bestowing Sewing. While they sewed, they talked about everything and everybody there was to talk about in Yarmouth County.

Of course, Rileigh hadn't wanted her to come, said yesterday's storm had done more than knock out everybody's cell phones and some people's land lines, it had washed out some roads and knocked tree limbs down on others. Lily had poo-pooed that, said the mains roads was always cleared quick — and she *had* to go to the grocery store on her way to church. What she did *not* tell Rileigh was that she was planning on making one *other* stop besides the grocery store.

Lily grinned, wishing she and her sisters could all do what she was about to do. They had never lived close enough to town or had enough money when she was a little girl to do such, but times was different now, and she was plannin' on taking advantage of that.

Lily was on her way to Red Eye Gravy. She had never done it before, but she was gonna walk right up to that counter and buy herself a vanilla milkshake!

And wouldn't it be fun if her sisters, the other flowers in her parents' bouquet, could be there, too?

Lily blinked, and Rose called out to her from the backseat. She looked in her rearview mirror and there little Rosie sat — in Jasmine's lap, between Iris and Della… for Delphinium. "Can we get a cherry on top?"

"Why sure you can, Sugar," Lily said.

"I'm not getting *vanilla!*"

Lily looked over and found her sister Daisy sitting in the passenger seat beside her. It figured. Daisy always had to be up front, and whatever everybody else wanted, she wanted the opposite.

"What *are* you getting, Daisy?" Iris asked.

"Strawberry," Daisy announced. "And I want a strawberry on the top, not some stupid cherry."

There weren't but a couple of cars in the parking lot of Red Eye Gravy, and none of them had local plates, so they was tourists. Lily shook her head. She hoped this place didn't catch on with the tourists. They'd elbowed locals out of almost every good thing in the whole county, and Red Eye Gravy was *their* diner.

Lily parked and went in the front door with a dinging bell above it and glorious smells wafted out to her, blown out into the world by the air conditioning: hamburgers frying on a grill, fried onions and, of course, *bacon.*

She looked around and went to the stool on the far end of the bar, away from the front door. It wouldn't do for somebody she did know to come in and then tell Rileigh they'd seen Mama at Red Eye Gravy when she wasn't supposed to be there.

She made sure to leave an empty stool beside her because little Rosie always wanted to sit right up next to her. And the other girls scattered all over the place, sitting wherever it suited them. She smiled at a stranger sitting with three other men at a table near her stool at the counter, but he didn't smile back. Tourists.

Patty Ann came over to take her order, chewing gum, popping it. "What'll you have, Miss Lily?"

Patty Ann had taken the place of … Mama couldn't find that memory. There was some young woman used to work here, a pretty young woman. She didn't work here no more, but Mama couldn't remember anything about her or why she left, and marveled that sometimes particular memories just fell right out of her head.

Lily told Patty Ann she wanted a vanilla milkshake with whipped cream and a cherry on the top.

"And just get the other girls whatever they want."

Patty Ann looked at her strange, then turned away. Big John came out from the kitchen then, spotted Lily, and came over to chat with her. He leaned over the bar and wiped it. The bar was absolutely clean, but he wiped it anyway. That's just what the man did. He carried a rag everywhere he went and wiped every surface he got near.

"How you doing, Miss Lily?"

Lily leaned over and whispered, "Shh, you got to keep my secret. John."

He made an X motion across his heart and held up

two fingers. "I swear I'll take your secret to my grave. What is it?"

"I ain't supposed to be here. Rileigh says I ain't allowed to do anything when I come into town, except what I come into town to do, but I wanted a milkshake."

John made a zipper motion across his mouth. "Lips are sealed. What are you supposed to be in town doing?"

"Well, I'm gonna make shrimp creole for Sunday dinner and I don't have all the ingredients."

"Shrimp creole? Sunday dinner calls for a pot roast with carrots and potatoes and gravy on homemade rolls. I bet your family would like something like that better."

"*They* probably would. But we got a houseguest. Nice young fella. Given where he's from, I figured he'd 'preciate a Cajun dish."

"Well, I'd ask you to save me a little bowl of it, but I've never fancied spicy food."

Big John turned away and Patty Ann came with the milkshake then, and Lily stuck the straw in it and sucked pure heaven up into her mouth.

"My goodness, but they make good vanilla milkshakes here."

She looked over and Rosie picked the cherry off hers and was sucking away. She didn't have no teeth in front, so it was hard to suck on a straw. Lily glanced around and saw the other girls, all of them had milkshakes. Well, except Daisy. She'd changed her mind, decided she wanted a banana split.

Lily shook her head. That girl was gonna grow up to be trouble.

She finished the drink and fished in her purse for her wallet and took out her credit card — plastic, gotta love plastic — and handed it to Patty Ann.

She made one final slurping sound in the bottom of

her glass, smiled at Big John, and stepped down off her stool. "Come on, Rosie," she said to the little girl who wasn't finished with her milkshake. "Time to go now. You can bring the rest of it with you. We got to get to the grocery store."

Taking Rosie's hand, she waved goodbye to Big John, then walked out the front door.

JOHN CLANCY WAVED goodbye to Lily Bishop as she walked out the front door, holding the hand of somebody who wasn't there. No telling who she thought she brought in there with her, probably her sisters. She came often to buy milkshakes, and every time she came, she told him not to tell Rileigh, although he done told Rileigh a long time ago. Rileigh had just shook her head and told him her Mama would probably bring imaginary people with her, "but she'll pay for whatever they eat."

The stranger seated with two other men at the table beside where Lily had been sitting on the stool, got to his feet and walked to the bar.

Jangle. Jangle. Jangle.

The sound came from the keys hanging off his belt.

"That sure was a sweet old lady," he said with a slight accent. "She reminds me of that character on the Andy Griffith Show a long time ago. What was her name?"

"Aunt Bee," John said and smiled. "Me, too. Or maybe Tweety Bird's grandmother."

The man chuckled, nodded toward the door with his chin. "What's her name?"

"That was Lily Bishop. She's lived here her whole life, I've known her ever since I was a little kid."

"Uh … maybe I'm mistaken, but it appeared to me, was she talking to somebody who wasn't there?"

"Aw, Miss Lily takes imaginary people with her wherever she goes. She's just like that."

"If she has mental problems, dementia maybe, can she make it home all by herself?"

Big John thought it was kind of a stranger to be worried about her.

"It's all right. Miss Lily lives on Bent Twig Road not too far from town and she's been driving that road for half a century. It's a straight shot, but she's not going home. She's got church tonight."

The man smiled and nodded, turned back to the other men at his table, and gestured for them to come with him.

Chapter Forty

J‌ILLIAN WAS IN HER STUDIO PAINTING LATE SATURDAY afternoon when she heard a knock on her door.

"Come in."

It was Rileigh. Jillian appreciated the respect that both Rileigh and Mama afforded her time in the studio. They never just marched right in, they always knocked.

For some reason, a random thought struck Jillian and she burped out a bark of inappropriate laughter.

"What?" Rileigh said.

"I don't know why in the world I thought about this, but are you sure you're not a vampire?"

Rileigh ran with it. "The last time I looked I wasn't, but I suppose since then I could have become one. Why?"

"Because a vampire can't come into your house unless you invite it in. So …"

"So you just invited me in, but I promise not to drink her blood."

Jillian could tell that Rileigh really wasn't in the mood for humor when she merely smiled wanly.

"I waited until Mama left to go to the grocery store."

"The grocery store? I thought she was going to her sewing group."

"She doesn't think I know she's going to the grocery store," Rileigh said. "She wants to get the ingredients to make some kind of Creole dish tomorrow for Lamar. I'm not supposed to know that either, but I saw the recipe book open on the kitchen counter … I know she doesn't have several of the ingredients. And after that, she's going to Bestowing Sewing at church. So I'm going to wait until …well, I don't really know when to tell her this."

"Tell her what?"

"When Mitch came by last night, he came to tell me that Jeremiah Johnson had been murdered."

Jillian felt her knees turn to bags of water, and she sat down quickly on the chair beside her easel.

"Murdered? Jeremiah Johnson? He's the man who…?"

"Found Lamar in the woods, yes."

"Murdered?" Jillian said again, trying to get it to fit inside her head somewhere. And as soon as she did, the rest of the files about the other murders downloaded into her head alongside it. "Was he? I mean, the other murders, did they…?" She couldn't finish the sentence, but she didn't need to.

"Yes, he was tortured just like the rest of them."

"Oh, my God."

Jillian put her elbows on her knees and her head in her hands and shook it back and forth. "It just gets more horrible and more horrible every second."

Suddenly Jillian's head snapped up. It had occurred to her, whoa, wait. "Did he know Lamar came here?"

"No, all he knows is that we took Lamar to Gus's."

"And they tortured him. They could have made him tell them about Gus."

As soon as she said it, she realized she wasn't telling Rileigh anything she hadn't thought of herself.

"If he talked."

"You said they did horrible things to those other men they tortured."

"And perhaps they broke Jeremiah. But maybe not. He's a tough old bird. He was a POW in Vietnam, and he hasn't said much, but he told Mama that the hardest part of the torture was listening to them coming down the hall and wondering which one of the prisoners they were going to pick to beat today."

"This nightmare just keeps getting worse and worse. Poor Lamar." Jillian's heart went out to the FBI agent who was caught up in the middle of it. "I mean, none of this is his fault."

"How sure are you of that?" Rileigh asked.

Jillian felt like Rileigh had slapped her. "What are you talking about?"

"Dr. Al-Masri and I had a conversation, not about Lamar specifically. She just pointed out to me that there are no better liars in the world than people who have something to hide."

"She thinks he's lying?"

"You're not listening. I didn't say that. I said that she was talking about patients in general and wanted me to be prepared for the possibility that none of this is the way it seems."

Jillian felt a big hole open up inside her chest.

"She thinks he's faking the amnesia." It was a statement, not a question.

"Jillian, she didn't say anything of the sort. You're so touchy."

"I'm not touchy."

"Yes, you are. she wasn't talking about Lamar. You're

too sensitive."

"I am not," Jillian said haughtily.

Rileigh just looked at her, and Jillian felt her face flush. "Me thinks thou doth protest too much," Rileigh said.

"What are you saying?"

"I'm not saying anything at all."

"All right. What are you implying?"

"I wasn't intending to imply anything, but since you asked." She paused. "Jillian, it seems to me that you have gotten really wrapped up in Lamar Devereaux and his circumstances — quickly. Am I wrong?"

Jillian opened her mouth to tell Rileigh she absolutely was wrong. But she didn't say anything for a few moments and then said instead, "I don't know Rileigh. I swear I don't know."

She heard the frustration and despair in her own voice, and so did Rileigh. And she responded to it. She got up from where she had sat down in the chair by the door, came to Jillian, and put her arm around her shoulders.

"I'm sorry this is so rough on you. We never planned to bring someone into the house that would make your transition back home even harder for you."

"It isn't making it harder."

"Yes, it is."

"No, it isn't. The situation isn't making it harder. Okay, well, it is, but—"

"Because you're certainly touchy about something."

"What's making it harder is everybody hovering over me." Jillian hadn't meant to raise her voice, but she had.

The remark seemed to strike Rileigh like a blow, and she stepped back. "I'm sorry."

"No, I'm sorry," Jillian said. Then she let out a sigh. "You and Mama and everybody else who know what happened to me have such compassion for me. Please understand that compassion gets old really fast."

"I never thought about that."

"I appreciate all your care and your concern. I would have nobody in my life without you guys. But the looks of concern on your faces every time you look at me, I feel like a bug on a pin."

"I hadn't thought about that either," Rileigh said.

"Sure, bring Lamar here has made it all worse, but it didn't create the problem. And there is no solution. I know you're compassionate, you love me and you're sorry for what happened to me … so *I'm* the one who has to figure out a way not be so thin-skinned that your sympathy is hard for me to take."

"It took guts to say that. Thanks for telling me."

Since they had both acknowledged the elephant in the middle of the room, Jillian went on.

"I don't know what is going on inside me about Lamar Devereaux."

"What do you mean?"

"I haven't had real relationships with people in 30 years. I don't know how to play the game anymore. I don't know what's normal and what's not normal."

"Normal is a setting on a dryer."

That's what their Aunt Daisy had always said. And Jillian could see that Rileigh was sorry she had brought the visage of Aunt Daisy into the conversation.

"I didn't say that," Rileigh added.

Both of them came close to smiling. It lightened the tension in the room.

"I don't want to believe Lamar Devereaux did anything wrong. I feel compassion for him, and it feels very good to be on the giving end of compassion for a change instead of the receiving end."

"I get that, but you have to accept that he might have done wrong."

"I thought in American jurisprudence a person was presumed innocent until proven guilty, and not the other way around."

Jillian's voice had an edge to it, so she backed off, said nothing else.

Rileigh was silent, too, until she asked quietly, "Is this causing problems with you and David?"

Again, Jillian felt like she'd been punched in the gut.

"Yes, and it's bringing up all kinds of feelings that I don't want to deal with right now. David doesn't understand what's going on, why things are mysterious. I can't tell him, and he's so possessive."

"David Hicks is possessive?"

"Okay, that was the wrong word. I just feels that way sometimes. I know I'm being too sensitive." Jillian let out a sigh of frustration. "I don't know how to do *people* things anymore." Jillian went to the window that looked out toward the northern woods and rested her forehead on the glass. "I just want things to be easy."

"I get that, Jillian," Rileigh said.

And she said something else too, but Jillian missed it because she was looking out at the trees. She froze, looked harder. Movement. Yes, there was movement out in the trees on the hillside. A deer? Yeah, it must be … no, *red!* She saw a flash of the color red and sucked in a gasp.

"Rileigh!"

Rileigh stopped in mid-sentence. "What?"

"There's somebody out there in the woods."

Rileigh was instantly at her side looking.

"Over there behind that big oak tree. Do you see?"

Rileigh gasped as well. There *was* somebody in the woods. More than one somebody.

Both women stood frozen for a heartbeat or two before Rileigh shifted gears and became a police officer right in front of Jillian's eyes. She might as well have stepped out of a phone booth wearing a Superman suit.

Jillian looked into her sister's eyes and was reassured by the sudden understanding that Rileigh knew what to do in a crisis. Jillian might be frozen with terror, but Rileigh was not. She was in full-on police officer mode, large and in charge. She grabbed Jillian's hand and squeezed it.

"Listen to me. We don't have much time. You have to get this right the first time. You have to get Lamar ... and *run.*"

Chapter Forty-One

Surely Jillian misunderstood what Rileigh said.

"Run? How? They'll see the car."

"You're not taking the car. You're taking the four-wheeler."

"What? I can't do that."

"Shut up and listen. You have to do what I say — without question — *now*. Get Lamar out, through the house and the yard into the barn. Put him on the four-wheeler and take off through the woods."

"But his leg is broken."

"A broken leg or tortured to death, pick one."

The sisters' eyes locked for what seemed like an eternity, and when Jillian looked away, it was almost as if Rileigh had given her confidence, courage, and determination like some kind of ray shooting out of her eyes and into Jillian's. She felt different.

"What are *you* going to do?"

"I'm going to create a diversion so you can get away."

"No!" Jillian cried, but Rileigh was already moving out the door and down the hall. "I'm not gonna leave you here," Jillian called after her, but Rileigh didn't turn around. Chasing her down the hall, Jillian yelled, "You can't do this, you *can't.*"

Rileigh never even slowed. She ran through the living room onto the porch, out into the evening darkening toward sunset and was gone.

Jillian stood frozen at the top of the stairs for a moment in indecision. Then she ran down them to Lamar's room, didn't knock on the door, just burst in.

"They're here!"

"Who's here?"

He was sitting on the bed with both legs over the side, just sitting there, and she wondered if that's what he'd been doing ever since Dr. Al-Masri left. Had he just come into the bedroom and sat down on the side of the bed, and stayed there staring?

"The guys who are after you, they're here."

"You have to get away," he told her.

"No, *we* have to get away. Rileigh has this all figured out, and we're going to do it her way. Now, put your arm around me, grab that crutch, and we're getting out of here."

Lamar sat a moment in indecision, then rose to the only foot he could put any weight on and grabbed the crutch. Jillian shoved herself up under his other arm, and together they crutch-walked out of the room, down the hall as fast as they could, across the kitchen, and out the back door. Lamar was groaning and grunting with the effort, and she knew that all this movement was hurting him, but he moved as fast as he could, and Jillian didn't waste time looking back. If they got caught, they got caught. She had to focus on getting the two of them out to the barn, onto that four-wheeler, and up the mountainside.

It seemed to take an eternity to cross the backyard.

Jillian hadn't counted on the fact that the uneven surface of the grass would make it hard for Lamar to seat the crutch tip. It slipped out from under him once, and he almost went down, but she grabbed and dragged and pulled as hard as she could until he was stable again, and they kept going.

"One step, just one at a time. You can do this. Come on."

"How many men are there?"

"I don't know. We just saw a flash of color in the woods."

Time did one of those stupid, loopy things then that it did sometimes, like a video played on slow motion. Jillian watched his crutch tip strike the grass and dig in, felt the weight of him lessen as he lifted himself to take a step, and then sag back down with a grunt of pain as he shifted his weight back to her and the crutch, and then started the whole process over again.

And in that rhythm, crutch, weight on her, step, weight off her, crutch — wash, rinse, repeat — they moved toward the backyard gate. Jillian reached out, flipped the catch, and kicked it. The gate banged against the fence with a cracking sound as loud as a gunshot, and she was suddenly aware of not just *hurry*, but *hide*. They couldn't make any noise or attract attention. Rileigh was doing something — Jillian didn't know what, and she didn't want to think about what — to distract the killers, to give her and Lamar a little window of time to get away.

Crutch, weight on her, step, weight off her, crutch.

Moving around the back side of the garage, they came out on the other side and froze when they heard a cry from the woods.

"That way, he went that way."

He.

Rileigh's distraction had worked. The killers thought she was Lamar.

The barn was rectangular. It had double bay doors on both of the long sides and a normal door in the end nearest the house. Jillian got them to that door and managed somehow to stumble across the threshold and inside.

Out of sight now, Jillian felt a momentary sense of elation — *we made it.* But that was before Lamar lost his balance.

And this time he couldn't catch himself with the crutch.

This time he crashed down to the floor, and she heard a terrible sound and a muffled scream, a shriek. His weight had come down on that leg, the broken leg.

Lamar rolled over onto his back, grabbing at his leg, and Jillian was horrified to see a huge lump appear on the side of his leg. The broken bones had moved, slid apart, and one of them was threatening to poke through the skin. Not a compound fracture yet, but just as bad as one.

Lamar lay on the barn floor, rolling around in agony, screaming without screaming. She could hear the horrible rumble in his throat that he wouldn't let out into the air, and she dropped to her knees.

"Lamar, oh God, no, Lamar."

He couldn't speak. All he could do was scream silently, snapping his head back and forth, shrieking with no voice. Then he opened his eyes and focused on her and ground out words.

"You have to go without me. Take the four-wheeler and go."

"I can't leave you here."

"*I* can't go with you."

"Yes, you can."

She got down in his face, her nose inches from him, and shrieked a whisper. "You *can*, and you *will*. I know it *hurts*. Deal with it."

He stopped flailing and she watched him try to grab hold of himself, grip his emotions, tamp down the pain somehow.

Jillian rose, reached down, and took hold of Lamar's left arm.

"Stand up."

"I can't stand up."

Jillian ignored him, dragging upward with every bit of her strength, and he began to rise off the floor. She pulled and pulled, and he began trying to help. He wiggled and got his left foot under him so he could stand with his weight on it and not the right leg that was a horror, bleeding inside and turning purple. Jillian couldn't look at it. She grabbed his crutch, shoving it under his arm.

He was panting, sweating profusely, but his skin felt clammy. His face was flushed beet red, and she could see his heart hammering by the movement of the T-shirt on his chest.

As quickly as they could, they crutch-walked across the barn to the four-wheeler. Jillian hadn't given a moment's thought to how she was going to get Lamar on the back of that thing. If she could get his broken leg over the top of the seat — as painful as that would be — and down on the right side, he could put his left leg behind hers on the footrest.

They got to the four-wheeler, and Jillian leaned him gently against it as he moaned in agony.

She ran to the back bay doors, moved the hasp, and eased the left door open wide enough for the four-wheeler to pass through. Then she ran back to Lamar.

"Okay, you have to sit down on this seat."

He didn't respond, but she could hear his teeth grinding to keep himself from screaming. He was leaning against the back right bumper of the four-wheeler.

"Put all of your weight on your left leg. Then I'll lift your right leg up over the seat and down on the other side."

He shook his head violently. "No, no, I can't." Tears were streaming down his flushed cheeks.

"Yes, you can." And without giving him time to consider it, she grabbed his right leg above the knee, and began to raise the leg upward.

"Don't! Stop, don't!" He was whispering, but it was almost a scream.

Shaking his head violently, he made a feeble effort to pull away. She couldn't wrestle him. The kindest thing she could do was get it over fast. She tightened her grip on his leg and, in a single motion, pulled it up over the saddle of the four-wheeler and down onto the other side, where it landed with a sickening whump.

He did cry out, then. He couldn't help it, but it wasn't loud. It was a shriek turned into a tiny mewl, like a baby rabbit run over by a threshing machine.

She had pulled on his body as she lifted his leg, and now he was straddling the machine behind where she would be sitting, so he could hold on to her. She glanced at his leg. Dear God, it was three times the size that it had been, swelling up into a horrible melon, where she could literally see the bones jammed up against the skin, threatening to push through.

She climbed up onto the 4-wheeler in front of him. "Grab hold," she said.

He wrapped his arms around her and laid his head over on her back, and she could feel his whole body shaking. He was sobbing silently.

The most dangerous part of it all would be the first thirty yards, because it was out in the open. They'd be totally exposed, and there was a big lump they'd have to bounce over. Then the trail led up through the trees, and she knew it well. They would be out of sight.

"Hold on," she said.

She took a deep breath, reached down and turned the key David had left in the ignition.

Nothing happened.

Chapter Forty-Two

RILEIGH MADE SURE THE KILLERS COULDN'T MISS HER grand exit. She exploded through the screen door to the front porch, stretching the squawking spring on the screen tight to exaggerate its shriek of noisy protest. Then she slammed it shut behind her with a bang as loud as a rifle shot.

She had to wrench her mind away from considerations of Jillian and how she could possibly get a man with a broken leg onto a four-wheeler. That wasn't Rileigh's concern right now. They wouldn't be able to do anything if she didn't distract the men who were in the woods hunting them.

Rileigh felt the narrowing of her vision and focus, a sign of a massive adrenaline dump into her veins. Her hearing became more acute. All her senses were heightened. The adrenaline gave her strength and stamina. She knew it would. It always did.

With no time to formulate a plan, one would just have to open up in front of her. And as she leapt off the porch, bypassing the steps altogether, and landed in the yard, an escape route appeared in her mind. It was dicey, chancy, but it was all she had. A BTN plan — better than nothing.

She raced into the front yard and turned toward the woods in the opposite direction from where they had seen the flash of red in the trees. She had short hair, was wearing jeans and a white t-shirt, easy to spot, and they were expecting to see a man running away. She could pass for that. They'd come here looking for Agent Devereaux, had no idea that he had been shot and his leg was broken. All she could do was hope that they would follow her in hot pursuit, believing she was the prey they'd been looking for, and she could lead them away from the house so Jillian and Devereaux could get away.

Racing up the hillside on the other side of the house and into the trees, she wasn't cringing away from a bullet that any moment might slam into her back. She knew they wouldn't shoot her. They wanted her alive. And then she began to sprint through the woods as familiar to her as her own hand. The BTN plan included no time for examination. It would work or it would not. And if it didn't … she kept herself from finishing that thought.

It would work.

As she dodged around familiar rocks and trees, the shadows under the trees began to puddle, and she realized how close to sunset it was out there on the flat. It would be true dark in these woods in a matter of minutes. And darkness was Rileigh's friend. If she could just elude capture long enough for her friend darkness to come to her rescue, she would be safe. She knew these woods. These men didn't. She knew five different ways to get out of the woods, go deeper into them, or hole up if she had to. She was running toward one of those places now. She was making for the Keebler Tree.

That's what she and Georgia had named it when they

were children. They played in these woods every summer of her remembrance until at some point in junior high school when it wasn't cool anymore to go out in the woods, get tick bites, look for grub worms and swing from monkey vines. But even then, she came out here by herself just because she loved it.

One day, when she and Georgia were playing hide and seek, it was Rileigh's turn to hide. Georgia stood with her eyes squeezed tight shut, her hands over them, counting to a hundred as Rileigh raced off through the trees, looking for a small bush she could hide behind or maybe a low limb that she could reach to climb up into a tree.

She spotted a large rock she was familiar with and raced toward it, but when she went around behind it to hunker down, she saw what she had never noticed before. Growing there was a huge tree, towering above her, and it had a big hole in the trunk near the bottom. To eight-year-old Rileigh, the hole was huge.

She had hurried to it and peered inside. If she had learned anything about the outdoors, it was that vacant spaces were often not vacant at all. This was a perfect place to build a den or a nest, and some wild critters probably had, or would. She didn't want to run across a wild cat, an angry raccoon, or heaven forbid, a grumpy skunk.

Peering in, she saw no critters. She inched her body slowly inside the hole and looked around. She could tell that it had been home to several different families of wildlife. She could see the nests — and turds of mice, the little gray kind that lived in the woods. Squirrels had made their home here, too, perhaps even a badger or a fox or a weasel. Any one or all of them could at one time or another have called the hollow tree home. But right now, it appeared that it had a vacancy sign out front. There was no evidence of a currently occupied tenant.

Unfortunately, as a hiding place, the newly discovered hole in the tree lacked the most important characteristic of such places. There was nowhere to hide. She could crawl into the hole in the tree and crouch down inside it, but if you spotted the tree, there she was. There was nothing to hunker down behind.

She was turning to leave when she chanced to look up and saw a shaft of sunlight on the inside of the tree. The hole where she crouched continued upward into the trunk of the tree. It appeared to get smaller and smaller as it went up, but there was a hole up there, too, where the sun was shining through. Rileigh began to climb up inside the tree, making her way through the opening that was like a chimney. Soon, the space got too small for her to go any farther forward, but now she was far above the space you could see from the outside. She hung there and waited. And waited. Georgia never came. She never even found the hole in the tree, let alone Rileigh's special hiding place in the hole above the hole.

Rileigh heard her distant cry that she was giving up, that Rileigh had won so she could come out. She hurried to Georgia and dragged her to the tree to show where she'd hidden.

Georgia squealed. "It's the Keebler Tree!"

She was talking about the Keebler elves, of course, who made the cookies. Though there were no cookies in the hole in the tree, and it was certainly not a cookie factory, the tree was a marvelously special place, and she and Georgia had returned many times. They cleaned the crud out of the bottom of the hole, the remains of various creatures' living spaces, and pulled down the stems and twigs from the inside part of the tree so it was easier to climb up into it.

Rileigh hadn't seen the Keebler Tree in two, maybe

three decades. She ran through the woods in the length-ening shadows, her breath heaving in and out of her chest, praying the tree was still there and that the property was still unoccupied. She didn't want to have to evict a skunk, porcupine, or bobcat to crawl in there and hide.

When she came around the large rock to the base of the gigantic tree, she groaned. A big hole to an eight-year-old is a small hole to an adult, but there was nothing for it now but to give it a shot. She got down on her hands and knees and shoved her head into the opening. If there were critters in there or the remains of critters, it was too dark for her to see. She crawled inside and slowly got to her feet with her arms above her head. There was not enough space to lift them with her shoulders almost touching the inside walls and she needed her hands and arms to climb.

Then she dug the toes of her shoes into the old bark and pushed herself upward, clawing with her fingers and shoving her way up through the hollow trunk. The sticks and stems and rough edges of the inside of the tree gouged her arms and sides as she climbed, but she kept going as high as she could until there was no possibility of squeezing herself up any higher. Then she pulled her legs up so they couldn't be seen from outside, holding herself in place with her hands and feet against the inside walls, looking down at the empty hole in the tree a few feet below her.

Then she waited. And waited some more, praying that it would be as it was with Georgia and her hiding place would remain secret. Suddenly, she heard a sound from outside. She concentrated, listened, her muscles straining and beginning to tremble from the strain of holding her body in place. Was it just some animal? It was past dusk now, so the deer were out and all the nocturnal creatures were beginning to venture forth. Was that all?

Crunch.

She recognized a distinct sound — feet on dried leaves.

But that wasn't the only sound she heard. As she concentrated, she heard a jingling sound of some kind.

Jangle. Jangle. Jangle.

At least one and probably more than one of the men were approaching through the trees. Then she saw light. They'd turned on the flashlight apps on their phones and were using them to light the way. Closer and closer they came, the lights growing brighter. She heard murmurs. The sounds of conversation grew louder, but they were in Spanish, and she couldn't understand what they were saying. It soon became clear that a group of men, two, three, five, who knew how many, had stopped in a small clearing by the rock outside the base of the Keebler Tree.

Then the sound of jingling drew closer and closer. Rileigh squeezed herself up into her hiding place as far as she could go and held her breath as she saw a beam of light shine into the opening at the bottom. The light grew brighter and brighter as the flashlight got closer to the hole.

Jangle. Jangle. Jangle.

She watched in horror as a man's hand holding a phone with a bright light came into view below her. Then she saw his arm, and then his head poked into the hole in the side of the tree trunk.

All the man had to do was look up, shine that light upward, and Rileigh would be caught.

Caught meant torture.

Caught meant bones crushed.

Caught meant being skinned alive.

The man's head began to move, his face lifting up toward her.

Chapter Forty-Three

Panic welled up like bile in the back of Jillian's throat. She turned the key again and again.

Still nothing.

They'd gotten this far, had managed to evade the killers, and escape sat right under them — and *nothing*. Not even the clicking sound a car makes when you turn the key on a dead battery. She drew in a shaky breath, struggling with all her strength not to burst into tears. It had worked fine Wednesday afternoon when she and David went riding in the woods! Started right up as soon as she turned the key…

And pushed the red button!

Relief washed over her was so warm and sweet, she wanted to giggle. She'd been so frightened and desperate that her whirring mind had spun right past that. You didn't start a four-wheeler by turning an ignition key. You started a four-wheeler by turning on the key and then *punching the red ignition button.*

With one deep restoring breath, she turned and spoke over her shoulder to the man in agony behind her.

"Hold on *tight,* this is going to be a bumpy ride, particularly in the beginning because I'm going to be hauling ass."

"Thank you" was all he could say.

She glanced down at his leg behind hers and wanted to cry again. The bone that had been displaced was so close to bursting through the skin that you could see it straining, like looking at the head of a baby moving in a pregnant woman's stomach. God how that must hurt!

"Okay, here we go."

She pushed the button and the engine sprang to life, growling and rumbling. Oh God, it was loud. She never noticed how loud it was before. Engaging the clutch by pulling the lever with the fingers of her left hand, she used her foot on the gear shift to put the four-wheeler in first gear and turned the throttle up. Then she popped the clutch and with a great lurch, the four-wheeler leapt forward out through the back door of the barn.

She didn't have time to warn Lamar again about the bump. They flew over it and slammed down on the other side. He squeaked out an uncontainable cry of pain and then they sped up the side of the mountain and into the trees. She didn't dare take her eyes off the trail to look back over her shoulder as they climbed the side of the mountain. Rileigh had led the killers off into the trees on the other side of the house, but if even one had remained behind, he would see her and Lamar flying out of the barn on the four-wheeler. And the engine was so loud, surely even the men in the woods searching for Rileigh had heard it. Would they give chase? They might try, but they were on foot and she had four wheels. She could outrun them.

But her terror was more than fear that the men would come after her. She was frightened for Rileigh. Her little sister had tricked them like a mother bird faking a broken wing to lead predators away from her nest. Had they caught her? Oh dear God, had they? She couldn't let her mind go there. Rileigh knew what she was doing. Rileigh had been a soldier in combat. She knew these woods like the back of her hand. She'd get away from them. She *would.*

Jillian gritted her teeth, determined to believe that, to hang on to that reality. And soon she had plenty of other distractions to keep her from dwelling on who might be chasing her and what might be happening to Rileigh. It was getting dark. But she didn't want to turn on the headlight quite yet. Neither did she want to crash into a tree. She knew the trail well enough that from the light fading out of the sky, she could feel her way along, but there were several places with ledges and drop-offs and really nasty stuff below if she missed a turn or swung too wide at a corner.

The trail forked in about half a mile. The left fork led to the top of Eagle's Nest Peak where she and David had gone on Wednesday. Before the peak, another trail branched off that went down to the Houlihans, who were not exactly borrow-a-cup-of-sugar neighbors. Rileigh called them the *hooligans.* Though she couldn't prove it, Rileigh believed that Aunt Daisy had paid one of their teenage boys to cut the brake lines on Rileigh's car. The right fork led to other trails that went up and over the top of Tucker Mountain. Regardless of which way she went at the fork, the terrain would become really rugged, and there was no way to maneuver over it without jostling and bouncing her injured passenger.

The trail was relatively smooth before the fork.

But even so, Jillian didn't manage to miss the huge pothole in the middle of the otherwise smooth trail. She hit it hard, and the four-wheeler bounced high. The two of them were thrown up out of their seats, and when Lamar came back down, he lost his balance and fell off the side of the machine, crying out in agony when he hit the ground.

Jillian hit the kill switch and ran back to where he lay and was horrified to see that the fall had shoved the displaced broken bone in his calf out through the skin. Now it was a terrible, ugly, white thing protruding from the melon-sized lump on his lower leg. Blood was oozing out all around it.

Lamar writhed in pain, his eyes squeezed tight shut, tears running down both cheeks.

"I'm so sorry," she said, unable to drag her eyes away from the horrible wound. There was absolutely nothing she could do to help him … except load him back up on the four-wheeler and get him to a doctor. She hadn't yet decided which of the forks in the trail she would take when she got to them, but now the decision had been made for her. She couldn't make for the nearest neighbor on this side of the mountain and hope the Houlihans wouldn't be so hostile they'd refuse to help. Hope they had a land line or a cell phone that worked to call Mitch or an ambulance. Hope they were even home, because if they weren't, she'd have to take the highway to reach the next neighbor beyond them, and she might just run smack into the killers on the way.

But the left fork to the Houlihans wasn't an option anymore. A compound fracture was life-threatening. Lamar could go into shock and die. There was no time to gamble on an iffy reception and a maybe cell phone. She had to take him where it was certain he would get medical care immediately, and that meant not turning left. That meant turning right at the fork and weaving her way over the top of Tucker Mountain. In the hollow on the other side, she could make her way across creeks, through meadows, and around tilled fields to the back of the property where Gus Hazelton's house sat on a hill at the end of a winding lane.

"You have to get back up on the bike," she told Lamar.

He literally whimpered in pain and shook his head in denial.

"You have to do it now. I know that's asking a lot. But you either get back on the bike or stay where you are — until the bad guys find you and torture you to death, or you die from shock and exposure. Your choice."

Without waiting for a reply, she reached down and grabbed Lamar's arm and dragged him on his butt to the back of the four-wheeler. There was no crutch now for him to lean on. She'd have to pull him up with his weight on his good leg and holding onto the machine for balance.

"Are you ready?"

He squeezed his eyes shut and neither nodded nor shook his head, just whimpered deep in his throat.

She pulled then as hard as she could. He got his left foot under him and somehow managed to stand, wobbling, holding onto the four-wheeler, his right leg a visage of horror with a bone sticking out of it.

He cried out in pain now, but there was no one to hear, shrieked when she lifted his leg up and over, dragged the rest of him into the seat and settled him there, and recognized immediately she had another problem. What if Lamar became too weak to hold onto her? Stepping around to the back of the four-wheeler, she removed two bungee cords attached to the frame. David had used them to secure the picnic basket. She climbed into the seat in front of Lamar, and he collapsed against her. She used the bungee cords to attach his body to hers.

The terrain where they were going was rough and treacherous. If Lamar passed out, he might drag her off with him when he went limp. Even if both she and the four-wheeler survived the fall, she would never be able to lift the dead weight of Lamar's unconscious body onto the machine and somehow go on.

Over her shoulder, she said to him, "Stay with me, you hear? If you pass out, we're both toast." Then she flipped on the headlamp that stabbed a saber of light into the gloom, put the engine in gear, and went on.

Chapter Forty-Four

ALL HE HAD TO DO WAS LOOK UP.

Rileigh was only a few feet above the man leaning into the hole in the hollow tree, looking around in the light from his cell phone flashlight.

All he had to do was look up.

Rileigh was as frozen as a stone statue, holding her breath. She watched in horror as his head began to tilt back, lifting his face up toward where she was crouched in the tree above him. Surely he could hear her heart hammering in her chest and smell her fear in her sweat.

She only had seconds before he—

Suddenly a voice called from outside. "This way, he went this way!"

The man instantly pulled back out of the hollow tree, leaving Rileigh there, trembling in terror. She heard the sound of his footsteps crunching leaves and twigs as he ran toward the voice that had called out. Then … silence. Her ears strained for even the slightest sound, but there was nothing. The woods were quiet.

She had pulled her legs up as high as she could so they

couldn't be seen through the hole in the bottom of the tree trunk. Now, she slowly relaxed her muscles and climbed back down, but she remained in the hollowed-out tree trunk. The killers could still be nearby, so she waited, still hiding. She wouldn't leave the sanctuary of the hollow tree until she was sure they were gone, wanted to give them a full ten minutes to get as far away as possible.

Unfortunately, she had no watch to time it. She'd taken it off to scrub the magnetic watchband and had left it on the kitchen counter to dry. With no watch, she could do nothing more than count seconds.

"One Mississippi. Two Mississippi. Three Mississippi."

Counting put her in mind of all the times she and Georgia had played hide and seek in these woods. Count to a hundred, that was the rule, and she strictly followed it, didn't try to find Georgia without counting all the way. Sure, she counted really fast, so fast her numbers ran together: *onetwothreefourfivesixseveneightnineten*. But even so, she gave Georgia a reasonable amount of time to find a hiding place, and she was sure that Georgia afforded her the same courtesy when it was her turn to hide.

When Rileigh was certain that she had waited at least ten minutes and hadn't heard a single sound, she quietly scooted out of the hollowed-out tree into what was now darkness. The men hunting her had flashlights, and she could see those coming a long way off and hide before they got to her.

As she waited, hunkered down in the hole in the Keebler tree, counting seconds, she had considered her escape options. She couldn't go back to the house, of course. Surely, they had left someone behind to watch it. And had that someone caught Jillian and Lamar before they were able to get away?

No. They wouldn't have kept looking for her in the

woods if they'd caught Lamar at the house. But there was the treacherous ride through the woods on the four-wheeler…

She couldn't think about that. She had to trust that when the chips were down, Jillian was strong enough and competent enough to get the job done. Rileigh had seen hints of that strength in her sister. Without it, she never would have lasted all those years in captivity.

Rileigh would have to cut a wide path away from the house through the trees and head for the neighbors where Jillian had taken Lamar. Rileigh wasn't likely to get any friendlier a reception than Jillian from the Hooligans, given that Aunt Daisy had paid one or the other of the teenagers to cut the brake lines on her car. But if they had a func-tioning cell phone or landline, Jillian would have summoned Mitch, and he might right now be on the way.

The thought that she would soon see Mitch warmed her heart. *Mitch to the rescue,* just like he had rescued Lamar from the mountain when Jeremiah Johnson…

Rileigh froze in her tracks.

Oh, god — Jeremiah Johnson!

Rileigh almost sunk to her knees as the full realization hit her like a wrecking ball in her gut. There was only one way the killers could have known Lamar was at Mama's. Jeremiah Johnson had told them. Rileigh didn't know that Mitch had told Jeremiah Lamar was staying with the Bishop family, but he must have. And if Jeremiah had told them about Mama, he had told them the whole story. How he'd found the injured FBI agent in the woods and how *Dr. Gus Hazelton* had treated the agent's wounds!

Since they missed capturing Lamar here, their next stop would be Gus. She was sure of it. They'd go there to get him to tell them where the agent might have run to.

Rileigh had to warn Gus! She had to get to the Houlihans and use their phone …. no, phone service might still be out. Then what? Commandeer one of their cars and drive to his house — all the way around the mountain? It would take too long for her to walk to the Houlihans and then drive...

No. Not *around* the mountain. *Over* it.

David Hicks had left his dirt bike in the woods! He'd hidden it so it wouldn't be stolen, but she knew where to look. She'd find it and ride it over the mountains to Gus's.

Except that bike had no front brake. David had broken the brake handle on the hill climb, and he was waiting to get a new one from the bike shop to repair it. That meant the dirt bike had only *one* brake, the back brake. She supposed that was better than just one brake on the front. But the bottom line was you needed *both* brakes on a bike to negotiate the trails through the mountains. To stop a bike on a slope, either up or down, you had to alternate between putting pressure on the front brake and the back. You only had control of a bike when the tires were *rolling.* Lock up either one with the brake, and it would slide right out from under you.

But a bike with only one brake was better than walking … if she didn't crash it and kill herself. She had no other choice. She had to get to Gus before the killers did, or they'd torture him to death just like they did all the others.

Rileigh carefully cut a wide arc around the house, keeping an eye out for flashlight beams, and then picked up the trail where she was sure Jillian had gone earlier on the four-wheeler. There was a full moon tonight and mountain-brilliant stars as big as chunks of ice — as much light as you were likely to get in the woods at night. Even so, it was harder than she thought it would be to find the bike. But she finally rolled it out onto the trail and inspected the damage. Yep, the front brake was totally gone. The brake handle dangled where it had broken off. But beggars couldn't be choosers, and she climbed aboard the bike, reached down with her right hand and pulled the kickstart lever away from the bike so she could get her foot on it. Then she leapt onto the starter a couple of times and it roared to life. She turned on the headlight and headed out down the trail.

Rileigh crashed the bike on the very first slope.

She came up on it too fast. She would have braked to a stop and eased her way down, but her momentum had carried her forward too fast. She pumped the back brake desperately, but it wouldn't slow her down enough and she kept gaining speed — downhill, faster and faster until she finally pulled the brake handle in all the way. The back tire instantly stopped moving — locked up — and started sliding. She took her feet off the pegs and put them on the ground, scrabbling to keep the bike upright, but she had no control over it now. It slid sideways out from under her, and she tumbled off.

Rileigh lay where she had fallen for a moment, stunned. She didn't think she was hurt. Oh, she *hurt* alright — all over! — was bunged up from head to toe. But at first blush it didn't feel like she was severely injured.

She sat up slowly. Unfortunately, she was wearing shorts and a sleeveless shirt. She'd never have gone dirt bike riding dressed like that! Jeans, riding boots, gloves, and especially a helmet would have protected her from all the scrapes, cuts, and bruises she had just incurred. Nobody but an idiot rode a dirt bike in a pair of shorts and tennis shoes with no helmet. An idiot or somebody desperately running away from killers.

She got to her feet and lifted the bike up, inspecting the damage to it. She had dented the gas tank and bent the back bumper, but she was able to bend it back into place. It was still drivable, so she cranked the engine and headed out, two emotions warring for dominance. The desperate need to get to Gus before the killers did. And the less desperate but more practical need to go more slowly so maybe she could get there in one piece.

She made it up the first big incline between her and the top of the mountain, a slope a hundred feet long and steep. Going up an incline was more about balance and momentum — fast enough to keep moving forward but not so fast you lost control — than it was about keeping the tires from locking up, and she made it to the top, scrambling with her feet, almost pulling a wheelie when the trail flattened.

She went on. Time blurred, became an endless tunnel of white light piercing the darkness, bouncing up over rocks and tree roots and down into holes and cracks in the rocks. She finally topped the mountain and started down the other side.

Down. Down was harder than up.

And then a steep slope appeared suddenly in the glare of the headlights, and she hit rocks that were slick where a spring poured out of a crack.

She was going too fast.

She pumped the brake and dragged her feet on the ground to slow down. But it was quickly clear that she couldn't possibly make it down a slope this steep. She held on as the bike leapt and bucked, slamming into rocks that came at her too fast. Then an outcrop of granite knocked her front tire sideways, and she went over the handlebars, flew through the air and landed hard. She and the bike slid together down the rocky incline. The bike banged along beside her. The skin on her arms and legs was instantly scraped raw. Sharp rocks jabbed and gouged her back and the back of her head.

She and the bike came to rest at the bottom of the incline, and she lay where she was, gasping, attending to the various parts of her body reporting in with damage assessments, breathing in the stink of exhaust and burned rubber.

Everything hurt and she was afraid to move, but she sat up carefully and tried to see where she might be bleeding — mostly everywhere she had exposed skin. Her whole body was a skinned knee. She found a pretty good-sized bleeding cut on her upper left arm and could feel smaller ones on her back.

When she stood, she found the real injury instantly. Her right ankle screamed in pain — badly sprained, cracked ... or maybe broken. Squinting against the glare of the headlight that was pointing right up into her face, she balanced on her left foot and picked the bike up, set it aright on the kickstand, and examined it. It appeared to be intact, nothing essential like a clutch handle broken or the rim of a tire bent. Dirt bikes were made tough.

But the engine had died. And that was a problem. The kick starter was on the right side. She'd have to jump up and slam all her weight down on the kick starter — *and on her injured ankle* — to crank the engine.

It might take two or three tries.

Would the engine start?

If it didn't, she'd have to walk down the mountain ... on an ankle already swelled to twice its normal size.

Chapter Forty-Five

There was no one home at Lily Bishop's house to hear Eduardo Perez jangling his keys as he walked up the front sidewalk to the porch steps and opened the screen door that squawked loudly.

Eduardo's men called him *El Tiburón*, Spanish for "The Shark," because he was as efficient, ruthless, and pitiless a killer as any shark that ever swam the seas. He'd never been anything else in his life, and he'd long since lost count of how many men he had killed. He didn't add to that total the women and the handful of children, too.

El Tiburón had worked for Guillermo Castillo for almost five years now, and those five years had been better than all the thirty years preceding them. Castillo paid well and expected absolute loyalty and absolute obedience, and if you gave him both of those, you were rewarded accordingly. The Shark lived in a beautiful hacienda in Mérida, Mexico, with white stucco walls, a red tile roof, two swimming pools, and a beautiful woman waiting there for him when he came home from a job.

Most of the people he was sent to kill were in Mexico, members of one of the other gangs, or in Central or South America. He had worked in the United States a couple of times; his English was good enough, but he'd never been sent there to stay until the job was done until now.

In years past when he had jobs in the United States, he'd had to come into the country across the desert in Arizona or New Mexico. He refused to chance hiding in a compartment in a truck and crossing at one of the designated crossings in El Paso or Nueva Laredo. It was easier to elude the Border Patrol in the wide-open desert spaces he knew well.

But now! He laughed about how easy it was to go back and forth across the border now. All you had to do was line up with the other people, thousands and thousands, crossing the border every day, mingle with them, look like them. He was, of course, a wanted man in Mexico, but the chances that they would catch him were almost none, because they didn't have the staff or the resources to investigate the hundreds of thousands of people a month. He always smiled when he thought of the United States Border Patrol agent who stamped a piece of paper and handed it to him, telling him that he would have to appear at a hearing in court to determine whether or not he would be allowed to stay in the United States.

The hearing date was April 9th, *2027!*

This job had kept him away from home for far too long, and he had in equal parts grown wearier and wound tighter. His boss expected results, expected The Shark to get the truth out of the people he captured. Someone had stolen a fortune in diamonds from Castilla the night of an FBI raid on a Walking Horse farm in Tennessee. Castilla had paid for a list of all the federal agents who'd worked that raid, and The Shark and his men had been going down that list systematically, one after another, to find the culprit and recover Castilla's diamonds. But as weeks turned into months and he failed to get what he had been sent for, his employer was growing impatient, and The Shark couldn't have that. If he failed Castilla and didn't get back his diamonds, it was a certainty he would not be present at that immigration hearing in 2027. He would be moldering in an unmarked grave with a bullet in his skull.

As the pool of possible suspects shrank one after another, Eduardo/El Tiburón/The Shark went from annoyed and stressed to desperate. This FBI agent was his last shot, the last name on the list, the only possible suspect, and Eduardo absolutely would get the agent to tell him where the diamonds were.

El Tiburón knew every method of torture that had been invented, and he plied the tools of his trade with both expertise and delight. He understood that he was a sadist, was gratified by causing pain to others. It had been that way since he was a boy. Catching a cat or a dog somewhere and torturing it had been a great sport for him and his friends. A professional now, he still enjoyed the sport of pain. He loved watching each victim arrive at breaking point, the point where they would tell you anything, pleading for their lives, begging you to stop hurting them. He had pulverized the hands of that last young man with a sledgehammer, and he had held out surprisingly long before he gave up his girlfriend's name. And out of some bit of respect for his tenacity, The Shark had put a bullet in his forehead.

But he was still bothered by the old man he had questioned a few days ago, the one who lived way back up in the mountains, the one called Jeremiah Johnson. The human body reached a certain point in torture where it could endure no more trauma. Everybody broke. Everybody. Everybody he'd ever questioned had reached a point where they would have sold their mother's soul to ease the agony he'd caused them. But the old man was different, and The Shark didn't know why. Oh, he answered The Shark's questions, but the answers were babble. They meant nothing, and he continued to babble on and on as The Shark broke one bone after another. It was as if he'd gone somewhere and left his body behind and didn't really care what The Shark did to it.

In the end, the man broke but never gave up information, he just *broke*. His mind shattered, and he answered every question with name, rank, and serial number.

The Shark had been shaken by that old man, and there was nothing better to relieve a sense of failure than success. He would find this agent, he would torture him, he would get the information, and he would get Castilla's diamonds back.

Trouble was, the FBI agent had slipped through his fingers, escaped, vanished like a rabbit in the woods, and they'd been tramping around out there for hours trying to flush him out. It was useless. They'd have to snag him somewhere else. And where else might there be? Maybe there was some clue to his whereabouts in the house where he'd been living, so he told his men to search it. When they asked what they were looking for, he told them they would know it when they found it.

It took The Shark no time to find the bedroom where the FBI agent had been staying, and it had been as he feared after all. He had been afraid that the agent had been hurt when they stormed the safe house. The Shark had been careful, had shot only at the agents outside. He had to get this man alive, but one of his men had sprayed the building with bullets before El Tiburón could stop him.

The Shark went into that house fearing he would find

the FBI agent he was looking for dead on the floor, and now it was clear that he had, indeed, been hit. He had taken a bullet. The bloody bandages were evidence of that. The Shark stopped then. How had he run like a rabbit into the woods if he had a bullet in him?

He didn't know the answer to that question or how he had hooked up with the crazy old lady, but somehow he had, and he had been staying here with her and at least two other women, obvious from ransacking their bedrooms. The old lady's name was Lily Bishop, and one of the women was Rileigh Bishop. The driver's license in the other woman's purse identified her as Heather Priest.

After thoroughly searching the house, El Tiburón had found nothing that would indicate where the FBI agent might have gone, and he was left yet again with "now what?" He could stay here and wait until the old lady came home and see what he could get out of her, but she was as crazy as a bedbug. He wouldn't be able to trust any information she gave. But before he packed it in, he decided to take one more look at the room where the FBI agent had been staying, and he spotted something under the bed. Kneeling down, he picked up an empty prescription bottle. So the old lady had found a doctor somewhere to treat the FBI agent's bullet wound, and that doctor had given him a bottle of drugs for the pain.

There was no patient's name on the label, just the handwritten words: "2 every 4-6 hours."

But the printed label listed the name of the prescribing physician: Dr. Gustav Hazelton, and his address. The Shark figured his cell phone's maps app might not be working to find the address since the storm had knocked out some cell tower somewhere. But he didn't care. He would just stop and ask someone where to find the doctor. These stupid people were totally willing to give out that kind of information to total strangers.

Pocketing the prescription bottle, he grinned, revealing the space where a front tooth had been knocked out once in a fight, and led his men out of the house, jangling his keyring as he went.

Chapter Forty-Six

THE STORM THAT'D KNOCKED OUT CELL SERVICE AND electric lines had ripped limbs off trees and dropped them across the trail. For Jillian, life became all about going around the broken limbs … about the next bump, the next pothole, missing the next rock. Doing anything she could to keep the ride as smooth as possible, because she could feel Lamar's arms weakening around her.

She hadn't wanted to, but she forced herself to take a good look at his compound fracture. It was bleeding, but not profusely. Still, bleeding a little for a long time wasn't good. And this was a man who had already lost too much blood from the bullet wound. How much did he have left? Going fast to get him medical care as soon as possible warred against making the ride as smooth as possible.

She climbed — bounced — her way up steep, rocky inclines and inched her way down the other side. One trail connected to the next, and she had to make the correct choice at each fork.

At some point, Jillian realized she was talking to Lamar, the way you'd talk to a little kid to reassure them. A stream-of-consciousness mumble in an effort to engage his mind to keep him alert enough to hold on.

"It's all right. It's going to be just fine. You'll see. We'll get there. It won't be long. I'm going as smooth as I can. Hold on now. You can do this. I know it's hard. I know it hurts, but you can do it. You're strong. You can hang on. Don't let go."

She hit the mist without much warning. It was just suddenly there. Mist had earned the mountains the name "Smoky" mountains, clung to mountaintops, lay in valleys, rose up from creeks and rivers in random places. Now, she had to contend with the headlights reflecting on the mist, obliterating the path in front of her. She had to go achingly slow, knowing Lamar was bleeding, knowing he was in pain, her hand so tight on the throttle that her fingers ached.

The slopes slowly grew less and less steep. And the trail began to smooth. She tried to picture what the terrain looked like in front of her, since she couldn't see it in the dark and mist. There was a meadow, a grassy meadow with wildflowers. Though she'd never ridden across it, she inched her way out through the mist, which slowly grew thinner and thinner until shapes began appearing in front of her in the dim dawn light, now ten feet away, now fifteen, now twenty. Then she came out of the mist altogether, down low enough that the mist was above her. And she could see where she was going, and gratefully the terrain was not rugged.

"Hang on now, hang on," she said and took her hand off the handgrip for just a moment to pat his hands wrapped around her waist. When she finally got to the field directly behind Gus's house, the sky above was turning blue and she had to fight tears of relief — her nerves were frayed all the way to the ends. Pulling up behind his house, she unfastened the bungee cords that kept Lamar's body attached to hers and slid down off the seat. His weight had been against her back, and as she slid, he began to fall forward, so she turned and supported his body, laying him gently out over. His eyes were closed.

"Lamar, we're here."

His eyes fluttered open briefly and closed again.

Surely Gus had heard the sound of the four-wheeler coming. It made such a racket. But no lights came on in his house, and she ran to his back door and banged.

"Gus, Gus, open up. Gus, it's me, Jillian. Open the door." She tried the knob, but it was locked. He wasn't one of those locals who never locked his doors. She was sure he kept his place locked up tight because he had so many guns in there, and maybe even drugs that somebody would want to break in and steal.

When he finally opened the door, she literally fell into his arms, sobbing. All she could do was point back toward the four-wheeler.

"Lamar, he's — the bone in his leg, it broke. It pushed through."

Gus pulled out of her grip and ran to the four-wheeler.

"Holy shit!" she heard him say, in a bedside manner reserved for patients who were already dead. "We have to get him to a hospital."

And then she heard Lamar speak the first thing he'd said since they left Mama's: "No hospital."

So he was awake and aware, after all.

Gus ignored him, of course. It was no longer an option to treat the agent's wounds. He needed immediate surgery on that leg.

"I have a portable gurney in the utility room ... don't ask."

Gus was dressed in pajamas, no shirt, barefoot, as he

ran back into the house. "Help me, come on," he said, and she went in behind him, helping him get the gurney unfolded and roll it out to the four-wheeler. The sun hadn't yet cleared the top of the mountain, of course, but it was past dawn out on the flat, and the darkness had faded away. It was going to be tricky to get Lamar off that bike with the bone in his leg exposed as it was. There was no easy, painless way to do it, as there had been no easy painless way to get him up off the ground and onto the seat of the four-wheeler. As she lifted up his arm, to wrap it around her shoulders, she heard something and looked up toward the mountainside, toward the mist at the top.

A rumble. The sound of a dirt bike.

Chapter Forty-Seven

STARTING A BIKE IS A LITTLE LIKE STARTING A LAWNMOWER. You have to snap a lawnmower starter cord exactly right for it to turn the engine over. Starting a motorcycle is even more challenging. It's a dance.

With the bike on its kickstand, Rileigh stood next to it, balancing on her left foot, then eased her right leg over the seat to straddle it. Carefully, she placed the foot protruding down from her swollen right ankle on the starter lever. She took deep breaths, summoning muscle memory to get the rhythm right, and gritted her teeth. Then, with her weight on her *left* foot, she jumped into the air, and slammed down with all her weight shifted to her *right* foot resting on the starter lever.

She cried out in agony. The engine turned over but didn't start. She leaned her head over onto the handlebars, gasping for breath, tears running down her cheeks.

She'd have to try again.

She performed the whole maneuver again; the engine sputtered but didn't catch. Third time had better be the charm … and when her right foot came down hard on the lever, the pain was so severe she screamed and almost lost her balance. The engine caught, though, sputtered, and she gently gave it gas to coax it to life, and finally it was humming beneath her. It was agony to stand on her right foot as she leaned the bike over and pushed up the kickstand with her left, then she drove slowly away with her right foot resting on the foot peg.

Every time she moved the ankle it was agony, but she had to move it. She had no choice. The rear brake was the only brake she had, and the pedal was on the right side, which meant she had to move that ankle, whether it hurt or not, whenever she had to engage the brake to slow the bike down.

Rileigh tried to be grateful that it wasn't the left ankle. The left foot operated the gear shift, and she was constantly moving it, downshifting to slow her speed going downhill and shifting back up into a higher gear to go fast enough to make it up the inclines.

The storm had brought its own challenges. Trees were knocked down, leaving limbs lying across the trail. She had to be careful how she hit each one, even if the limb was no bigger around than her arm, a size the tires could easily roll over. She had to hit every one straight on. If the front tire was turned slightly to the right or left, the tire would slide along the limb instead of bouncing over it, and the bike would crash over on its side.

She came to the top of the ridge — the hardest part of this trail lay ahead of her. It was downhill at a steep grade for half a mile, and then it dog-legged to the left. The trail was narrow, with a rock wall on the right side and a drop-off on the left. And if a rock knocked her tire sideways or she got off balance, she would either slam into the rock wall or careen off the edge of the rock face, in an almost vertical drop down to a rocky slope fifty feet below. The bike most certainly would be totaled. She most likely would be as well.

Half of the glass on the headlight had broken off in one of the crashes, so it cast a distorted beam down the slope where the trail snaked around lumps and rocks. She took a deep breath, swallowed, then swallowed again. Then she eased her foot off the back brake, turned the throttle gently, and began to edge down the incline. Oh, how she needed a front brake! She'd already downshifted into first gear to use the engine drag to slow the bike, so she had nowhere else to downshift to. It was a dance to keep the only brake, the back brake, steady, applying enough pressure so the bike didn't go hurling down the incline, but not so much that the tire stopped moving entirely. If she locked up the brake, the back tire would slide … and on this narrow trail, a slide would carry her off the edge.

Time did one of those strange things. It elongated, stretched out like a rubber band. She watched the front tire move down the trail in slow motion, sliding between rocks and bumps, holes and cracks, bouncing up over what she couldn't miss. Down, down, down.

Her heart slammed into her chest wall so hard each beat throbbed in her temples. She was getting close to the bottom, but she had been gaining momentum as she descended, going faster and faster. Finally, she was going too fast to steer the bike. She couldn't control it as it bounced and bucked. She pulled harder and harder on the brake handle until her pressure on the back brake finally locked it up. The tire stopped rolling and the back of the bike began to slide toward the drop-off.

Rileigh took a desperate chance then, a life gamble. She turned the front tire *toward* the drop-off. The bike was momentarily crossways on the trail and at that moment, she threw all her weight onto the uphill side of the bike and laid it over on its side. Its momentum carried it skidding on its side down the trail between the rock wall and the drop off, not off the edge. Fifteen feet, twenty, and then the frame hit a big rock and the bike stopped.

Rileigh gasped for air, heaving in great lungfuls of it, so frightened that it was a few moments before she realized that *she* had slid down that incline too, further shredding her left leg and arm.

Nobody but an idiot would ride a dirt bike in a pair of shorts. Nobody but an idiot, or someone desperate.

When she finally caught her breath, she pulled the bike upright. Miraculously, the engine hadn't died, so she gave it a little gas, steered around the rock that had stopped her downward slide, and soon she reached the bottom of the slope, and the trail leveled out.

She felt a wave of relief wash over her. It lasted only until she saw the mist forming in front of her.

Oh, shit. As if it weren't hard enough to come down the mountainside, now she couldn't see more than ten feet in front of her. It wasn't thick, just wispy. And every time she thought she was running into mist so thick she would have to stop, it thinned out again, like driving through the edges of the clouds. The sky above was no longer black. The sun had come up, and it was dawn beyond the mountains.

When Rileigh finally rode down off the trail onto the backside of a field, she stopped, took great healing breaths, and for just a moment allowed herself to feel all of her injuries. The places that didn't hurt were far outnumbered by the places that did. She could feel the warmth of the blood running in tiny rivulets from dozens of cuts, scrapes and scratches. But she'd made it.

When she made the last curve, she could see Gus's house down below her in the dawn light. The lights were on, glowing golden in the brightening gloom. She quickly squelched the temptation to peg the throttle and go roaring down the hillside and continued slowly, negotiating her way around a field and into a meadow. As soon as she got close enough, she could see a four-wheeler parked behind the house. squeaked a cry of delight, watching Gus and Jillian move Lamar off the four-wheeler onto a gurney.

And then Rileigh noticed the two dark-colored vehicles on the road down the mountain from Gus's house.

They pulled off the main road and onto the end of Gus's lane and stopped, and men poured out of both of them. She didn't count how many. Surely there were half a dozen or so in each vehicle. They gathered around the van in front for a moment and then split up, fanning out in both directions.

So they could come at the house from three sides when they attacked.

Chapter Forty-Eight

Rileigh came roaring across the meadow and into Gus's backyard with the throttle pegged. She cut the front wheel sharply, like a slalom skier at the bottom of a slope, and slid to a stop only a few feet in front of a stunned Gus and Jillian. She leapt off the bike, let it drop in the dirt, and hobbled toward them.

"Rileigh!" Jillian squealed in delight, and then dismay. "You're hurt!"

"Get him back in the house!" Rileigh barked.

"You're all torn up!"

"Two carloads of gunmen just pulled into your driveway, got out, and scattered," she told Gus. "They're gonna come at us from all sides. We've only got a few minutes. Get him back in there."

Jillian's mouth dropped open, and her face went pale so fast that Rileigh could see the blue veins in her temples. Rileigh grabbed her sister by the arm and shoved her to get her moving, and the three of them pushed Agent Devereaux on the gurney into the house and slammed the door.

"Where are your guns?" Rileigh asked Gus.

"Which ones? What kind?"

"Got any AR-15s or AK-47s?"

Gus shook his head to clear it, then focused.

"Sure, all my weapons are upstairs. I got a hit on the prints from the body found with Jeremiah's. He was one of Castilla's personal bodyguards." He gestured with his chin toward the outside. "Safe money says every man out there is an experienced killer."

"Go, *go!*" Rileigh cried.

Gus ran up the stairs with Jillian behind him and Rileigh in the rear, hobbling. He went into the second-floor man-cave — an absolute armory, with gun racks on the all the walls, floor to ceiling. Gus wasn't just a hunter. He was a gun connoisseur, had an arsenal of weapons, all different kinds. Military weapons, historic weapons, hunting rifles — you name it, Gus had it. He went to the rack on the wall on the far side of the room and turned and pointed.

"AR-15s." Then he pointed to different rifles on another rack. "AK-47s. Which do you want?"

Rileigh was mentally sorting through all the information her firearms instructors, both in the military and the police, had given her over the years, trying to determine the best weapons for the situation they were in. Rileigh didn't know if Jillian had ever even fired a rifle. Being proficient with a handgun and hitting a target with a rifle were night-and-day different.

An AK-47 delivered a powerful round, what her instructor called "a bone crusher," a projectile that hits a leg and doesn't just break bones when it passes through, it *explodes* the bones. Rileigh once saw a soldier take an AK-47 round through the shin, and the bottom portion of his leg had to be amputated because his tibia lost six inches out of the middle of it. The AK-47 was designed for moderately close-range fire, absolutely devastating, lethal rounds. But the sighting system on the rifle sucked. You couldn't hit the broad side of a barn at a distance greater than fifty or sixty yards.

The AR-15, the civilian version of the military's M4, fired a far less devastating round. It would kill, but it didn't pulverize bones, and you could stand next to one goal post and accurately sight in on a target in the other end zone.

"But I've never fired this kind of weapon," Jillian began.

Rileigh took an AR-15 from a rack, placed Jillian's hands on it properly, and told her to jam it into her shoulder to absorb the kick.

"This one has an LPVO and magnifier," Rileigh said to a blank look on Jillian's face. She backed up and simplified. "All you have to know is there are crosshairs in this sight." She pointed to it. "Look through the sight at the crosshairs. There's also a red dot. Put the red dot on the target and pull the trigger."

Rileigh grabbed four magazines of 30 rounds each and shoved them at Jillian, then took four more for herself. Rileigh was impressed with the fact that her sister was not panicking. She was upset and frightened and confused, but she wasn't in panic mode. You could look in her eyes and talk to her and know that she understood what you said and would do what you told her to.

Rileigh picked up one of the magazines and took the rifle from Jillian.

"Step one, press the magazine release," Rileigh said, and showed Jillian where it was located, pressed it, and watched the magazine drop to the floor. "Step two, insert the new magazine in the opening. Make sure it locks in place. Do you hear it?" The magazine audibly clicked into place. "Step three, release the bolt catch." She demonstrated the simple movement. "That's it. Step four is start shooting." The AR-15 would expel the spent casings as it fired.

Rileigh stopped then and quieted herself, looking first into Gus's eyes and then into Jillian's. "I'm not going to ask either of you if you've ever killed anybody. It's none of my business." She paused. "But if you haven't, you're about to today — because if you don't, they're going to kill you."

She let that sink in for a beat.

"They've got us outnumbered, but I'm banking on the fact that we've got them outgunned." She hoped. When she saw them from the mountain, Rileigh couldn't tell for sure what weapons the men were carrying, but she could take a safe bet.

"Outgunned?" Jillian asked. Her voice was soft, but firm. It didn't quaver.

"It depends on whether the men I saw get out of those vehicles were cartel members or Sicarios."

The difference was that cartel members recruited random thugs off the streets in Central and South American countries, shoved AK-47s in their hands, and said, "You work for me now." The goons knew nothing about the weapon, except maybe which was the dangerous end. Sicarios were Mexican assassins, from the Hebrew word Sakari — Jewish assassins who rebelled against the Romans and assassinated their leaders. Mexican Sicarios were employed by the cartels for contract killing — like Castilla's bodyguard that Jeremiah had killed. Rileigh was sure there were Sicarios among the men approaching Gus's house. But she was equally sure most of them were simple goons.

Heading off Jillian's question, she said simply, "The Sicarios might be packing *anything.* All the rest will have AK-47s — with a very limited range."

Of course, she knew that Gus had killed countless dozens of animals, all shapes and sizes, but she seriously doubted he'd ever put the crosshairs on a human being. And Jillian was a crapshoot. What she might know or might not was anybody's guess.

"Our strategy is very simple, but it will work if we can pull it off. We have an unlimited amount of ammunition; they've only got whatever they're carrying. They're used to getting the job done with thirty rounds. I'd be surprised if they've got even one spare magazine. Certainly not two. We have an elevation advantage; we'll be firing down on them from above. And we're firing long-range weapons, while they're firing short-range. We have to pin them down, pick them off, lay down a constant barrage of lethal fire to keep them out beyond the range where their weapons are accurate. Do that, and they're not likely to land a shot on any of us. We just *keep* firing, a deadly hail of bullets that goes on and on. We will keep it up, keep shooting … until they're all dead."

It really wasn't that simple at all. There were dozens of variables — like how the Sicarios were armed — and multiple scenarios that could go down. But Gus and Jillian didn't need to know that.

"Gus, you take the front windows — move from one to another. Jillian, you and I will take the two corner bedrooms on the back." Both bedrooms had two windows — one facing the side of the house and one facing the back. "We'll alternate windows. I'll start at a side window, you start in a back window. When I yell 'Switch,' you go to the other window. That way we can cover all four sides of the house with only three shooters."

She paused.

"Clear?"

For the second time today, Rileigh wished for a watch.

It had seemed to take forever to arm and position Jillian and Gus. She knew that in reality, it had taken only a handful of minutes. The gunmen outside would approach slowly, stay in hiding as long as possible, intent on getting close to launch a surprise attack.

Rileigh led Jillian into the back bedroom on the north side of the house, hopping on one foot.

"Rileigh, your ankle," Jillian began.

Rileigh silenced her with one word. "Later!"

Jillian opened the windows on both sides of the room, then knelt in front of the one facing the back yard, dropping a pile of magazines on the floor beside her.

Rileigh handed her the rifle again, fitting her hands on it properly.

"It's just like a pistol in that you *squeeze* the trigger, don't pull it. Look through the sight, see what you can see." Jillian put her eye to the sight, moving the barrel of the rifle around, and then squeaked, "There's one of them, there's a man."

"Shoot him!" Rileigh commanded, and Jillian pulled the trigger without hesitation. That was the shot heard round the world. Now, the men would stop sneaking and storm the house.

"Showtime," she said, then turned and hopped down the hall to the other back bedroom, knelt in front of the side window, and began scanning for targets.

After that, Rileigh fell so totally into combat mode that time unraveled in the way it often did in a battle. Each individual shot was a separate event that played out with excruciating slowness. She'd come out of a firefight one time in Afghanistan and discovered to her amazement that they'd been at it for more than two hours. If you'd asked her, she'd have said fifteen minutes.

Now that they'd opened fire, the men outside did, too.

The air filled with the sound of automatic weapons as the men opened up on Gus's house from whatever their position, raking sprays of bullets back and forth. Rileigh, Gus, and Jillian, on the other hand, selected targets and picked them off, one by one. With their home team height advantage, the men outside couldn't tell exactly where they were concealed. Bullets pelted the house, slammed into the outside walls, firing splinters off the doors and frames in the shoot-enough-bullets-and-you'll-eventually-hit-something tradition that seldom hit the target you were aiming at.

Rileigh settled into her own shooting position and put her eye to the scope, spotting a man creeping forward through the brush heading toward a tree with bushes around it. She put the crosshairs on his chest and pulled the trigger and watched him fly backward. She heard Gus and Jillian, the booming of their rifles joining hers in a constant cacophonous chorus that went on and on.

At some point, she yelled "Switch!" and hopped to the other window in the room, the pain in her ankle seeming to come from a long way away. The men ran at the house just like in every other battle Rileigh had ever been in, dashing from one piece of cover to another. You sighted in on one and followed him, took your shot when you had one, and moved on.

"Lay down a lot of fire," Rileigh cried. "Keep them away from the house."

Twice gunmen strafed the window where she was firing, stitching seams of bullet holes in the walls behind her. She kept her head down, waiting for a shot before she pulled the trigger, then she dropped the man who'd fired.

Over and over, automatic gunfire smacked into the house, shattering every window as the three shooters inside kept their heads down. *Go on, use up those bullets!*

She'd only seen one rifle as it flew out of the hands of the man she'd just shot. It was an AK-47. A man stepped out from behind a tree and let loose a blast from his AK-47, and Rileigh took him out, saw him drop, but wasn't sure it was a kill shot. She didn't care whether she killed them or wounded them. She was just determined to put bullets in everybody out there.

"Switch!"

Rileigh hobbled back to the first window, squeezed off two shots, and heard a click. She deftly ejected the magazine and slammed another one into its place. If she had emptied a magazine, that meant the men firing back were getting low on ammo now, too. She crouched down and a single bullet whizzed past her head so close she could feel the air rearrange itself around its passing. Lucky shot. Or a Sicario using a better weapon than an AK-47? She knelt, sighted, and pulled the trigger again, sending a man creeping around the bush diving for cover behind the rock. Gus began firing rapidly, semi-automatic, and Rileigh didn't know if several men were rushing the house or if he was simply trying to keep the ones still in hiding as far away as possible.

The gunfire from the killers had been brutal and furious in the beginning, but as Rileigh, Gus, and Jillian picked off one after another of them — and as their ammo began to run out — the gunfire aimed at the house slowed dramatically, while the gunfire coming *from* the house never missed a beat, was constant and deadly … and seemingly endless. With the ammo Gus had stockpiled, they could keep this up all day. And perhaps the gunmen were beginning to figure that out. The strafing ceased, but individual bullets still smacked into the walls around the windows. One sending splinters that dug into Rileigh's right cheek. If they ever got close enough to aim properly … but they didn't.

There was a lull in the gunfire. Then it stopped altogether. Gus fired two more rounds, Jillian one, Rileigh saw no targets of any kind out either of the windows she was covering. And the killers had never gotten closer than fifty yards from the house.

The silence was profound and scary. Nothing moved.

"Sound off," she yelled.

"What does that mean?" Jillian asked.

"You just did," Rileigh replied.

"I'm here," Gus called out, then said, "They're gone."

Rileigh wanted to be sure. She swung her sight around, but saw no movement. Then she lowered her weapon, closed her eyes, and listened.

A few bird calls in the distance. What could be a truck jake-braking miles away, the sound echoing around, making it impossible to tell how far away. The tinkling of a wind chime, or maybe it was someone jangling keys, although there were no close neighbors. A few muffled thumps like someone easing a car door shut, although that also could have been pieces of Gus's ruined house falling.

It was impossible to see the highway from anywhere in Gus's house, nor could you see the lane below the house where the vehicles had pulled in to park. You could see that road from higher up on the mountain, but it wasn't visible from the house. But from the front window on the top floor, it *was* possible to see the road as it twisted back around the mountain, maybe half a mile away.

"I just saw two similar vehicles going around the curve at the top of the hill," she heard Gus say.

"What were they?"

"One was a black SUV of some kind. The other was a dark blue van. Maybe. Hard to tell."

Those were the vehicles Rileigh had seen from the mountainside pulling off the road in front of Gus's house.

They *were* gone.

Rileigh felt the air sigh out of her and was overwhelmed momentarily by the post-battle exhaustion that hit every soldier, a result of fear, tension, and the aftereffects of the adrenaline dump that had kept them going. Rileigh slowly got to her feet — *foot* — and avoided moving directly in front of the window. She hobbled out the door and hopped down the hallway to the room where Gus was still squatted, his rifle out the front window.

"I think we can stand down," she said. Gus turned around and she saw that his face was almost white — which was a neat trick for a Black man.

He placed the rifle carefully, almost reverently on the floor in front of the window, then stood up. "I hope 'stand down' means party time," he said, trying for humor and missing by a mile. Jillian came into the room then, unarmed.

"They're gone, aren't they? It's over?"

Rileigh hopped to her sister and put her arm around her shoulders.

"Yeah, it's over."

"We need to get Devereaux to a hospital!" Gus said, "Into the back of the SUV and haul ass into town."

He merely gestured at Rileigh, who was beat up and bunged up, had cuts and bruises and scratches and probably a broken ankle. "And you…"

She waved him off. "Later."

When they came down into the hallway where they had left the gurney with Agent Devereaux on it, Gus rushed to his side, put his fingers on his neck, and Rileigh could see that Jillian was holding her breath until he said,

"Pulse, weak and thready, but there's a pulse. Let's get the hell out of here."

Chapter Forty-Nine

WITH RILEIGH STILL HOPPING ON ONE FOOT, THEY maneuvered the gurney out into the garage where Gus's SUV was parked. Jillian and Gus pushed the gurney down along the side of the SUV toward the back, and Rileigh hit the button on the wall to open the garage door. She started hopping toward the back of the vehicle to help them load up Lamar when Jillian suddenly squeaked out a cry, and Rileigh looked toward the door that was going up. When it opened all the way, it revealed a man standing there, holding a pistol on them.

Rileigh knew instantly who he had to be. Chad Gregory, Lamar's not-dead partner.

"God, what happened to him?" Gregory asked, gesturing with his chin toward Lamar — without taking the gun off the others.

"He was in a wreck," Rileigh said. "What do you want?"

"Somebody needs to put him out of his misery," he said.

"What?" Jillian asked. "What do you mean?"

"All three of you — turn around and go back into the house." He took two sudden steps and grabbed Jillian by the arm, shoving the gun up beside her head.

"In the house, now. Anybody tries anything, she's dead. Go on, move."

Gus shoved the gurney back down the side of the SUV and Rileigh grabbed hold of it for balance as she hobbled on the painful ankle.

As soon as they got the gurney into the house, Gregory commanded, "Leave it here." Gus helped Rileigh down the remainder of the hallway to the living room.

Gus eased Rileigh down on the couch in front of a coffee table where Gus had been working on one of his trophies. It was a set of horns of some kind mounted on a plaque, and apparently the plaque had fallen off the wall and broke off one of the horns. It lay on the table beside the plaque along with a small tube of glue. Gus sat down beside her.

"What do you want with us?" Gus demanded.

"Actually, I don't want anything at all with you, but I don't have a choice, because you're here and you have to go away."

"How can *you* be here?" Rileigh said, not because she really wanted an answer, but because she wanted to engage him while she frantically tried to figure out a way to jump him — unarmed and with a broken ankle.

"Yeah, I'm supposed to be dead. And I *was* dead officially. Have been since my car blew up and I became another person entirely. I had my fingerprints altered on my permanent FBI record, had my retinal scan swapped out for somebody else's. I've had my exit planned for years, just waiting for the right score. Then — boom! Seventy-five million dollars' worth of diamonds dropped in my lap — and nobody but the bad guys even knew they existed.

Suh-weet! I grabbed those babies and boogied." He laughed cheerfully and pointed to his face. "I had some significant plastic surgery. Acquired dimples and a cleft in my chin. Lost the prominent Adam's apple I've hated since I started growing the thing in junior high. Colored my hair black. Been sitting on a private beach, getting a tan and drinking Mai Tais — somewhere I'll never cross paths with anybody from my former life."

"So why didn't you stay dead?"

"I buy information, just to keep tabs on what's going on. But I let things slide — I was busy. I found out Castilla was murdering agents at the same time I found out Lamar wasn't in a coma anymore, so I high-tailed it back. But I was too late, Lamar was already in protective custody. I got here and found out the safe house was raided the night before, with Lamar in the wind. I've been scrambling ever since, trying to find him before Castilla did."

"Why were you trying to save Lamar?"

"I wasn't trying to *save* him, I was trying to kill him. I still can't believe he didn't die when I bashed in the back of his skull with that shovel! I don't know why he never told our superiors about what we saw that day, but I knew if Castilla got his hands on him, he'd torture the truth out of him. Then Castilla would figure out I had a powerful motive — and the means — to *fake* being dead. And he'd track me down — seventy-five million dollars, yeah, he'd track me down. I didn't get this far to spend the rest of my life looking over my shoulder." He sighed dramatically. "And the rest, as they say, is history."

Gregory gestured toward the outside. "Spotted one of Castilla's goons in town yesterday and I've been shadowing him. I just about shit my pants when I followed him here to the shootout at the OK Corral. So I'm on the outside, looking in. I figured they'd eliminate the rest of you. The best I could hope for was to get a shot at Lamar when they dragged him out. I brought a sniper's rifle, but that'd be one helluva shot … and then I'd have to get away after. But damned if you didn't kick their asses." He sighed. "Well, if you want a job done right, you have to do it yourself."

He held tight his grip on Jillian's arm with the gun pointed at her temple.

"But why?" Rileigh was scrambling, trying to buy time.

"No more questions. Surely to God the neighbors heard all that gunfire and called the law. I'm out of time. I never intended for any of you to get involved in this, and I'm really sorry for what I have to do. But when that sheriff comes roaring in here and finds those bodies outside, he's going to find four more inside. And I'll go back to my private beach and my Mai Tais. At least I'll be putting Lamar out of his misery."

Suddenly, there was movement in the doorway behind where Gregory stood holding a gun on Jillian. He let go of her and started to turn as someone lurched at him, crashed into him, knocking him backward, and the two of them fell to the floor, wrestling for the gun.

Bang!

The gunshot exploded in the small space. The figure on top of Gregory collapsed.

Rileigh grabbed the horn that was lying on the coffee table and launched herself at the two men on the floor, slamming the horn into the side of Gregory's head before he had a chance to move. He went limp.

Gus got down on one knee and rolled Lamar off Gregory to reveal a gunshot wound in Lamar's chest. Lamar opened his eyes and looked at them, searching … and then he found her, Jillian. She dropped to the floor beside Gus.

"Lamar!" she cried.

He could barely speak. And when he did, blood bubbled out of his mouth.

"I thought I did it." He gasped for another breath. "Thought I stole ... them ... couldn't remember." He coughed then and blood spewed everywhere, splattering Gus's and Jillian's faces. "It ... wasn't me."

And then his eyes slowly unfocused.

"Lamar, Lamar," Jillian cried. "Gus, do something."

Gus looked at her compassionately. "I'm sorry, Jillian," he said, then reached up and closed Lamar Devereaux's dead eyes.

Jillian began to cry. Rileigh marveled at what had just happened. Lamar Devereaux had gotten off that gurney with a bleeding gunshot wound and a compound fracture, came all the way down the hall with the bones sticking out of his leg, and jumped Gregory from behind. He had saved all of them.

Chapter Fifty

RILEIGH HAD AN ACE BANDAGE ON HER ANKLE WHEN Mitch got to the house, and he looked questioningly at it.

"No, no, no, no. I'm good. This is just a precaution. It doesn't hurt. I've already practiced walking in the shoes."

The smile that lit his face would have melted frost off a windowpane in the dead of winter. She had been determined that she was going to wear those beautiful matching shoes with her green dress when they went to Ruth's Chris Steakhouse on the Tennessee River in Knoxville. The outfit looked so good together, she wasn't going to break it up. The date had become such a "thing" that she wanted it to be as fairy tale as possible, though she didn't use that terminology with Mitch, of course.

Her other injuries had healed up well enough that she wasn't self-conscious about them — stitches out of the cuts, scratches mostly healed, bruises large and small an ugly shade of dark yellow. Her ankle had been the only matter of concern when it came to the big date. Gus told her that she might have been better off if she'd actually broken it instead of spraining it so severely. She adamantly disagreed, of course. She'd suffered through two weeks on the little scooter, where you rested your knee and your injured foot stuck off the back. It was a sight better than crutches. She had taken off the Ace bandage three days ago, walked around without it for a day, and then tried on the high heels. And she was five by five, good to go.

Mitch had come over for dinner tonight, but Jillian hadn't invited David, and Rileigh didn't bring it up. Jillian had "stepped back" from that relationship. At least those were the words she used. She said she needed distance. David had honored her request and backed off. Rileigh understood the why, or thought she did, though Jillian had never explained it. Jillian had had some relationship with Agent Devereaux when he was here. Rileigh wasn't sure what it was. And maybe Jillian wasn't either, but it had somehow caused Jillian to question her involvement with David. Not that there was anything wrong with it, but it was too much too soon. Rileigh understood that, but it did make her sad. It had been such a perfect story. Jillian comes back home, finds the man she left at the altar. He still loves her, and they live happily ever after. And maybe that would still end up being the final result. Rileigh hoped so.

As soon as Rileigh was settled in the porch swing, Mitch said, "Had a visit from the *dis*Honorable J.P. Rutherford this morning."

"Oh, no. Is he still…?"

"Yep, he's still."

The Yarmouth County mayor had decided to insert himself into the investigation of the five dead men Jillian, Gus, and Rileigh had shot on Gus' property. The prosecutor had declined to prosecute the case, but Rutherford was getting desperate with the election coming up, and it was becoming more and more clear that Sundeep Singh was going to win it in a landslide.

Rutherford wanted publicity, so he'd glommed on to the horrible situation with the FBI agent and made it a crusade about law and order, or the lack thereof, in Yarmouth County. He was demanding a federal investigation, but nobody was listening. What was there to investigate? Other than the fact that of the five dead men, four of them were in the country illegally, and one had even been on the terrorist watch list.

"He'll get tired of pontificating and making a general ass of himself eventually," Mitch said. "I'm already looking forward to the election and Sundeep's victory. I have not yet had the good fortune of having a good boss, a man who's reasonable. It sounds like heaven."

Everyone looked up when they heard the sound of a vehicle turning off Bent Twig Road and up into Mama's driveway. It was the UPS truck.

"My Cousin Art is here!" Mama squealed.

Rileigh, Jillian, Mitch, and Gus had tried to tell her had that the word was pronounced Cuisinart, not Cousin Art, but in Mama's head, she *was* saying Cuisinart. She had begun to obsess over getting herself "one of them food processors like Betty Ferguson has" after she came home from a church potluck raving about Betty's guacamole, and how Betty had told her that the whole secret was the food processor. Mama was off to the races. She got Rileigh to help her look up online food processors, had spent days deciding which one she wanted, and finally ordered it on Monday, promising to have guacamole for Sunday dinner.

Rileigh wasn't terribly interested in what might be on the menu for Sunday dinner. Her eyes were fixed on Saturday night. Just thinking about it gave her goosebumps.

The UPS truck bounced up over the lump at the top of the driveway, and Mama hurried down the porch steps and out to greet the driver, who was opening up the doors of the big brown truck.

"You got a box for me, don't you?"

"I do indeed, Miss Lily. What's in it?" he asked as he picked up the box and handed it to her.

"It's a food processor," she said proudly.

"What does it do?"

"Why, you can slice vegetables faster than you can with a knife, whizz herbs for a garnish, or mix bread dough — or mash avocados for guacamole. It'll do all kinda stuff like that."

Rileigh hoped that Mama would do exactly that — would cut up vegetables and make bread. And she might. But it was equally possible that she would use the processor once and either forget that she had it or forget how to operate it.

"I'll have to stop by here and get me some of that homemade bread," the driver said as he went back around to the driver's side of the truck. "Maybe get some when it's still hot so it'll melt a pat of butter!" He stopped before he climbed back into the truck behind the wheel.

"One more package," he said, and his words froze Rileigh's heart.

"Another package? Why? What is it? That's the only thing I've ordered," Mama said. "Maybe it comes in more than one piece."

"No, this package is for Miss Rileigh." The driver pulled out a manila envelope, the kind with bubble wrap in it so that whatever is inside is protected, and started up the sidewalk with it.

Rileigh rose from the swing, an involuntary movement, and wanted desperately to run into the house, out the back door and up the mountainside and not face whatever was in the envelope. Julian and Mitch, of course, understood. Mama didn't.

Mitch stepped forward quickly and snatched the envelope out of the driver's hand. When he'd held it out to Rileigh, she stood had stood frozen and mute.

"I'll be back over here for a piece of that homemade bread," the driver said to Mama. "You just let me know when it's ready." He got back into his truck and pulled out of the driveway and down to the road.

Mama put the box with the food processor in it on the floor of the porch and was trying to get it open. "Rileigh, honey, will you go get me a knife to cut this tape?"

Rileigh didn't respond. Mama looked up into her face, then into Jillian's and Mitch's. "What's the matter?" she asked, looking from one to the other, confused, and then her eyes lit on the envelope in Mitch's hand and her hand flew to her mouth.

"Oh no, no, no," she said, shaking her head back and forth.

"Rileigh, I can take this with me," Mitch began.

"It's addressed to me."

"You don't have to do this."

"Yeah, I do. I have to."

She reached out her hand, and Mitch reluctantly laid the envelope in it. As if in some kind of dream, she tore the sticky end of the envelope off and opened it. She took a deep breath before looking inside, then just turned the envelope upside down over the coffee table and let the contents drop out.

It was some kind of fabric, a piece of something that looked like thin cloth, and she couldn't figure out what it was. Beside it, was a folded piece of paper and a key that made a clunking sound when it hit the top of the table.

Mitch figured it out before Rileigh did and snatched the piece of cloth up off the table.

"I'll take that."

"No, wait, what is it?"

"You don't need this. I'll take care of it."

"What is it?" she demanded and reached to grab it back out of his hand. Instead of giving it to her, he put it back down on the table and spread it open. Then she knew.

Mama didn't.

"What is that thing?"

There was an image on it that was hard to see, but Rileigh wouldn't touch it to move it so that she could get a better look. Just stood back gawking at the piece of dried and tanned human skin. Then she realized that the mark on it was a tattoo, but she couldn't make out the image.

"What is it?" Mama asked, looking from one to the other.

Jillian gasped when she figured it out and said, "Mama, we need to go in the house."

"No, we don't. I want to know. What is that thing?"

"I thought you wanted to open up that food processor," Jillian said. "Don't you want to see how it works?"

Mama's mind flitted to what Jillian said, like a butterfly going from one flower to another. "Why, I sure do."

"Let's take it inside then." Jillian picked the box up off the porch and shooed Mama into the house in front of her, closing the front door behind her.

"It's … it's…" Rileigh couldn't make herself say the words.

"It's skin," Mitch said. "We need to get this into an evidence bag and send it off to the lab for a DNA sample."

She looked up into Mitch's eyes, and her own filled with tears. "What kind of person does a thing like that?"

Mitch reached down and picked up the key and examined it. "I think this may be a locker key."

"Locker." The word was airless.

"You know, like in a train station. A locker."

Rileigh reached down and picked up the piece of paper, even though she knew what she'd see there. It was the antithesis of a smiley face. A horribly frowning drawing with the lips curled down. She turned the piece of paper over, and on the back was a number. Not a number six like the card she'd gotten right after Jillian came home. Or the number five like the paper inside the box with the finger bone. Or the number four written beside the frowny face on the card inside the envelop with the thumb bones.

The number written on the paper she held now in trembling fingers was the number three.

What would happen when the countdown got to zero?

THE END

About The Author

Lauren Street has always loved a mystery. As a kid growing up in bible belt country she devoured every whodunit book she could get her sticky little hands on and secretly investigated all of her (seemingly) normal boring neighbors. Sometimes their pets and farm animals too. All grown up now and living in the UK with her thoroughly unsuspicious (and often unsuspecting) husband, she writes domestic psychological thrillers about families torn apart by secrets and lies. And she sometimes still peers over garden walls to check up on the neighbors.

Also By Lauren Street

The Bishop Smoky Mountain Thrillers

Hide Me Away

Fuel To The Flame

Closer By The Hour

A Gamble Either Way

Calling My Children Home

Too Far Gone

Here You Come Again

A Friend Like You

The Company You Keep

One By One

Replaced with Nolon King

Replaced

In Her Place

Irreplaceable

The Salazar Redwood Forest Thrillers

The Girl Who Couldn't Stop Dying

The Girl Who Couldn't Get Out

The Girl Who Couldn't Be Found